the
honorable
correspondent

henry scholder

the permanent press
sag harbor, ny 11963

Library of Congress Cataloging-in-Publication Data

Scholder, Henry, 1948-
    The honorable correspondent / by Henry Scholder
    p. cm.
    ISBN 1-57962-085-X
    1. Illegal arms transfers--Fiction. 2. Middle East--Fiction.
    3. Hostages--Fiction. 1. Title.

    PS3619.C4535H66 2003
    813'.6--dc21

                     2002030309

Printed in The United States of America

THE PERMANENT PRESS
4170 Noyac Road
Sag Harbor, NY 11963

For Arrelle, and for Renee and Jordan.

For Imoneke & Steve:
A new and an old friend.
Warmest Regards,
Hugh Schildm

Chapter One

November 1973, Junieh, Lebanon.

Claude Harouni's thirty-eighth birthday fell on a freakishly hot day in late November. The heat's parched breath left Claude dazed and made his wife Naama fretful and short-tempered.

They had taken refuge in hammocks on their back porch, where they lay sprawled, limbs distanced from trunks, eyelids tacky with dried sweat. Naama considered her party, her grand party for him, and slowly retreated into hopelessness. The big event was now only hours away, yet so much was left to be accomplished: tables to be set, chairs placed for more than two hundred people, the carousel to be installed, a van-load of food unpacked, the children bathed. Remembering the carousel, she smiled; it had been Bobo's find, in the dusty warehouse somewhere in the south, near Beirut airport, where they had made love for the first time. She quickly looked to see whether Claude had noticed her smile. As if he could know from a smile!

"People barely move today," she said to him in a dispirited way, meaning their staff. "How will they do it all, Claude? We have two hundred people coming." She clucked her tongue with self-pity.

He ignored her. "How strange for it to be so hot," he moaned. "Only last week I had the men change over to their winter clothes."

"Please make this sun go away," Naama whispered to the pale sky, and thought, Screw him and his men's winter clothes. She propped her head on her slender hands, gazed out onto the sizzling world beyond the terrace, and thought of Bobo.

The encouraging screech of a table being dragged across the floor somewhere in the house recalled her. Thank God my cretins are at work, she thought.

With two fingers she gingerly lifted a chunk of ice from her drink and rubbed it along her lips as she squinted at the dusty glare reflected off pines and cypresses, earth and rocks, all baked into an ashen color by the sun's scowl. Through the saddle between their hill and the next, she could see the Mediterranean and a bit of the port of Junieh. The sea was limpid and coppery, the yellow shore shimmered like burning desert shrubs. From roasting Junieh itself, a vapor rose. Naama sighed and wished

5

mightily for an infusion of the rash enthusiasm that had inspired this party.

"I refuse to accept this," she said in a sudden flare-up of chagrin, speaking to no one in particular. "Yesterday I rushed out to buy coat hangers—well it's fall, isn't it? Everyone I spoke with was breaking out their furs, so we'd need hangers. Today? Today I had to order the beach club to send up lounge chairs for guests to sun themselves at the pool. Impossible, just impossible." A thought cheered her. "Don't you think I was clever to do that, Claude, getting the beach chairs? Don't you think so? Claude?"

Claude lifted his empty glass with some effort, as if it had become enormously heavy, and rolled it back and forth against his forehead.

"A pool party in November," Naama muttered. "In Beirut they will make jokes at our expense."

"Who cares what they think in Beirut?" Claude growled, sparked into anger. He was touchy about living in this relative backwater, where he felt better able to protect himself, but where Naama sometimes felt in exile. He emitted a gurgling chuckle, putting her on notice that his patience, never abundant, had run out, that he had had enough of this hot day, of the fracas surrounding his birthday, of her chatter about furs and beach chairs. Also, he'd been irritable over some convoluted gun deal he'd been negotiating with Palestinians down in Sidon—she had heard him speak with Bobo about it.

Naama knew it was best to keep still now; Claude was basically a crude man and it was no use goading him. Even after a dozen years of marriage and the birth of two sons and a daughter, he remained what he was: the autocratic head of a clan from the remote hills of Tripoli, a backward region up north near the Syrian border, a man used to having his word obeyed. After a few moments, however, she felt safe again. "Now Claude darling," she said, "don't you dare be in a bad mood, not on your birthday." She smiled brightly and wrested away his empty glass. "Have some more tamarind drink, sweetie," she counseled.

Eight years earlier, Claude had unexpectedly inherited his father's militia. Before it was known that he, and not his older brother Awal, would assume leadership, the men used to tease him for his excess of good looks. They called him "Mr. Profile," and "Bebe Delon" because of a supposed resemblance to the French film actor. They thought him frail, because his raven hair made his pale skin appear sallow. An expression of perpetual affability, a sort of priestly simper, also encouraged misleading impressions. In time, however, these men and many others learned that,

6

expression to the contrary, Claude was capable of great ferocity.

When the time came for the guests to arrive, they went down to the gates at the foot of the hill. Carefully, Naama inspected the huge bouquets of roses and carnations fastened to the gray and cream marble gate columns, ordering the shoring-up of some flowers that had come loose. This party was important to her. "Tout Lebanon" was coming, its proprietors and financiers, its politicians and top soldiers, heads of other clans, ranking Militia officers, churchmen of five sects, the diplomatic corps, her coterie of fashion, art, and entertainment friends.

She sat on a folding chair at a small table placed on the grass near the gate and sipped more of her chilled tamarind drink, her dark eyes staring up the winding road that led from the Beirut highway. She thought of Bobo and giggled; several militiamen loitering nearby looked to see what caused her laughter, and she stared back at them. The truth was, she had, at one time or another, fancied some of them. Now they looked somehow different, and suddenly she realized why: they were not carrying their weapons, and that made them appear younger than usual, more their true age, really. Teenagers, she thought, not much older than my Antoine, Claude's army of teenagers, looking as if they belonged in classrooms or on the beaches, but deadly all the same. Most had been hired from small villages near Tripoli, where Claude's father Suleiman and brother Awal held sway. She looked to see where they had placed their guns. Life around Claude had taught her always to know the whereabouts of people's weapons.

The militiamen avoided her gaze, and she chuckled inwardly. It was always the same with them: first a brief acknowledgment, then a refusal to look more. "No matter," she once told her best friend Chantal. "By the time they look away I have seen their desire. They say to me, 'I alone would love you as they love in paradise.'" She should write poetry Chantal said. "But then," Naama had continued, "they remember they are on earth still, and near Claude, and they shit in their pants," and she'd laughed uproariously.

For the party, and for Bobo, she was wearing her new Givenchy suit, light blue, trimmed with darker piping. Actually, she wore only the skirt and blouse. Fortunately, these went well without the jacket, which of course had proved impossible in the heat. Her dark blond hair was gathered up from her neck and fixed by gilded clasps. Her neck and bare arms were deeply tanned.

She heard the clank of metal; the men were picking up their weapons.

7

A plume of dust rose along the unpaved road from the Beirut highway—the first guests were arriving. When the car was about fifty meters away, two of the men signaled it to halt. "Oh Claude," she protested, "for heaven's sake, it's Chantal and Maurice."

"All right. All right, there. Let them by," he barked at the men—as if they should have anticipated his coming change of mind.

Since his now notorious assault on the Forjieh clan's compound in Baade, north of Beirut and within sight of the Presidential palace, Claude was taking no chances. Although the raid, brazen and daring, had been a success (he and his men having annihilated the Forjiehs—men, women, and children— leaving him uncontested overlord of Maronite militias), he would not permit himself to forget that a single Forjieh, a man named Atrash, was still alive somewhere abroad.

Chantal, wearing a flowing gauzy turquoise dress with matching green shoes and fabric handbag, emerged from her car with a flourish. Maurice, who fancied himself a wit, said, "I simply adore November swimming parties, Naama." Chantal rolled her eyes upwards for Naama's benefit, fanning away at herself with her hands. Naama bussed her cheeks. "I'm so glad you are here before the others," she whispered.

Soon the hillside road was jammed with vehicles, throwing the militiamen into a frenzied struggle to carry out Claude's order, which was to maintain the area in front of the gates clear of cars and potential car bombs. But when they became overzealous, hurrying guests along in a none-too-dignified manner, Claude took his adjutant aside. "Tell them to go easy," he hissed. "I'm having a fucking birthday party here, not a war."

Naama and he stood patiently in the heat to receive a seemingly endless line of well-wishers, many of whom insisted on embracing and kissing them and of making a prolonged show of their presents. There was a lifetime's supply of dates from an Iraqi businessman, thirty-eight (for Claude's years on earth) cackling white hens in cages from a Druse elder and his wife (she impervious to the weather in a crimson velvet gown), numberless expensive cigarette lighters, one embedded in the stalk of a scimitar.

Naama's face already was aching from too many forced smiles when she saw him—tall and redheaded, regal in his white French navy dress uniform, sunglasses in one hand, a gift in the other. His green eyes twinkled at her, at everyone, and through her weariness a smile true, wide, and happy appeared for her special friend, Claude's friend too, the French military attaché, Bertrand de Bossier, "Bobo" to all.

As it turned out, he had brought two gifts: an elaborately wrapped book, a photographic history of the French navy—"an official gift, you see," Bobo said somewhat apologetically; and a small package of the size that often holds expensive jewelry. "This is from Gaspar and me, Claude," he said. Naama craned her neck as Claude eagerly tore away the wrapping paper and snapped open the small velvet box. It contained a Rolex diving watch. Claude's face took on the particular grimace that was his expression of delight. "By my all, I swear this is something I've always wanted!" he exclaimed.

Naama smiled. "Thank you, Bobo dear." She gestured at his uniform. "You look wonderful," she said, then caught herself. "But your friend Gaspar, the nice one from Belgium, where is he?"

"Gaspar...oh, his holiday ended. He went home yesterday." Bobo said, then, turning to Claude, "My oldest friend, Gaspar Bruyn."

"What a pity!" Naama cried. "And I was so hoping to show him our beautiful Lebanon."

Bobo smiled his enigmatic smile. At least, Naama thought it enigmatic because she was certain Bobo was a man of many secrets. Her intuition had led her to suspect that he was more than just a naval officer. She had asked about it once, and he had lapsed into a teasing silence which only stoked her fond suspicions.

She had run her hunch about de Bossier by Claude, whose disingenuous grunt of denial had only confirmed it to her: Bobo was engaged in secret doings; her lover was a spy. With this certainty she had considered herself the luckiest woman on earth: her lover was French, a count, smart, aloof, attractive in an unconventional way—and a spy! How much more exciting could things get!

Noting the few guests still in line, Claude said to Bobo, "Wait until I'm done, then we'll walk back together to the house, okay?"

He is so unaffected, Naama thought, so charming, with his military hair cut and the wire-rimmed glasses he ordinarily wears, and his endless curiosity and ability to speak with the lofty and the lowly in the same easy way. In his simplicity he was more elegant than all the dandies of Beirut put together. She grew warm recalling his thin, long body against hers, his freckled face and elongated lips pressed against her naked stomach, recalling how she had nearly gone mad with abandon that first time, pleading with him to remain in her afterwards and for a few moments caring about nothing but his love, fearing nothing except having it taken away.

"Thank God," Claude muttered to Bobo when the line of well-wishers finally came to an end. "One more gift and I would have died."

Bobo smiled. "Not just yet, please, Claude."

Naama took the watch from Claude and instructed a servant to take it to the house and place it on the mantle in the living room, "so that we may admire it later when this is over." Then she excused herself to be driven with Chantal up to the house in a golf cart. As they started off, Chantal stole a look at de Bossier over her shoulder, and Naama squeezed her hand to make her stop. They giggled in unison.

"I've wanted one of these for a long time," Claude said as he and Bobo embarked on the uphill climb, "but I thought it silly, you know, for someone who does not dive. But as you're a naval officer, it makes it all right."

"You're lucky I settled on the watch, Claude." Bobo said. "It was a toss-up between that and a bunch of chickens." Claude exploded with laughter and swatted Bobo on the back. After a short silence Bobo said, "I think we found your missing Forjieh. Atrash?"

At once somber, Claude said in a near whisper, "Yes, that's the one. Where is the runt?"

"Last seen somewhere in Paris, last known to be traveling. We'll be more exact by tomorrow."

Claude placed his hand on his chest. "I am most grateful, Bobo," he said earnestly. "It is the best of feelings to have you, to have France, for a friend."

"We've appreciated your past help too, Claude."

"Thank you for saying so," Claude said. Lebanon's Maronites were closely allied with France, and Claude had from time to time done Bobo small favors, stealing people past borders, providing security for others, and the like. "I hope, my friend, you do not still hold it against me," he went on, "this little gun deal of mine with the Palestinians. I just couldn't let a competitor get in with those guys, they're getting richer every day—you know how it is."

Bobo shrugged to indicate the insignificance of the matter.

The huge white Harouni home came into view with, on its front lawn, the carousel, now surrounded by chattering guests. Claude shook his head in admiration. "Naama's idea," he said.

"I know, I was there when she found it," Bobo said.

"Ah, that's right, Bobo." Claude smiled magnanimously. People talked about his wife and this Frenchman who, in any event, he did not think particularly attractive. He had made certain there was nothing between her and Bobo; his informants followed them everywhere. Even when de Bossier had taken her swimming down near Naqra, at the border

10

with Israel, and they had been together on the rocks there practically an entire day, he was assured by his man, who had pretended to be a fisherman, that nothing untoward had taken place.

Naama came towards them in something of a huff. "They are all supposed to be down at the pool," she said, gesturing at the crowd milling about the carousel, "but they are like children with a new toy. Please Claude, Bertrand, can you help me get them down there?"

Bobo looked toward the carousel, then smiled at Naama. "Remember how grimy it was when we first saw it?" he said.

"Unbelievable," she confirmed to Claude. "It must have been in that warehouse fifty years."

Bobo had discovered the carousel and had brought her to see it. Naturally, Claude's sleuth followed, but as soon as Bobo had ushered her into the huge, dim building he'd shoved the metal gate shut behind him, seized her, and brought her against him. "He'll tell Claude," she had protested, but by then Bobo had lifted her skirt and she was taut with desire. "Wrong analysis, Naama; he won't dare admit he let us out of his sight," Bobo had whispered, and laughed. After the warehouse incident, the hapless sleuth became their cover; whenever he was on the job, they made love.

Her feast, her immense Levantine banquet for Claude, started when the sun, huge and dark orange, finally slid into the Mediterranean. Endless offerings were stacked atop twenty long tables for the guests to help themselves at will, aided by the Harounis' staff and by servants hired for the evening. Dozens of huge tureens were filled with finely chopped tomatoes, onions, cucumbers, peppers, and parsley bathed in lemon juice and olive oil, to go with the shashliks and kebabs continuously broiling on upright spits. There were four varieties of fish and three of fowl; bowls laden with spiced rices and trays stacked high with kibbeh (balls of fried semolina wrapped around chunks of mutton); platters heavy with dips of humus and baba ghanouj; jars of pickled peppers, cucumbers, tomatoes, and beets; tureens filled with leban (yoghurt spiced with mint), others with cardamom and garnished with sliced cucumbers.

Between courses, entertainers performed. Naama had worked hard on the variety and pacing of the acts, from a dancing Circassi, terribly dignified in his tall black lamb fur cap, flowing dark gray robe trimmed in black, glistening black boots, and a gleaming saber in his hand, to a slithery, belly-bumping, breast-quivering Egyptian dancer, to a poet reading passionately from Khalil Gibran, to a stripper imported for the evening from Athens. As Naama had expected, the stripper drew the most inter-

11

est. When the last of her bright silk scarves sank to the floor, men rushed to stuff currency and calling cards under the ornamental string she was left wearing. She rewarded particularly generous givers with embraces and small kisses to the forehead, at which the women guests shrieked and ululated.

For dessert, pastries and fruits were paraded around by the smiling staff on trays of beaten copper before being set down. Then Naama introduced Danny, the Maronites' favorite funny man, whom she had chosen for the closing act. "This is the only man I can think of in Lebanon—no, in the world," she said, her audience already grinning in anticipation, "whose insults Claude suffers, laughs at, and, would you believe it, pays for."

Danny then came on to lampoon and harass, to point out those who were rich, yet miserly; ecclesiastic, yet riddled with earthly vices; powerful, yet timid; stylish, yet in yesteryear's fashions. He shifted from subtleties to raunchy jokes, then cupped his hands around his mouth, trumpeted a screechy imitation of a racetrack trumpet, and asked for silence.

"Ladies and gentlemen...," (a pause). "Oh yes, I see one there," he said, and had to quiet the crowd again with spread and downturned hands. "We are so very fortunate to have Naama Harouni for our hostess. Not only has she given us all this free food and drink, and tamed Claude for one whole evening so that we might consume all these goodies in peace, but she has arranged the most wonderfully original after-dinner fun for all. Naama has thought up for us not one, but two diversions: carousel rides, and a simultaneous prize raffle drawing, which will be held in the lower gardens behind the house. Ladies and gentlemen, Naama Harouni!"

Naama stood to tumultuous applause. She thanked them all for being there and for their generous gifts to Claude. At this, Danny did an uncanny imitation of cackling hens, at which all but the Druse guests laughed.

"We have decided, Danny and I," Naama continued, "who goes first to the carousel and who goes down to the garden. It is only fair that Danny got to pick, because that way everyone is certain to be equally offended." She and Claude, she explained, would take the first ride on the carousel, then the first group of guests. "And then, the groups will switch."

Danny fussed for long minutes designating people to their groups. There was much shouting, laughter, and mock and not-so-mock protests. In an effort to mollify the garden group, Chantal and Maurice, as the Harounis' close friends, were designated to the latter. Finally, all the lights in the house and grounds were turned down and everyone headed, giggling and whispering in the darkness, out to the lawn.

12

When anticipation had finally stilled them, Naama raised her arm, then dropped it. At once hundreds of light bulbs, blue and green and red and white, lit up the carousel, winding up and down the poles and around every curving line of its circumference. The horses, black— spotted, white, and brown—had tiny light bulbs running up and down their manes; even their nostrils glowed red. The crowd was enthralled, applause broke out, and gushing compliments flew Naama's way.

Claude made a pronounced showing of his appreciation. He embraced her, raising and holding her arm above her head, like a boxing champion. Naama was moved; then, regaining control of the proceedings, she asked everyone to find their designated group. Some balked, and Danny screamed in a high falsetto, a standard tool of his comedy routines, "It will be better this way, really, darlings, I promise."

When at last the garden group had cleared the area, he turned to the others. "Now, our hosts will ride first, to show us how they do it in Junieh, you understand," he squealed, stressing the "they." After a pause and a giant wink, he added, "I mean of course, but of course, how "they" ride the carousel, I mean nothing else, you filthy minds." He led Claude to a white horse, made a show of demonstrating how to mount, and tumbled farcically to the ground, tried again, and tumbled again. "Let me show you how 'we' do it in Junieh, Danny, my friend," shouted Claude, brushing away tears of laughter. Danny feigned anger at the white horse that had so shamelessly betrayed him. He slapped its rump with a loud sound and shrieked in pain. Squeezing more laughter from the crowd, he ran towards the house, howling and blowing on the offended hand all the way until he disappeared inside.

Now in the saddle, Claude beckoned Naama to him, lifted her, and installed her before him. She turned to look for Bobo, but could not see him. Claude mistook her movement for an invitation and promptly kissed her on the lips. The crowd cheered and whistled and hooted. At last the carousel's operator, who had been quietly standing by throughout, pushed a lever and the horses started to spin as a Nino Rota tune came over the loudspeaker.

On its second go-around, just as the white horse came into view again, the carousel disintegrated. With a terrific din and an explosion of jagged orange flames, it fragmented into a thousand bits. There followed a second of utter silence, as if the world held its breath to learn what was to come. Then the silence too was smashed, by howls and screams from the dozens of broken bodies strewn about the wreck. Those who screamed did so from torn throats choked with blood. Those not screaming lay on the lawn, cut down by the savage storm of shrapnel, bits and pieces of wood, metal, and glass that had so recently been their promise of pleasure to come. Others stumbled around as if in a final giddy dance, their faces and bodies slashed. From the bodies closest to the wreck there came only low moans or silence. Blood was the dominant substance on the lawn, red the prevailing color. Somewhere in these puddles of red were the remains of Claude and Naama, together in death more than they ever had been in life.

Gunfire came from down the road, from the gates, and from nearby— from the house itself. The hired servants, still in their service whites, were firing automatic rifles both into the air and in the direction of the carnage on the lawn. Those of the second group of partygoers, who were just making their way to the scene from the garden, fell screaming to the ground. The servants, shouting in French—the Maronites' preferred language— and in Arabic, ordered everyone to stay where they were and to keep their eyes down. The gunfire ceased.

A large blue Mercedes taxi scampered up the drive and onto the lawn. From its front passenger seat a well-dressed man emerged. Deliberately, he walked the blood-soaked lawn, pointing with a small black pistol at one or another of the surviving wounded from the carousel group. A militiaman following the newcomer and fired a fusillade at the designated person.

Finally, the dapper executioner arrived at the doorway of the house, where the Harouni children were being held by a couple of the sham servants. Danny the comedian held Antoine, the eldest, in a cruel vice, his forearm tucked forcefully under the boy's chin, making him gag.

The man gave the children no more than a glance. "I am told your father has been looking for me," he said. "Well, when you see him, tell him I found him first." He spat in Antoine's face, then raised his pistol and when the muzzle was level with the boy's head, fired. Then he shot the younger boy. The baby had been propped against the doorway because she could not yet stand on her own. He looked around as if to make certain there were no more children, then shot her too. Because of her small size, the bullets lifted her body off the door.

The man stood there another moment, a finger resting lengthwise on his closed lips, as if contemplating things past and future. Then he walked to the blue taxi and resumed the front passenger seat. Some of the servants piled in the back seats, others headed down the hill on foot, their rifles held behind their necks like so many shepherds carrying their staffs, at peace after bringing in the flock at day's end.

14

As the Mercedes started to move, Chantal, her green dress now red and yellow tatters, made a frenzied dash forward. "You will die in the sewers, Atrash, in buckets of pig shit, you mad son of a filthy whore, Atrash Forjieh," she screamed, at each word pounding her clenched fists against her bloodied thighs. Atrash Forjieh leaped out of the slow-moving car and in two steps stood in front of her. He slapped her face hard, with the palm and back of his hand. "Be careful what you say about my mother, you fancy slut," he said in French, then aimed his pistol at her belly and fired twice. When she lay on the ground, bucking and thrashing as if in the culminating throes of love-making, he fired a third bullet into her head. He resumed his seat and the car drove away.

In the living room, Bobo de Bossier warily lifted himself from behind the table he had used for a shield. He listened for a moment, then, satisfied that the action had at last subsided, walked to the fireplace mantle and reclaimed his gift to Claude. Pleased to see that the watch was still in its velvet case, he pocketed it and left.

Chapter Two

Eighteen years later. A car is traveling north, away from Beirut's airport. The men who had earlier forced Gaspar Bruyn inside are making no attempt to keep him from observing the way. Their nonchalance makes him ill. He feels feverish, his bones and joints ache, his mouth and eyes are dry. They are permitting him to see the way because they know he will never describe it to anyone. They intend to kill him.

The car is small, a European-made Ford, Gaspar thinks. The young men at either side press against him, their thighs hard and unselfconscious against his, as if they were all school chums returning from a football match, their comradery having long since dissolved any male queasiness about being touched by other males. They are lean, with dark hair and eyes and skin. They wear jeans, casual shirts, Puma running shoes.

Next to the driver—a young man, like those on either side of Gaspar—sits a man different from the others, a man whose posture and demeanor are those of a patron, a man of power. He is older than they, in his late twenties or early thirties. His skin is pale, unusually so for the Levant. He wears beige slacks, a white dress shirt, its sleeves folded halfway up his forearms, brown loafers, and dark green socks.

It was the young men now sitting by Gaspar who had come up to Sarah and him in Beirut airport and lured him to the car.

Sarah and he had been depleted, so very weary there in the grimy, worn-out lounge that had only recently been reopened to air travelers. They had joked about doing a coffeetable book on airports that had survived wars: Kuwait, Kabul, Beirut. Their humor had been designed to make them immune to the place, to reassure one another that they had regained their capacity for levity.

The mangled streets and buildings of Kuwait City had dampened their good cheer. The eyes of its citizens broadcast a blend of rage and bewilderment, like the eyes of well-heeled travelers on a luxury ocean liner suddenly set upon by pirates whose ferocity and rapaciousness the genteel travelers had not imagined possible.

Gaspar and Sarah had gone to Kuwait just after Saddam had been thrown back. Sarah had accepted a <u>Sentinel Sunday</u> magazine assignment to do an article on the place and Gaspar had come along, as he had on all her working trips following the final events at Belle Marais.

16

After Belle Marais, they had agreed to be apart as little as possible.

The two young men had approached them in the passenger lounge wearing expressions of familiarity and friendship, their easy demeanor placing them in a world far away from the one inhabited by the edgy, grim-faced travelers awaiting transit in the ruin of an airport. Sarah had just removed a cigarette from its box and one of the men promptly fished out his cigarette lighter. She accepted the light, smiling gratefully. The same man then bent down to whisper to Gaspar, to tell him how pleased they were that he was in Beirut and that an old friend of his and Bobo's wished to greet him.

Gaspar was unperturbed that these strangers knew of his presence in Beirut. To the contrary, it only served to lend them credibility: friends of his and Bobo's from the old days had been in the business of knowing such things. It had, however, been sixteen years since Bobo had been stationed in Beirut, since Gaspar had joined him there for that brief holiday.

"Which friend?" Gaspar inquired.

"Forjieh. Atrash Forjieh's boy." The man whispered the answer, glancing at Sarah as if the trust implicit in his willingness to confide the name extended to her too.

The other man made a quick survey of the sullen travelers as Forjieh's name was mentioned. A better-safe-than-sorry survey, a you-never-know-who-is-listening survey.

Things in Beirut still being what they were—risky, in flux—Atrash's son could not leave his car, the man explained. So would Gaspar accompany them? Atrash the younger had not had the opportunity to speak to anyone about Bobo, about his father, about the loss they had all suffered upon Bobo's and his father's sudden deaths three years earlier.

The Ford pulls off the road at a point high up the side of a hill. The top man turns to face Gaspar and says in accented French, "Nice view, what?" His intonation is heavy with sarcasm. His eyes, large and black, shine brightly. But for the thinness of his lips and the way the upper covers part of the lower when at rest, he would be handsome.

The view is indeed nice. They are looking west, onto the Mediterranean. The blue sea is speckled with flakes of sunlight, small patches of gold that dance to the rhythm of the gentle waves beneath them. All the long way to its vaporous vanishing point, far off in the west, the sea is open, unhindered, in the way that evokes in men the certain knowledge that the soul is real, that freedom is possible.

17

"My brother Claude used to see a nice view from his house," the top man says. When Gaspar's face betrays his incomprehension, he elaborates, "Harouni. My brother was Claude Harouni. You and your pal Bobo blew him and his family to bits sixteen years ago."

They drive on higher into the hills, then through a rusted wrought iron gate which is opened for them by two armed men. They drive past a house, whitewashed, iridescent in the early afternoon sun, and onto a dirt track that stops at a shed made of corrugated metal once shiny, now dulled by time.

Gaspar is taken out of the car. One of the young men clamps a rough hand around his wrist and pulls him through the shed's door, a sheet of metal framed by roughly hewn wooden planks. The shed's vertical center supporting beam, a steel I-beam, is anchored in a concrete cone embedded in the damp earthen floor. To this, the second man fastens a chain about a meter and a half long with a shackle at one end. The man holding Gaspar's wrist forces him to sit, placing his free hand on top of Gaspar's head and pressing downwards hard. Gaspar's muscles comply even as his comprehension lags and he drops abruptly to the dirt floor. They fasten the shackle around his ankle, over his pants leg.

Harouni enters the shed. He scrutinizes the arrangements, tugs at the chain.

Gaspar grunts in pain, then blurts out at Harouni a single word: "When?"

The question's tone and finality leave no room for doubt as to its sense: Gaspar is asking to be told his time of execution.

Harouni's glare turns indignant, as if by posing the question Gaspar has presumed too much. Why should I tell you? his expression says, You will die in my own good time.

Resigned, Gaspar asks for pencils and paper. The request somehow breaks through to Harouni, altering the prevailing rhythm in the shed. The implicit daring and optimism seem to touch Harouni's goodwill.

"What will you write?" Harouni guffaws and turns to his men to make certain they are getting the full measure of this entertaining hostage.

"Thoughts for my wife. Perhaps you will let her have them one day."

"Which wife?" Harouni demands.

A chill runs through Gaspar. At that moment he understands fully the fierceness of Harouni's desire for vengeance. To have known that Gaspar had married twice, known that he would be passing through Beirut airport, has required focus, dedication. Gaspar is reminded of Bobo's similar dedication to his own pursuits.

18

Harouni speaks briefly in Arabic to his men. They leave the shed. Harouni lights a cigarette and stares at Gaspar as he smokes it down. One of the men returns with several sheets of paper and a sharpened pencil, both of which he hands to Gaspar.

Gaspar searches for a suitable place on the earthen floor. He chooses a spot where a ray of sunlight falls, no thicker than the pencil he has just been handed, with glowing bits of dust floating in it. He places himself so that the light illuminates the paper.

Suddenly Harouni lunges at him and yanks the pencil from his fingers. He tests the pencil's point against his thumb, strolls over to the shed's wall, places the point against the wall and scratches back and forth several times. Then he tests the point once more.

He hands the pencil back to Gaspar. "So you don't do bad things to yourself," he explains.

The executioner's tenderness, muses Gaspar.

Harouni and his man leave. Gaspar listens as a lock is snapped shut on the door's other side. The light that had come through the open door is gone now. Only his writing ray and a few more like it drill though, shards of clarity in a murky darkness.

He huddles in this light-perforated darkness and soon falls into a depression so oppressive that it makes his breathing fall shallow. He succumbs to a paroxysm of self-blame, blame for everything from that first time when as a child of six or seven he had obeyed Bobo, to all the ensuing years of compliance, to his failed marriage to Laura, to his complacency at the airport. He berates himself for having married Laura in the first place, for having remained with her as long as he had, for not having made their marriage work. Others would have, he silently howls at himself. You couldn't, but others would have.

He is rescued from his abyss by an image of Sarah. Her name and face become a gentle but irresistible crane that fastens onto the scruff of his neck and lifts him until he is clear of his black mood. He is back in the reality of the gloomy prison shed.

Now he attempts a rational evaluation of his situation. He examines the shackle and chain, the I-beam. He smirks as he tells himself, with his architect's perspicacity, that all are sound and would resist all means he could invent to challenge their structural integrity.

He switches to considering Harouni, to pondering why Harouni didn't have him shot immediately. Perhaps, he postulates, it's because Harouni wishes to exact a ransom for him! That's it! As soon as Sarah pays up, Harouni will let him go.

Then the heart-wrenching thought lances through his mind that both will be true: that Harouni will collect, then kill him. Just as quickly, he dismisses the thought: Sarah will be too smart to let that happen, too wise for this Maronite brigand.

Maronite. He remembers Naama, whom he'd met very briefly during that long-ago visit to Beirut. Perhaps, he now thinks, he ought to have known back then—well, if not just then, later when he found out that it had indeed been Bobo and Forjieh who had done in Claude and Naama and their children. Perhaps he ought to have known then that Bobo didn't play by the rules he had claimed to follow, that someone capable of arranging the killing of his lover, as Bobo had done, didn't accept any rules. That the first rule of Bobo's and his world had been to disregard the rules—for the good of the cause, of course. "We break laws so that France can remain a place of order and civility," Bobo had explained.

It had been Forjieh who told him about Harouni's birthday party. After Bobo had left SEDCE, and SEDCE ceased being SEDCE, after they'd gone into business together, Bobo suggested that they bring in a Lebanese chap he'd known, worked with, and trusted for years, Atrash Forjieh by name. Bobo arranged for Gaspar and Forjieh to meet over lunch so that Gaspar could assess the candidate. The idea was that Forjieh would represent their business in Middle Eastern countries where they themselves could not—due to time constraints, they were likely to spend most of their time with their client in Baghdad. The business, Bobo pointed out, ought to have clients other than Saddam, if only for the sake of appearances.

Forjieh turned out to be a small, pleasant person, over-dressed in a manner that hinted at a yearning to appear grander than his physical dimension permitted. His double-breasted light-blue blazer was of an imposing cut, too little waist, too much chest, with golden buttons that would have done an admiral's uniform proud. He wore a crimson and silver tie and soft grey slacks that flared at the bottom.

When Forjieh noticed Gaspar's gaze resting on the blazer's buttons he smiled and pointed out that they were made of eighteen-carat gold. "If I have to bribe someone I just pick a button off my jacket and hand it over," he said with a grin.

During the lunch they discussed the job, its requirements, the territory Forjieh would cover. Forjieh sounded competent and eager—understandably, since his commissions could run into the millions. Forjieh insisted they drink Dom Perignon, not Gaspar's favorite.

Before long, and quite naturally, the conversation turned to Bobo.

Forjieh spoke about Bobo's regard for Gaspar which, Forjieh said, evidenced itself continuously. There was a time, before Gaspar had gotten used to the Middle Eastern propensity for hyperbolic and ornate speech, when this sort of thing would have embarrassed him. Now he only smiled and thanked Forjieh.

Then Forjieh turned to his own ties to Bobo. He became sentimental. He recalled for Gaspar how Bobo had helped him restore his family's honor at a time when enemies back home had all but erased the Forjieh name. How this stranger from France had come through, extended a helping hand and made it possible to set things right.

How had Bobo done this? Gaspar asked.

At the time, Forjieh explained, Bobo had been an attaché stationed in Beirut while he, Forjieh, was in hiding in France. Bobo had contacted him and offered him the opportunity to settle the score with the Harounis (may the earth spit out their bones).

By lunch's end Gaspar had learned new aspects of what had taken place at Claude's birthday party. He had of course known about the slaughter. Bobo had told him at the time and there had been accounts in the press. Bobo had described it as the outcome of a Maronite blood feud, a case of those living by the sword dying by it. It was a pity, he'd said, about Naama.

Evening falls, the sun retracts its slender emissaries to the shed. Gaspar lies on the fast-cooling earth, tucked into himself, his hands, pressed between his thighs, clasped as if in prayer. Every bit of exposed skin is cold, the shackle radiates cold into his ankle. He shivers and tears well in his eyes, but he does not retrieve his hands from their nest to wipe them away. He heaves himself over and searches for the places in the wall where the sun had earlier come through, hoping to see into the night beyond, to glimpse anything at all but the darkness that now envelopes him, but there is nothing. At least the futile search serves to point out to him that it is possible, if only for brief spells, to forget his numbing discomfort.

Deep self-reproach denies him sleep. He harangues himself. He ought long ago, at the beginning of their relationship, told Sarah about Bobo and the Harounis. Now she will find out for herself in a way that will sour her heart, that will convince her that Gaspar has been loyal all the while to another of Bobo's sanctimonious lies. How stupid that he had kept this from her, even after all the rest became known.

Sleep comes on the sly, mysteriously, without his willing it.

21

Gaspar is awakened by the sound of a key being turned in the lock. It is just barely a new day. He attempts to sit up but fails, his body refusing to obey him. He is rigid from the night's distorted sleep, from having lain in an envelope of damp frost. His bladder is stabbing at him from within, and he says as much to whoever is at the door. When no answer comes, he painfully flips himself to face the door.

Silhouetted against the pure blue sky, the shrubbery and trees of the exterior world, stands one of Harouni's young men. An M16 is slung on his shoulder, and in his hands is a steaming saucepan. The man steps inside and places the saucepan in front of Gaspar.

"Piss. I need to piss," Gaspar says insistently.

The man looks on and doesn't betray the slightest sign of comprehension.

Gaspar reaches down for his groin, cups his hands, and makes a motion and sound to illustrate and underline his need.

This angers the man, and too late Gaspar realizes that his pantomime is taken for an attempted slight, for a depiction of his opinion of his jailer. Abruptly the man bends down, reclaims the saucepan, and splashes the hot liquid it holds onto Gaspar.

Gaspar urinates standing at the end of his tether. The shed takes on the odor of a movie house men's room.

Of the five sheets of paper Gaspar has been given, two are soaked by the overly sensitive young man's emptying of Gaspar's intended breakfast. Gaspar lays these out on the floor to dry. During the remainder of the day he moves them around so that light, and possibly drying warmth, fall onto them.

Gaspar writes for Sarah, not to her; he doubts she will ever read his words. He thinks long and hard before he writes—there is only so much paper, so much pencil.

"As I consider my life, I realize that for much of the time I did not own it, that it belonged to Bobo, and that he has a claim on it still. I wonder whether this belated realization qualifies as redemption. Was it you who told me that redemption only postpones the inevitable?"

Chapter Three

The irony was that, dead as he was, Bobo still pulled strings, reached out from the past and imprisoned Gaspar, made him hapless and unknowing in this godawful tin-walled prison. The pity was that Gaspar had never severed the strings when he might have.

Ten years ago, Gaspar thinks, early summer. He calculates carefully: June of 1981, a Thursday afternoon. (In the shed Gaspar is developing a mania for precision—there are forty-seven perforations in the metal wall, so many millimeters apart. Why this particular distribution? Where is the highest point on the earthen floor?—as if with precision he can defeat his new and oppressive circumstance, as if in precision he retains his self.)

On that Thursday afternoon Bobo called him into his office and had him put on an ear phone to listen to a tape cassette played on a small, hand-held Sony recorder. He heard two male voices discussing Osirak. One voice was French, the other spoke with an accent Gaspar couldn't place. He glanced at Bobo, who brought a finger to his lips, then scribbled on a sheet of paper the word "Juif," and underlined it. Gaspar understood that the second man was Israeli—Bobo had long ago taken up that penchant of their Arab friends for referring to Israelis as Jews.

The Israeli was making the case for France not to rebuild Tamuz 17, Osirak, Iraq's nuclear facility which Israel's airforce had three months earlier obliterated in a spectacular bombing raid. Osirak had been built by France, an early and pivotal gesture in her relations with Iraq.

Saddam, the Israeli argued, had no purpose for Osirak other than to construct nuclear weapons, no use for such weapons other than to terrorize his enemies: Israel foremost, but also Iran, the Saudis, and others. And when this inevitably happened, France too would suffer.

The Frenchman, whose voice sounded familiar to Gaspar, was sympathetic. He spoke of his determination to forestall another holocaust, of the immorality of helping Saddam in this endeavor.

Then the Israeli switched his argument to grounds other than Israel's interest, to wit: that if Saddam had the bomb he would surely use it against Iran (the war between Iran and Iraq was then in its first year) and thus render Iran's oil useless to the world, including France. "Sir, the previous president pretends to accept Saddam's claim that Osirak is for research. If that reactor is for research then my grandmother is a bus."

The Frenchman laughed briefly. He said he would do his utmost for all concerned, after which there was a long silence. Gaspar glanced at Bobo to see whether something had gone wrong with the recording. Bobo shook his head, indicating more to come.

From the tape came the sound of someone clearing his throat. It was the Israeli. "Excuse me, sir, I do not wish to sound impertinent, but when you were a candidate for your office and we spoke, you promised not to rebuild Tamuz 17. It sounds to me now as if you are less certain that you will be able to keep your promise."

A third voice interjected to say that the president's schedule made it necessary to end this meeting, that another would be scheduled soon. The conversation ended with an assurance by the Frenchman that he would not be the one to rebuild Saddam's reactor.

Bobo switched off the Sony. He and Gaspar left the building together and went for a stroll on a busy street.

"That was Mitterand, you know," Bobo said. Immediately Gaspar matched the voice he'd heard on the tape with Francois Mitterand's puckish face— Mitterand, leader of France's Socialist Party who had in May 1980 won the presidency.

"The Jew is Peres, Shimon Peres, another Red," Bobo continued. "You heard them. He's going to pull the rug out from under us. Before long he'll make it impossible for us to go on with Saddam, and without Saddam France will go down the tubes. Which is of course what he and his cabal want."

"You're raving, Bobo," Gaspar said. "And just how did you get this recording?"

He received an annoyed look. "How does that matter?" Bobo demanded tersely, which meant that Gaspar had touched a raw spot.

"Spying on the Socialists will sink you, Bobo," Gaspar admonished. "Domestic spying is a great big no-no, you know this to be the law, Bobo. If you are ever found out it will mean a couple of years of unpaid vacation on Devil's Island for you."

"Cut the crap, Gaspar," Bobo demanded. "Did you hear clearly what I said? This little man of the Left is going to ruin everything. If he indeed goes on to deny Saddam his reactor it will mean curtains for us. You're not quitting now, I want you to stay on, I need you."

"Not a chance in the world, pal," Gaspar said.

"You don't understand, Gaspar, this Mitterand is going to close down our shop. He's going to dismantle SEDCE."

"You're inventing things, Bobo. Fibbing doesn't become you."

24

"Tell you what, my high-minded friend, you stay on another year, just one more year. It'll go by faster than you can say 'Bobo is a liar.' And if by the end of it the prediction I'm about to make fails to materialize—to its last letter—I'll let you sleep with Deadeye."

"I don't want to sleep with Deadeye, she'll shoot me if I don't perform. So what is going to happen within this year?"

"Just this: the little Red man in the Élysée Palace will set out to dismantle our Firm. He'll remake it and rename it, and France will have a counterintelligence operation run by pinkos and pansies."

"You're raving, Bobo. I'm not staying on, I've had enough. I've done plenty, you've said so yourself. I want to rest, I want to sit at my drafting table and draw up boat designs, I want to sleep with my wife more than once every fortnight. I'm sick of going to Baghdad, of Iraqi food, of chills running down my spine every time some stranger walks too close to my table at a restaurant. I want to be able to hold conversations on subjects other than the wiring on this rapid-fire cannon or the blind spot on that radar."

A familiar expression came over Bobo's face, the look of a dreamer of perfect dreams, of flawless visions, of the man from whose dictionary the word "doubt" had been omitted. The look Gaspar had known since forever, since their boyhood days on the riverbank at Belle Marais.

"The same friend who provided me with the tape you just heard also told me what I will tell you now," Bobo said, sincere as a preacher closing in on a would-be convert. He grinned. "I too would like to rest, you know. I too would like to sleep with your wife more than once every two weeks and go live at Belle Marais and walk my lands, only I cannot, and neither can you. I need you with me right now every bit as much as I did when I first talked to you about becoming an HC. I give you my word on this."

"So what did your informative friend tell you that will cause me to forego what I intend to do with the rest of my life?"

"The Socialists have drawn up secret contingencies for dismantling SEDCE, redoing it top to bottom in their image. This isn't just fanciful talk, Gaspar. Want to know what they'll call this...whatever it will become? 'Direction Générale de la Sécurité Extérieure.' DGSE, Gaspar, get it?"

"Sure I get it, Bobo. Mitterand is pissed off, tired of being treated like a Fifth Columnist by you and SEDCE."

"Undoubtedly he'll get much better treatment from the director he intends to appoint in my stead. You ready for this? Gilbert Valancien."

Despite himself, Gaspar was taken aback. Valancien had been director of France's railway system in the last Socialist government. "Surely you're joking!"

"Not a syllable of humor here, Gaspar; dismally serious. Gilbert Valancien. Eminently qualified, don't you think?"

Gaspar's incredulity persisted. SEDCE was France's eyes and ears in the world. It made no sense that the nation's leadership, whatever its political colors, would play fast and loose with so essential a component of its national interest. He continued to challenge Bobo, to argue that such a thing was hardly possible. SEDCE was beyond party politics, a sacred cow if ever there was one, and the nation would not stand for tampering with it.

"Tell you what," Bobo said. He had resumed his air of missionary zeal. "Take me up on my offer. Let's wait and see what these guys will and will not dare. Stick with me and then we'll see, ok? If things go otherwise, if they leave the Firm alone, I will personally paint your ship's architect shingle."

His passion flowed on, the desperate passion of a man whose mistress is being courted by another. "You don't know these people as I do, Gaspar, you think you do, but you don't. They're zealots; they intend to castrate the army, turn it into a troop of show soldiers, ushers for their May Day parades. They mean to cut back on shipments to Saddam. Gaspar, God and you know I have nothing against Jews, but this man Mitterand is surrounded by them. The Élysée Palace will soon become a veritable synagogue under him. His Jewish advisors have their own agenda: Saddam is the enemy of Israel, therefore their enemy. Well, I won't permit anyone to tamper with this relationship, not while I live. Oh, Mitterand and his gang will camouflage their intentions with exalted words, the Reds always do. They'll say that France ought not to profit from blood money, they'll concoct horror stories, they'll besmirch us and our friends. Their stable of intellectual whores will eloquently decry our misdeeds on television and in their rags. And you and I will know what they'll really be up to." Bobo rammed an angry fist into an open palm. "And you and I and ours will not permit them to get away with it."

It was nearly a year later on an April evening in 1982 that Bobo was proven right.

He brought Gaspar for drinks to a restaurant owned by a former honorable correspondent nicknamed Tintin. There they sipped their whiskies and listened as two SEDCE section heads sputtered their bilious discontent because SEDCE, their beloved Firm, was about to be massacred.

That was the word they used—massacred. SEDCE was to become DGSE, Valancien its new Director. Valancien, a man expert at drawing up train schedules and at wining and dining travel agents. The only sort of agents he knew his way around, observed one of the two.

"I thought you ought to hear it from someone besides me," Bobo said.

Gaspar was overwhelmed by a powerful indignation, the fury of a man who has been out hunting and returns to find that his cabin has been torched.

He had turned over his life to Bobo when he'd agreed to become an Honorable Correspondent. He was swept up in the honor of having been asked, the pleasure and importance of being part of a great and good secret. He would be a member of the SEDCE's cadre of far-flung private operatives, pure operatives, not sullied spies like those in the pay of, say, MI6 or the CIA or the KGB and GRU.

Nothing like them, Bobo had stated emphatically, his voice thick with derision. Nothing honorable about those, indeed not. Those others purchased harlots' favors, put Judases on their payrolls. Gaspar and his fellow Honorable Correspondents worked out of love for France, not a single coin crossed their palm, never a numbered account was opened on their behalf. Agents got paid, operatives got paid, Honorable Correspondents spied for love. HCs were decent folk—a schoolmarm, for instance, in South Africa, a woman from Nice who taught high school French to the children of the ruling class. As coincidence would have it, one of her students was the son of a general officer in the South African defense forces. One day, for example, the son told her, his favorite teacher, that his dad was traveling on business to Taiwan. The teacher HC passed the information along to her SEDCE handler back in Paris at the headquarters on the Bvd. Mortier, the information was collated, cross-referenced, put to use. Meaning was made of it.

Another HC owned a button-making factory in Argentina where his family had immigrated from Lyon a hundred years earlier, bringing their button-making skills with them. He was a substantial person, cultured and respectable, a pillar of the community. When a uniforms-maker ordered brass and other buttons from him, buttons for such-and-such quantity of military uniforms, this information too ended up on the Bvd. Mortier.

Every bit counted. France was a solitary traveler, going its own way and therefore needing to know about all whom it encountered along the road. HCs helped the motherland from their disparate stations all along its demanding course.

27

Gaspar became an HC, but with a difference. Unlike the others, who had a trade, a profession, to begin with, he took his on at Bobo's behest: he became a dealer in naval vessels, frigates, destroyers, patrol boats, fast missile boats, and their attendant electronics and weaponry. As a matter of fact, his trade ended up making him very wealthy, but that had been unavoidable. As it turned out, his wealth, too, proved useful to Bobo.

Bobo had been given his walking papers. Mitterand, who had been forced to tolerate him for a full year after taking office, finally felt sufficiently strong to bring their uneasy coexistence to a close.

Gaspar spent moving day in Bobo's office, leaning up against an ornate mahagony file cabinet, a gift to Bobo from a Middle Eastern counterpart. Perversely, he had enjoyed the moment, enjoyed that Bobo once again had been proved right.

That it had taken Mitterand a full year to implement his plan had been a function of France's military leadership's distrust of him and of the promise he'd had to make them to keep Bobo on for a while. Things were too delicate abroad, they'd explained, this was the wrong stream in which to change horses. And Mitterand, nothing if not a patient man, one who had waited a very long time to become president, understood and accepted. Probably he understood only too well that it was the wrong moment, when he was about to go to war with France's economic elite. Leading banks would be nationalized, major industrial concerns were on his targets list. He would get to de Bossier and his crypto-fascist friends in the army soon enough.

But once the year was up, so was Bobo's tenure. As Gaspar watched him pack, together they laid out their future. Retirement was forgotten.

In the stifling shed, the conversation of that fateful day echoes in Gaspar's mind.

A ship was needed, Bobo said, a very large container ship. "Something around five or six thousand twenty foot equivalent units" he explained, and grinned because he was showing he'd gone to the trouble of educating himself about container ships.

Right there, Gaspar, he now jeers at himself, right there, right there was the when of it, was when you ought to have cut loose, when you ought to have walked. He clasps his hands, fingers locked against fingers, his fury at having been wrong so many times expressing itself in the force of the grip.

I could have gotten out, gotten away. I could have refused to go with those two at the airport to see Atrash Forjieh's son. If I had gotten out, I wouldn't have known Atrash Forjieh. Who was I trying to impress, anyway? I ought to have said to them, Go away, you and your Forjiehs. Slime, that's what he was, why should I want to see his son?

"That's a leviathan you're talking about, Bobo," Gaspar said. "What on earth do you need with a ship that size?"

Gaspar shifts his place on the shed's floor so as to keep up with his shifting light source. He hears Bobo's voice clearly, the voice disputing his recollections.

"You are having a bad time just now, Gaspar," Bobo's voice points out patiently. "I can't blame you for being angry with me. I'm sorry for what has happened to you, but this too is the price we pay for serving. Mine was temination. You, my friend, are at least still breathing."

Don't bullshit me, Bobo. Serving whom? France? Or France according to Bobo.

"France according to us, not just me, us, from day one, since you and I first started to speak of such things, pal. People were out to turn our France into an ugly little place where excellence would be a sin, ambition a felony. Where the glories of the past would be skewed into the perversions and follies of the ruling classes. This little man in the Élysée Palace who fired me was Red through and through, a proponent of the economics of envy, a founding member of the society for the promotion of class warfare. Fuck him and his, Gaspar! Never, not while I was alive, would he get away with it!"

Bobo's voice rises, fills the shed. The dead, it seems, are capable of reciting in loud, jolting voices.

"Have you and I, Gaspar, struggled all these years, from Beirut to the Safari Club, from the Shah's secret medical exam to where we bested all the others doing business in the Gulf, for nothing?"

Liar, liar, liar Bobo, self-serving liar, master of selective recall. "You and I, Gaspar!" You used to say 'you and I' a lot. As if your Deadeye didn't exist, as if you hadn't turned others who did your bidding to fishmeal on the Gulf! I had nothing to do with their deaths, with your bloody birthday in Beirut, with that poor woman at the Gallery Lafayette, nothing! That was all you. And about all the rest, I know things now, Bobo, no need to charm me. I was at best a spectator, a willing audience to your terrible brilliance. You told me what you wanted me to know only because you wanted me along, because you were lonely. Brilliant and lonely, that was you, so you said "you and I, Gaspar." You were lonely because you always believed you knew best. Being best necessarily means being alone, Bobo. You told me so yourself.

Then to endorse his furious thesis Gaspar invokes Sarah, Sarah the wise, the dispassionate, the loving.

She liked you, Bobo, you know she did, and you liked her. And she saw as I do that you were lonely, that you lied, that you thought you alone knew best. She said so at the time.

Gaspar had done much on SEDCE's behalf. He had lectured ignorant arms shoppers on France's sophisticated naval electronics and on hulls that best suited their needs, his credentials in the field going a long way towards convincing waverers that a French-made Thompson radar was superior to an English Racal or an American GE. And when the task had been to supply a captive client, a SEDCE stooge who had no option other than to buy French, he still labored at making the man feel he was that proverbial customer who is always right, who was getting to pick and choose.

As he visited the word's navies and its ports and bases in his capacity as a prominent Belgian dealer, as he met his brother merchants and client defense ministers and captains and admirals, front-line sea soldiers and submariners, he made mental notes. He memorized names, counted ships, guns, harbors, and docks. And he listened. Much was to be gathered from listening, and all that he gathered, remembered, sketched, surmised, counted, was recorded in the proper and useful files at SEDCE.

Before and after Saddam attacked Iran, Gaspar was the Iraqi's second-favorite naval expert, the first being Saddam himself. Bobo had first introduced them as one introduces one's oldest son: "When I need to understand about ships I turn to my pal Gaspar here, Mr. President," he'd said, and patted Gaspar's back. Gaspar had smiled in embarrassed confirmation.

"Then so shall I, my friend," Saddam replied.

Saddam made Gaspar his consultant, his conversation-mate about naval warfare, a field about which Saddam was even less informed than he was about land and air warfare.

As it turned out, naval weapons were the least category of France's military trade with Iraq, lagging far behind aircraft, missiles of all sorts, tanks, armored vehicles, electronics. Yet when Saddam turned to Italy for his first substantial naval order away from his traditional Soviet supplier, he retained Gaspar to oversee the contract.

Saddam used to engage Gaspar in theoretical naval discussions:

30

where was Iran likely to use its Wellington and Winchester hovercraft? Ought Iraq to have some of its own? No, Gaspar countered, these are toys full of show and bluster. There are better ways to get around the shallow waters of the Shatt al-Arab.

On occasion, Gaspar argued with the ruler, which Saddam appeared to enjoy, probably because he was being treated as an equal by the expert. Once Gaspar heatedly opposed Saddam's choice of an Italian-made rapid-fire cannon for the ships he had ordered ("Sir, it's no good being called 'rapid' if it won't fire when asked to"). Saddam of course went ahead, and the guns of course proved a headache. But Gaspar's consultant's fees were paid anyway, and on time, which was more than many of the others doing business with Saddam could say.

Soon after Gaspar was made an HC, Bobo sent him his first client, an official of the Ivory Coast police in search of a patrol boat. Later, dining with Bobo (this was before his marriage to Laura, when he and Bobo spent virtually all their time together), Gaspar asked the patrol boat's purpose.

Bobo turned on his generous smile, at once mocking and concerned, and posed a question in return: Did Gaspar really wish to know? Did he realize that knowing might prove burdensome, that the information might alter the way Gaspar felt and behaved, that others might sense his knowledge and attempt to force it from him?

Then, smiling still, Bobo told him the patrol boat's purpose, which was straightforward enough. The rule, though, had been established. Gaspar learned what Bobo chose to tell him. Otherwise he accepted that it was best not to know.

"I thought it best for you not to know," Bobo said quietly after Gaspar's lunch with Atrash Forjieh, that lunch after Bobo had left SEDCE and he and Gaspar were in business for themselves. "I did what I had to do. I didn't personally shoot anyone at Claude's party and I certainly didn't know Naama and the children would die. I only wanted Claude out of the way and so did Atrash, so we got together on it. I'm sorry you had to find out, Atrash was wrong to tell you. I suppose he assumed you knew. Just goes to show I too make mistakes. I was at war then, Gaspar, I'm at war now, SEDCE is always at war, always, always. I take no pleasure in it, I didn't render this world as it is. I only mean to try to save France from being devoured by it. Claude Harouni was a greedy, stubborn bastard. For him, the gun deal with the PLO was just another sale, to me it was an essential stepping stone to a relationship with a rising star in the Levant. I'm sorry about Naama, truly." He covered his face with his hands and wept, and that had been good enough for Gaspar.

They'd gone into business for themselves because the little Red man in the Élysée Palace intended to keep from Iraq certain goods that it required. They established Boulevard Consultants because Bobo was not about to stand by and watch Mitterand's Jews sour France's best-ever business relationship. That was why, Bobo explained, they needed the gargantuan container ship. It would be used for deliveries all the way from the manufacturers to certain ports in the Gulf. If this President and his cabal intended to deny France's great friend in the Gulf what he required to win, then Bobo, his people, and Gaspar would step into the breach, would deliver to Iraq what it required.

Still Gaspar had been dubious. No man despised France's Left more than himself, that was a fact, his father's legacy to him. But wasn't the new President on record as being committed to the Arabs in their fight with Iran? Hadn't he said so in his recent Cairo speech?

Yes, he had said so, and yes, he was a liar. He would say anything to help him retain the office from which he would eventually behead France and give it a new head in his image.

After the tumultuous dinner with the section heads, Gaspar went home to Belgium, to Laura, where he told her the news and griped some about the ever-demanding Bobo. That was expected, that he would gripe and that Laura would offer little sympathy. That she would uphold her adored pal Bobo, telling Gaspar he was the most fortunate of men to have such a friend.

A few days later, Gaspar began the search for a suitable container ship.

To Sarah he writes with his dulled pencil: "Besides, had I then refused Bobo, I would never have met you. You would have practiced your wiles on some other fortunate victim."

32

Chapter Four

In the shed, two weeks pass under the same harsh conditions as on the first day. Then without warning there is a significant alteration for the better.

One morning Harouni enters bearing the saucepan of sweet, hot tea that has represented Gaspar's only meal until evening when he would be given raw vegetables—a cucumber or turnip, a kohlrabi, a few carrots, a couple of tomatoes—along with a pinch of salt wrapped in a bit of newspaper and half a pita.

Harouni hands Gaspar the saucepan and when Gaspar extends his hand Harouni bends down and scoops up Gaspar's letters. He departs with the letters and one of the militiamen enters, bringing with him a folding military cot and a brown wool blanket. He sets up the cot and drops the blanket on the floor next to Gaspar. He unlocks Gaspar's shackle and leads him out of the shed to a spot behind it, where he stands and watches as Gaspar relieves himself. Then he returns him to the shed.

An older man in tattered clothes and unlaced shoes, decidedly not one of Harouni's militia, comes into the shed pushing a wheelbarrow filled with fine yellow sand. He goes off again and returns with two buckets of water. The old man proceeds to clean up two weeks' worth of excrement from the shed's floor. That done, he spreads the sand in a circle around the supporting I-beam.

Later Harouni returns with the letters he has confiscated, along with more writing paper and pencils. "You will be in plenty of hot water when your wife reads these," he observes laughingly, one man offering to another good-natured advice about women's propensity for jealousy.

"I've gotten used to being doused in hot stuff. Your man broke me in on the practice as soon as I got here, what was it, two weeks ago?" Gaspar retorts wryly. He considers a moment, then adds, "Besides, at this juncture I would far prefer a scolding by Sarah to being here. Nothing personal."

Gaspar concludes that Sarah, or someone, has managed to establish contact with Harouni, that a hint of a ransom payment is in the air, that he has therefore taken on a value missing before. This has to be the answer. He glimpses the light of hope for the first time since leaving Sarah at the airport.

In fact, a message inviting Gaspar's kidnappers to speak up, whoever they are, has been circulating in Beirut and has been transmitted to Paz, with whom Sarah has been in contact.

Harouni's friendly admonition about getting into hot water has presumably been prompted by Gaspar's recounting in the letters his brief affair with a ship's broker's assistant in the port of La Spezia outside Genoa. Her name was Agatha, and she was pretty and likable.

La Spezia was the third port Gaspar had visited in his search for Bobo's container ship, and there he found it: the <u>Hydra</u>, a German-built, forty-nine-hundred TEUs vessel with a thirty-eight-meter beam, length of two hundred seventy-five meters, draft of twelve meters. It could carry sixteen rows of containers abreast above deck and fourteen below; it also had two state-of-the-art gantry cranes and superb electronics.

Agatha had deftly and discreetly handled the negotiations on his behalf. She'd appeared to take pleasure in the bargaining, to share with him her pride in her accomplishment, and had suggested they celebrate when the deal was done, and so they had. He'd spent two days with her at the Cipriani in Venice—a honeymoon without prelude or aftermath.

After taking possession of the vessel, Gaspar had it ferried to a Yugoslav port and its name changed to <u>Twanee</u>, a Carib Indian word that stuck in his mind from a visit to the French West Indies.

"It wasn't that my escapades with Agatha and others were without meaning," Gaspar wrote, "for even fleeting encounters can be visited by moments of love, tenderness, passion, abandon. Only these affairs of mine were demarcated, like meals with strictly timed beginning and endings. When it was time to return to Laura, I was left sated but no more than that. Until I met you. You left me famished. (For this bless the traitor Chardeau"—had he actually written "traitor"? He erased the word— "bless Chardeau for having set you on Bobo's trail in the first place.")

"When I studied at MIT, one of my professors used to tease me about glib European mores—'hypocrisy with a fetching accent,' she called them. I always felt she was at once disapproving and envious. When I was married to Laura I thought it did no harm to chase and I assumed she felt and did the same. That's life, I thought. Certainly that had been life as I'd seen it in my parents' household, and for that matter in Bobo's. But meeting you changed me. I only wish I'd changed sooner. But then you probably wouldn't have remained near me for as long as you did, I wouldn't have been the man you suspected of knowing Bobo's juicy secrets. You would have done a different article about another mystery man, and that would have been that."

Chapter Five

After waiting fifteen minutes in the passenger lounge at Beirut airport for Gaspar to return from speaking to Atrash Forjieh's son, Sarah becomes concerned. She walks out of the terminal building to look for him, but sees nothing but travelers coming and going and a number of armed men whom she assumes are guards and who regard her with great curiosity.

She stands for a while looking at the grimy, broken walkway leading into the terminal, at the guards who lounge against parked cars, cigarette in one hand, assault rifle in the other. Their eyes squint as they watch her; they make comments to each other, smirk, and chuckle.

Out there alone she begins to feel the fear of an abandoned child much like, could she have known, Gaspar's fear in Harouni's Ford that is at that moment carrying him to his prison shed.

She walks up to a couple of the armed men, who slide off their perch on a car and stand at near attention as she addresses them. She describes Gaspar: not quite tall, broad-shouldered, dark blond hair, hazel eyes, wearing a khaki photographer's jacket and jeans, beige hiking boots, perhaps sunglasses.

No, they haven't seen any such man. One shouts over to a colleague still slouching on his chosen car fender. No, he hasn't seen Gaspar either.

Even as she feels herself slipping into panic she notes how they have altered once she confided her problem, once they've seen how distressed she is. By speaking to them she has become more than just a pretty foreigner in a white and yellow cotton sweater and white slacks, a subject for lascivious conjecture and fantasy. They seem embarrassed at not being able to help.

She thanks them and walks back to stand closer to the entrance of the passenger terminal.

How could she not have been sharper earlier about the situation! She ought to have been more aware, more suspicious. How could she have accepted those men's slick routine in the passenger lounge? Where was her head? Still, it seems, in Kuwait. The trip there had left both her and Gaspar drained, not only by the horrific scenes of Iraqi destruction, but because for both of them Iraq continuously evoked Bobo.

She brings her clenched fists to her mouth. Bobo! That has to be it! Every ounce of her considerable intuitive force flashes his name at her.

Wherever Gaspar is, whoever these men are who have taken him, it has something to do with Bobo.

She begins to think rationally. There is little she can accomplish here—she knows no one in Beirut and the British diplomatic representation in Lebanon is minimal and in any case ineffectual. Her best course is to continue on to London and try to sort things out from there.

In London she telephones Robin Colechester, the Sentinel's editor, from a Heathrow telephone booth. Colechester is immediately sympathetic and promises help, which he delivers. By the time she arrives at her Cresswell Gardens home, crazily hoping that she'll find Gaspar waiting for her on his favorite bench in the garden, reading the evening papers, there is a message from Colechester. He has arranged for her to meet early next morning with the Foreign Secretary.

The Foreign Secretary is also sympathetic, and transparently insincere. She is shown into his office by an assistant splendidly adept at the nuances of correct step and proper gesture. He walks behind her just so, steps ahead and to the side in time to open and hold the door for her.

The Secretary also excels at step and gesture. He comes out from behind his sizable desk and guides her, his open hand slightly touching the back of her upper arm, to a small, ornate table in the midst of his sumptuous office, where he offers tea and biscuits.

A dreadful thing to have happened, he says, an awful place, Beirut. Of course this business of people disappearing is hardly new, at this very moment British subjects are being held there. Perhaps now that the shooting has abated things will become easier, Beirut will make its way back to civility. Personally, though, he has his doubts. Too many disparate interests willing to pull the trigger.

Of course he will put the right people on notice about her husband's disappearance. He does not say who these "right people" are, thus signaling to her that they are people whose work and methods one does not speak about. He opines that this is a bit of very bad luck, the whole thing, and that the kidnappers will soon contact her or someone to demand money, or that one of theirs being held in Europe be released in exchange for Gaspar's freedom.

The Secretary's problem, made clear by his pained expression as he talks to her, is that Gaspar is not British. There is only so far he can go with this matter since Gaspar is, as Mr. Colechester has informed him, a Belgian subject.

Her periodic awareness that Gaspar is Belgian unfailingly startles Sarah. She has always considered him French, since that is his ancestry and he has lived his life as if a Frenchman. A pain as acute as a bone fracture shoots through her—the dreadful realization that Gaspar may have forfeited his life because others, too, think of him as French. Because he has been Bobo's friend, and therefore assumed to be French himself.

The Foreign Secretary reminds Sarah of someone—not a specific person, but the small group of polite, polished people who, with Deadeye, had been waiting for her and Gaspar in the living room at Belle Marais just after Bobo died. Just after Sarah and Gaspar had finally understood everything. The polite, polished people who had explained that while it was fine for Gaspar and her to understand, the world at large was not ready to do so, and would not be ready for, say, thirty or so years—whatever was the time period of an Official Secrets classification. (Did France even have such a classification? she'd wondered, and been told that the answer to that, too, was classified.) Throughout they had addressed her as Mrs. Tillinghast. That she had become Mrs. Bruyn was for some reason not yet acceptable to them.

Sarah shivers as she remembers the scene. She sees in her mind the expression on Deadeye's face as the smooth-talking officials delivered their pronouncement—a look of lethal endorsement.

The Foreign Secretary has thus tightened, as it were, the straps of deadly constraint by which she and Gaspar were bound at Belle Marais, where they were given the opportunity to live, albeit in silence—an opportunity not extended to others.

She is reduced to making small points to the Secretary: that Gaspar is in fact a resident of Britain, that he has lived in London as her husband for the past several years. She leaves unsaid that Gaspar likes his acquired English anonymity, London, their garden, his small boat design jobs. That even when he sinned in the past he was under the impression that he was doing righteous work.

The Secretary chats her up about her work. He is an admirer, being an investigative reporter must be ever so interesting, and working for Robin Colechester, what a good chap he is. They were at Magdalene together, read the Greeks.

Back at Cresswell Gardens she thinks furiously, sifting through the past, Gaspar's past, names and places, people he knew when he was an HC.

Paz.

Recalling his name brings her immediate and immense relief, as if a persistent ache has suddenly been expunged. Paz's name is in itself a solution, it is right. Paz is the one. He knows the Levant, he lives in it, he's known Gaspar forever. He likes Gaspar and did not like Bobo. And Paz too has served, has been a warrior in civvies.

She sits and ponders how to make contact. Paz is not someone they've kept up with. His name pops up once in a while when Gaspar reminisces...when he sent them an announcement of the birth of his first grandchild!

She dashes upstairs to Gaspar's study, to the shelf with a large tin that once held shortbread, but now is filled with postcards, magazine photographs of boats he likes, and finally a small envelope containing the announcement of Paz's grandchild. The return address reads: Kfar Ha'Vradim, Upper Galilee, Israel.

Chapter Six

If the nights are cold, the days are oppressively hot. While the blanket Gaspar has been given goes far to alleviate the cold, nothing can be done about the effects of the sun on the shed's metal walls. By midday the air in the shed has turned into the searing exhaust of an unseen giant engine with Gaspar the man forced to sit in its fiery path. The best he can do under the circumstances is to sleep.

On the evening of one such torrid day, during which Gaspar has slipped in and out of a sickly, sweat-soaked sleep that leaves him weak and dehydrated, the chimerical avenging Harouni walks in. He unlocks Gaspar's shackle and beckons him to follow.

Like a newborn colt on untried legs, Gaspar stands and trembles. Harouni, who has left the shed, returns to see what is keeping him. Once he grasps the reason, he looks at him with genuine puzzlement, as if Gaspar's frailty is not something he has counted possible.

The pleasure of being outside makes Gaspar lightheaded. He has to stop and lean against a tree and once again Harouni looks upon him with puzzlement. After a moment they continue.

Harouni leads Gaspar onto a small trail that peels off the main dirt road. They come to a gathering of cypresses, where the path slips between two trees to lead to a clearing at their center. Here a large boulder juts out from the earth, brown and spotted with moss. The boulder is striking, smooth and bulbous, its curves round and full. No sharp line or crease disrupts it, except that the top has flattened into a natural table.

"Our forefathers used to make sacrifices here, so the legend tells," Harouni says, with a certain evident pride of ownership. "We Maronites are of Phoenician origin, not at all Arabs, you know," he reassures Gaspar, and adds with the haste of a man anxious lest he misinform, "Of course we are Christians, not pagans like the Phoenicians."

His explanations are wasted on Gaspar, who has slipped into a dimension of delight from which he excludes Harouni and his self-conscious babble. Gaspar is relishing the evening, the scent of Cypress sap, a mélange of the world's smells that have been excluded from the shed.

"He was a pig, your friend Bobo," Harouni says, as if informing Gaspar of a fact only just come by.

Without reflection, Gaspar replies, "He was a difficult but a great man. He foresaw things others could not comprehend even after they happened."

Because they are now conversing, they have eased into a casual stance. They both lean against the boulder and look out into the moonless evening as they talk.

Harouni says, "My brother was also a great man. He had many businesses, he commanded our militias, many men obeyed him." As if spurred on by the truth of his own assertions, he says forcefully, "You tell me how your friend was so smart."

Gaspar considers, not so much what Harouni has demanded but his shifting tone and the underlying rage in that closing demand. He recognizes Harouni as a man continuously shuttling between ordinary discourse and searing anger. He remembers how Harouni had needlessly caused him pain by jerking the shackle around his ankle. He thinks of his own anger, which tends to flare, burn bright, and then be extinguished. Harouni's rage appears to be structural. The words about his brother had been ordinary, the ones about Bobo like lava combusting on reaching the surface of the earth.

An inner voice cautions Gaspar to respect Harouni's temper, to keep these thoughts to himself, to simply tell his tale and with it buy time.

"Do you know about the Safari Club?"

To his surprise, Harouni answers, "You mean the one at Mount Kenya?"

"Actually, the one I have in mind was named after it, but it had nothing to do with big game hunting. Well, it did, sort of. It was Bobo's big game."

Gaspar now sets out to fascinate, to awake in Harouni a craving that cannot be sated at a single sitting. (Like Scheherazade to Harouni's Caliph he thinks later, back in the shed, and chuckles. Even Harouni's name evokes that of Haroun el Rashid, Scheherezade's creator. Then he reminds himself that unlike el Rashid's protagonist he has no wish to remain in this place for anything like a thousand and one nights. Still, before falling asleep later he congratulates himself for having succeeded as well as he has.)

Gaspar unfurls the Safari Club tale at a flowing pace, easy about sharing what he knows, devoid of airs of superiority. Yet his composure is an artifice, a sham born of desperation. As he talks he is continuously aware that his survival rests in the hands of this one-man audience who at any second could decide that he'd had enough, that the time for blood was at hand.

At the outset, Gaspar fears most the moment of having to fix his tale in a time context relative to Bobo's days in Beirut. He dreads the mention of Bobo and Beirut in the same breath, lest this cause Harouni's rage to combust.

"As you undoubtedly know," Gaspar begins, "Bobo was much more than a Naval Attaché. He was in fact SEDCE's man in the area."

Harouni nods, he had indeed known. "My brother tried to be helpful to him in some of his operations," he says.

That he says no more spurs Gaspar on; he sees before him the hope of a licence to live. "When Bobo returned to Paris in late 1974," he continues, "he was promoted and put to work on the burning issue of the day..."

"Because he had done such a good job here," Harouni interrupts, somewhere between grim and sarcastic.

"France, Europe, indeed the whole industrialized world had been handed a huge problem back then. The price of petroleum had multiplied tenfold, a thousand percent. Mr. Harouni, can you imagine what effect this had?" Gaspar resumes, the skillful plasterer smoothing putty over a fissure to prevent it from becoming a rupture.

It had turned Paris, the City of Lights, dark. Gaspar crossed one of the Seine bridges just by the Louvre after the sun had set, the bridge's lamps were unlit, everything was dim and depressing. Once on the Left Bank he turned and walked toward Notre Dame and the Isle de la Cité beyond it. He was to sit in on an informal crisis management meeting at Bobo's place. The participants were associates and sympathizers of Bobo's from the military, the Foreign Ministry, and from Elf, France's petroleum monopoly, also the heads of a giant bank and of an equally imposing industrial outfit, SEDCE's head of Research Branch and its in-house psychologist, a specialist in group behavior whose topic that evening was France's citizenry.

Along his way Gaspar mused about the darkness imposed by the soaring price of petroleum, a darkness that had spread across Europe as governments struggled to cope with vastly greater expenses. He and all who walked the quay had always known night as merely the time zone that was electrically illuminated; the sun in the sky set and was replaced with a myriad of tiny artificial suns. Darkness made people appear less sure of themselves, caused them to move along a bit faster, bracing themselves as if the winds of winter were upon them, which they were not. Darkness stripped streets and buildings of a certain magnanimity, made them into places and objects of uncertainty, even menace. Gaspar hurried on to Bobo's place.

41

"Gentlemen, France is being made to atone for Yom Kippur," said the man from Elf, his play on words lost on several of the others present.

"What in the hell does that mean?" demanded General Georges, a former fighter pilot who had gone on to command France's fleet of Mirage IV strategic bombers.

"Pitou means that since the Israelis have managed to snatch victory from the jaws of defeat we are being made to suffer for it. Yom Kippur is the Jewish Day of Atonement. It was on Yom Kippur past that the Egyptians and Syrians launched their surprise attack on Israel, my dear general, only to be eventually turned back on the battlefield. So now the Arabs are furious because the Americans resupplied Israel during this Yom Kippur war, and we are all being made to pay; that was what Pitou meant, my dear general."

"We call it the October War," Harouni informs him dryly.

Gaspar nods and thanks him for the point of information.

"To put it simply," the banker said, "we are being bankrupted. We have been running the business that is France on the assumption that a barrel of oil will cost four or five dollars per forever. Well, we were wrong, it is now costing us forty per. Large problem, gentlemen, you see my point?"

"And it isn't as if we have available the time to try and fix things, to tinker with solutions. I have sixteen manufacturing business that are gagging, that will not survive this nonsense much longer," said the industrialist, "so I suggest someone think something up, very soon."

"We have drawn up a list of scenarios," Michel de Beaumont, head of Research Branch, offered. "Also, Alex here has put together a paper on the possible repercussion to the citizenry, you know, how the man on the street will likely respond to a prolonged deprivation..."

"Let me guess," Captain Hoch, head of procurement for the Mediterranean Fleet suggested with a chortle. "We all move back to live with our parents, we sleep with our mother and knock off our fathers, like that, de Beaumont, or what?"

"Unnecessary that, Captain," de Beaumont said dryly. "Why don't you sit back and let someone who has actually considered their words speak!"

Captain Hoch's face reddened. "Listen you asshole," he said, "you watch what you say, or I'll knock your boyfriend the shrink there on his cute little ass."

"Stop, now," Bobo commanded. "You are out of line, Hoch, sit back and you may learn something. What have you got Dr. Necker?"

"Simply put, collective stress will before long render the nation susceptible to extremes of analysis of the situation and of proposed remedies. Deprivation causes great insecurity, self-doubt, self-loathing, guilt, and it causes people to project onto others blame for their own hardship. It is likely that on the one hand people will undertake an unreasoned search for scapegoats. On the other they will be receptive to insensible solutions offered up by demagogues and opportunists. In short, we are in danger of severe instability."

"I could have told you that, pal," Captain Hoch grumbled.

"As to possible solutions, as far as I can see, our best option under the circumstance," de Beaumont said, "is to attempt to militarily secure sources of petroleum in Africa, where we are not likely to meet much local armed resistance from the locals, and where we are not likely to arouse much opposition from abroad, assuming that we manufacture a plausible, reasonable-sounding cause beli."

"That is preposterous! We do that and we will have a crisis on our hands such as you cannot imagine," an indignant Maurice Behar, the chap from the Foreign Ministry, observed.

"Sounds reasonable to me," the man from Elf replied.

"Not bad, de Beaumont, actually not too bad, but not good enough," Bobo said. Then he turned to the banker. "Let me ask you something, Henri. What exactly will happen here? I mean, we are paying OPEC a thousand percent more for its oil than we did in the past, so what will they do with all this money? Let me be more specific. Let me leave Venezuela, Nigeria, and the others who were only to happy to join in with the Near East petroleum producers, out of it for now. What will the Arabs and Iranians do with all that new money? How is the press calling it?"

"Petrodollars," Harouni says with a grin, his "p" sounding more like a "b." He is pleased at his contribution. "That was what they called it, right? Petrodollars."

"That's right," Gaspar confirms.

"We have been ejected from the driver's seat, Bobo," Henri said rather mournfully. "Not only that, we are at risk of being run over by the new driver. We are witnessing a sudden and drastic transfer of wealth, and it is causing great dislocations, tumultuous financial markets, great political flux, long lines at the gasoline stations."

"That is not what I asked Henri," Bobo said, and Gaspar could see

43

that Bobo was no longer in the room with them, that Bobo's mind had wandered off to that place where it thought up thoughts faster and further than the others present were capable of imagining.

"They will take all that new money, Henri, and do what with it? They will either save it or spend it, right? Right. And what will they spend it on? Not on us here in France, right? Isn't that really the problem, that we can offer cheeses and wines and couture evening gowns and perfumes, and that these will not make a difference, that we will not be able to offer Rolls Royces or Mercedes cars, Sony televisions, nor will our Renaults measure up against German M.A.N. trucks in the marketplace, big ticket items? And with all due respect, Henri, neither will our banks stand a chance against the Swiss, nor will our franc favorably compare to the American dollar and the Swiss franc. That is really why we are in trouble, right? The others will repatriate their money; we will not do nearly as well." His question had been rhetorical; he hardly intended to consider their answer.

The upshot of the meeting was that an informal committee of four was formed and charged with proposing an approach for France to expand its trade with the oil-producing nations, then the gathered dispersed.

Afterwards, Bobo and Gaspar retired to Bobo's small cluttered office where Gaspar poured two shots of Chivas, which they downed in one fell swoop.

"You have worked something out, I know you have," Gaspar said. "I have a thought, a realization, yes indeed, I realized that the answer to our dilemma is, so to speak, the Horn. De Beaumont sent me thinking. Africa, but not as he saw it. Here, reach under your chair and hand me the atlas, Gaspar, will you?" Bobo said.

Bobo opened the atlas to the Arabian peninsula and Persian Gulf. He placed his index finger on the blue of the gulf and slowly pushed it along southward, stopping when his finger reached the brown of land. "There, the Horn with which to prod the rich into spending more of their wealth in France." he said.

"Somalia and Ethiopia?" Gaspar asked. "Who in the hell cares about them? A couple of tribal hangouts who have lately taken to flirting with the Russians."

"Here, we will play a game, Gaspar. I will be France, you the rich Arabs and Persians, OK Gaspar? OK. I come to your palace with my atlas and I say the following: You have disliked me for some time I say, to the Arabs at any rate, and I can see how you got to feel this way. I gave your

44

kin the Algerians a very hard time back when they sought independence, I ganged up with the Israelis in 1956 and I occupied Egypt's Suez Canal, I armed your nemesis the Israelis who then used my Mirages and AMX 13 tanks to trounce you in the Six Day war of 1967 and I sold them a nuclear research reactor. Now I am here to tell you that you are in danger, and to propose that you hire me to stave it off. Here my friends, consider the Horn of Africa. In Somalia and Ethiopia the Russians are making friends, are arming the locals, are building a naval base, and are placing themselves in the position to choke you. See that? Virtually all of your oil makes its way down the narrow watery funnel that is the Arab Gulf. Mind you, Gaspar, when I go to see the Shah about this matter I will, of course, refer to it as the Persian Gulf. Every tanker ship has to pass through that narrowest of passages before it reaches open water, and whoever sits on the Horn will control transit through this choke point. You will say to me 'I fear not, I am the friend of the Americans, I will ask Washington to help.' Fine, I will answer. And when was the last time Washington succeeded in keeping the Reds out of Africa? Never, that is when. And what will they do this time, these heavy-handed Americans? Go to them and you will become the staging ground for a nuclear conflict. Your countries will become the playing fields for a contest between Washington and Moscow. That is what will happen, my friends. We in France, on the other hand, have done very well keeping the Reds out of the back yards of our friends in Africa. SEDCE had always had a strong presence in Africa. France's former colonies in west and central Africa retained strong ties to Paris—"

"You are not speaking to a moron, you know," Harouni observes quietly. "France owned those places. So don't bullshit me."

"You're right," Gaspar admits readily. "That was in fact the reality. And within that context SEDCE worked to keep the Russians and other troublemakers out, to secure the seats of power held by France's friends..."

"Puppets. Say it, puppets."

"France's puppets. So Bobo went to the heads of counter-intelligence in Saudi Arabia and Iran..."

"Their names?"

Suddenly, Gaspar's confidence in his raconteur skills plummets. An array of fractured thoughts mixed with messages of fright and confusion race through his mind like sparks from a severed electrical main, with hardly time to try to splice things together.

45

"It's been a while," he says, "But I think the Saudi was Sheikh Rahman Ibn Mafouz al Tallal and the Iranian was General Assiri. Yes, I think that's right." He waits for confirmation, approval, or some less agreeable response, but Harouni is silent.

"You see Gaspar, I, France, do have a line of products with great potential appeal to the newly rich: weapons. High-quality arms, war-tested and proven aircraft, tanks, missiles, electronics, big ticket items all. And ours are both less expensive than America's and clear of the political encumbrances of dealing with both the Americans and Soviets. Try and sell an American made weapon to an Arab and you have a hundred powerful angry Jews cluttering your days with determined efforts to make you stop. Buy something from the Soviets, a T55 tank, a Mig 21, or a Komar class missile boat and you also have technicians who came to live in your country, half of whom were not technicians, but KGB operatives who promptly set out to see to it that your country too avails itself of the benefits of Marxism. We, on the other hand, don't bother you unless you wish us to, cash and carry, we..."

"Why do you say 'we'?" Harouni asks, a sharp edge to his words. "You are supposed to be Belgian. "You said 'we.' Why?" Within seconds a fury takes hold of Harouni; his forehead takes on several furrows and creases, his eyes blaze.

Why indeed? Gaspar wonders. "I'm not denying that Bobo and I were friends, nor that I worked with him," he explains, "only that I had anything to do with what happened to your brother. At that time, while Bobo was stationed in Beirut, I didn't have any association with SEDCE. That began only after Bobo returned to France.

"This, then, is my proposal to you, my Arab friends, I will next see the Shah about this, I will convince him too that France is indeed who he should chose to keep the Horn from becoming a thorn, and this is how it will work. You, the Saudis, and the Iranians would assemble a military force composed partly of your own people, but mostly of African-Arab troops, Moroccan, and Egyptian. I will see to it that they accept this idea. SEDCE would remain in the background, supplying intelligence, transport, communications, coordination, logistics. This alliance will serve your purposes in several ways: it will bring you and the Shah closer; you have always had your differences. What better way to become better friends than to find yourself serving a common cause? You will get to look after your own security for a change, not a bad thing to lessen dependence on far-off Washington, right? And you will do so without overly upsetting the Soviets."

"Now, Mr. Harouni, this was a brilliant stroke. Bobo had invented an alliance that shrewdly circumvented potential pitfalls, that rectified France's relations with the Arabs, and enhanced its ties to the Shah. He had managed to loosen America's hegemony while at the same time denying the U.S. a pretext for making too great a fuss about it. The Shah and the House of Saud were, after all, proud monarchs. If Bobo's plan offered them the opportunity to look after their own vital interests, the U.S. couldn't very well object. And the composition of the Safari Club task force robbed the Soviets of any excuse to howl about imperialistic adventurism. Here, after all, were Egyptians, Moroccans, and Africans. Simply tending to their own back yard.

"In the end, Bobo convinced the relevant parties of the logic of his analysis, the rightness of his plan, and the Safari Club strike force came into being."

"Why did they call it the Safari Club?" Harouni asks. His manner is that of a person suddenly fascinated.

"At one point during the negotiations leading to the agreements (formal agreements were signed, you understand, treaties for all intents and purposes) the Saudi representative said that the villa where they'd been meeting, near Jeddah on the Red Sea, reminded him of Kenya's Safari Club. The name stuck and after that they were always referred to as the Safari Club agreements."

"So, did this invention of Bobo's achieve anything for the others? Or only for France?"

"Oh no, it did very well for everyone. And with a minimum use of force. As I recall force was used but once, down in Zaire's Shaba province. A Leftist general there, whose name was Bomba, honestly, that was his true name, attempted to overthrow Mobutu, who was a long time friend to France. Also, Shaba province produced oil; the fact that it did went a long way toward making the point to the Saudis and Iranians that France would be helpful in defending their own oil production means. In the end, Bomba was defused."

"What else?" Harouni says, his face deadpan; the pun failed to register.

Gaspar shakes his head in confusion.

"What else did the Safari Club do?"

"Oh. Well, it stopped cold the Russian threat at the Horn."

"By using force?"

"No, by using money, bribes. The Saudis and Iranians put up lots of money, around thirty million dollars just for the current Somalian head man. There was more cash for others, and arms and money for Ethiopia. That was what made the Safari Club work."

"You think money can buy anything, can buy your life back for you?"

"I hope so."

"I never said that your friend was a fool, only that he was a pig," Harouni announces. Then he marches Gaspar back to the shed.

And I only told you the half of, the lesser half at that, Gaspar muses, for at about the time of the Club, and as an outgrowth of having impressed the Shah, Bobo eventually accomplished exponentially greater feats.

On the way, Gaspar actually considers making a run for it. So far as he can see, Harouni is not armed and is alone, although Gaspar can't be certain they are not being shadowed by one of the guards. The temptation to flee takes on a concreteness, becomes a part of him like his limbs, his faculties. The struggle to resist the temptation is so intense that he wonders whether Harouni senses it.

Thoughts and counter-thoughts:

It's dark, he'll never see you once you're off the path.

Who is this saying 'you'? We're in this together. If I am proven wrong, you and I are dead. We're in the same body, we both want to keep it from being turned into a corpse.

Take off. Go, run. Once you're away from here you can make your way to Beirut. It isn't far, you were driven barely an hour to get here. Run to a Western embassy, they'll shelter you. Harouni is not the law, he's a criminal. Run, Gaspar, and you will be free!

They reach the shed. One of Harouni's men, armed of course, comes from somewhere off to the side, where he had been shadowing them all the while, and stands by while Harouni undoes the lock.

Gaspar lies in the darkness and congratulates himself for a victory of sorts. He has come away from the evening with a feeling of success in establishing something of a rapport with Harouni, a connection that may make it a bit harder for Harouni to shoot him. He laughs aloud thinking of himself in the guise of Scheherazade, telling tales about Bobo to the Khalif.

In Baghdad Gaspar once heard an Arab aphorism: "Better to be the head of a donkey than the tail of a lion."

Pretty, but not quite true, he'd thought at the time. Donkeys live donkeys' lives, they are beasts of burden that struggle along in unrelenting

48

misery, go where they're told, are punished harshly when they fail. Lions go where they wish when they wish. They have no master.

Bobo went places and did things which most people could not conceive. And so, by extension, did Gaspar. The aphorism about the donkey and the lion must have struck a chord in him since he remembered it so clearly. Invariably, he always stood a step— –if only a small step, no more than a shoe's length—behind Bobo.

Whenever they went together to meet someone, when they submitted to the opening rituals of introductions and the crisp small talk of their trade—quips and gossip and rumors and rakish humor—Gaspar, unfailingly, waited for Bobo to respond first, to establish that he was the head. Then he chimed in, acknowledged the humor or insight or noteworthy information that had just been offered, confirmed it on his own behalf as well as Bobo's. For Bobo never failed to turn to him for confirmation, a gesture that never went unnoticed. It was meant to be noticed, it broadcast to their interlocutors that Bobo and he worked in concert. That Bobo might be the head, but that Gaspar mattered.

Chapter Seven

"In Israel, however rich you are you cannot own lots of land," Paz says to Sarah. "Lots of land is available, but where no one wants it—in the desert, in the savannah."

They are on his back porch admiring the view, the open, unspoilt terrain which Paz has hastened to assure her is not all his property.

"When I was a boy in this country, it used to be that rich was unacceptable. This was a socialist country and if you were rich there was something dirty about you. Now everybody is chasing the almighty shekel. Still, the rich here have to make do with fancy homes and no land. I mean, you can have a large back yard, a few trees, maybe even a swimming pool, but nothing like the estates you have in England or Scotland. In Israel, even if you are rich you can always see your neighbors from your house, and they you. That is a real disincentive to make money."

Paz appears to be the outcome of a process of creation that got out of hand. He is short and inordinately broad, his hair white and cut close to his head. His face is like a good leather jacket that's gone for too many seasons without saddle soap and mink oil and has so many lines and creases that it seems doubtful it has ever been smooth. And yet his movements are abrupt and energetic, as if to be languid was to be at risk. He is deeply tanned—from gardening, he tells Sarah. He wears khaki shorts and a golf shirt that once had an emblem on the breast pocket.

"Polo," Paz explains, "it used to have a horse and a polo player here. When my wife gave it to me, she said, 'it's Polo,' like she expected me to melt just from letting it touch my skin. I cut off the horse and the guy with the stick and I said to her, 'Shula, when Mr. Lauren walks around with my picture on his shirt pocket I'll wear his horse on mine.'"

Paz's home perches on the rim of a promontory, a peninsula of mottled white and brown limestone that juts out sharply and narrowly into a valley. But for the limestone, all is green: pines and shrubs, grass and cultivated gardens. The valley continues some distance, then melds into a hump of land that becomes hills, high hills running east and west.

"There," Paz points to the north, toward the hills, "is Lebanon. If it were possible, I mean if our border with Lebanon was open, we could be in Beirut in less than two hours."

They go into the house where Shula, a small woman with bright eyes and a shy manner, has lunch waiting. During lunch, Paz translates for her.

Shula speaks no English.

"Shula wants you to try the burakas, she says they're the best in Israel. Everyone here says that about their burakas, or that they know where to get the best. It makes people feel like they're expert at something."

A burakas, she finds, is a patty of grated potato, an immigrant-introduced food that has become one of Israel's preferred snacks.

At one point during the meal Shula says something to Paz, punctuated with a grin. His answer is also marked by a grin. "Shula says that you are very beautiful. She said to me, 'Wouldn't you like her to take my place in bed tonight?'"

Sarah bursts out laughing. "And what was your reply?"

"I told Shula that her estimation of my prowess is based on memories of long ago."

After the meal they return to the back porch where they have coffee, strong and sweet. Just as Sarah is about to mention Gaspar, Paz says, "Did Gaspar ever tell you about the time I advised him to retire?"

No, she says, he hadn't. She wonders where Paz is heading. "You must understand, Mr. Paz, that in recent years Gaspar has had nothing to do with the work of the old days. Not since before Bobo died, really since he and I met. If you're assuming he was kidnaped because he'd been doing intelligence work, you're off the mark."

"Doesn't matter what I think, matters what they think," Paz replies.

His tone has become hard. She isn't certain whether it is meant for her or for the 'they' who have taken Gaspar.

"I assume you know this used to be my work, too," Paz says.

Yes, she had known.

"Well, I told Gaspar once, oh, maybe ten or eleven years ago, that he had wandered far afield. You see, when I first met Gaspar he was just a boy, mad about boats. He wanted only to be a ship's architect."

Sarah wonders whether Paz is trying to stave off her inevitable plea that he find Gaspar. She seeks to draw him out, to appear to ease him off the hook of compassion and thus sink it deeper. She asks him to tell her about that first long-ago meeting.

"My goodness, that was when Methuselah was still around," Paz says, "so long ago I have to think about it." He fashions with one hand a rest for his chin, wraps fingers and part of the hand around it, squeezes a little, and finds his memories.

"I was a kid myself then. In Europe, maybe 1947, something like that. No, it was later, maybe forty-eight because the war here had just ended—

51

the one we call the War of Independence, the one the Palestinians call their national tragedy—and I went to Europe on a shopping trip." He chuckles, "Not a real shopping trip, you know, not the kind where you go to Harrod's to look for bed sheets and the like. No, this was military shopping. We needed goods desperately. So I stopped off to see old man Bruyn, Mathias Bruyn, Gaspar's father, may he rest in peace. He had helped us before when we needed ships to bring survivors from the camps to Israel—well, Palestine, then. Bruyn owned a shipyard in Antwerp, been in the family for centuries. When we were doing our research we found out that Mathias Bruyn was a very religious man, a devout Protestant."

Yes, she'd known that, Gaspar had told her a lot about his father. She wonders whether Paz also knows of Mathias's regular disregard of the Good Book's admonitions against lusting after one's neighbor's wife.

"It was because of the Second Coming, you see, old Mathias was of the belief that it couldn't take place until the Jews had been returned to the Holy Land. He ended up selling us a couple of ships for practically nothing, was very generous, very helpful. Anyway, on that second visit, in forty-eight, he brought in his son Gaspar, couldn't have been more than five or six years old, to meet me. Good-looking boy he was."

Sarah murmurs that Gaspar has grown up to be a good-looking man.

"The next time I met Gaspar was right here, in Israel, about ten or eleven years ago at a certain large airbase. He'd been sent by his friend de Bossier to coordinate the transporting of arms and spare parts to a SEDCE airbase in France."

He pauses, apparently mired in recollections. He nods his head with a certain chagrin. "Some mamzer—bastard, Hebrew for bastard—this de Bossier was," he mutters at last, his tone somewhere between approbation and disapproval. Did Sarah know, he asks, of Gaspar's involvement with this particular transportation of arms?

She knew some, she says, and asks him to tell her more. She has wondered at intervals whether she knew all there was to know about Gaspar's past. Now she wonders whether she has asked to be told more because the journalist in her needs to cross-check the story one more time—even a story that has come and gone and will never in her lifetime see the light of day.

But first he wants to double check—to trip her up? She is to tell him whether she knows that Paz had in his day graduated from the refugee transport business to a career with Mossad?

She does know. Gaspar once told her that Paz had reached the highest echelons in Mossad, Israel's counter-intelligence service.

Okay then, he will now tell her about having run into Gaspar at that air base.

Why did he first have to be assured that she knew about his work with Mossad?

"Because you're a newspaper person. I figure that since you haven't written about it thus far you won't from here on out."

The overwhelming roar of jet engines shatters her thought, a massive sound from quite nearby. Two fighter aircraft painted in brown and cream and grey camouflage patterns are flying just above the valley floor, lower than Paz's house. She can see the pilots' helmets and the tips of the clumps of ordnance protruding from under the wings.

When they are gone Paz laughs and says, "They must have heard us at air force headquarters speaking about bases and the like."

It is obvious that she has failed to get his joke. He explains that Israel is extremely security conscious, that even the location or name of an airbase is classified. "Those were ours," he says about the planes, "on their way to bomb something in the Bekaa, the valley in eastern Lebanon where the terrorists who regularly give us a hard time hang out."

"Perhaps Gaspar is being held there," she whispers in alarm.

"I can't say no with certainty," Paz says, "but from what you've told me, I doubt it. Doesn't sound like the work of fanatics. Just a professional guess, mind. I'm sorry you have to worry so much, Mrs. Bruyn."

She thanks him and takes a moment to recover her composure.

"About seeing Gaspar that time," Paz continues. "In 1980 an American came to me, a man with heavyweight credentials in the business—our business, I mean, although at the time he was in politics. This man..."

"May I know his name?"

"Kirney. Jerome Martindale Kirney. You know him?"

"Not personally, but I should think anyone who reads newspapers or watches television knows of him."

"True. Anyway, Kirney was at the time managing the Republican Party's presidential election campaign. He came to me because we'd known one another over the years. I liked him, sort of. He was a rough guy, a little arrogant, a lawyer by training. Had done some good things in the OSS in France during World War Two, was even decorated for it by de Gaulle."

He hesitates, and as if feeling obliged to justify himself explains that in his business people necessarily feel kinships of sorts, even for people

53

they're ambivalent about. Spies, too, need to talk, and for the most part they can talk only with other spies, which automatically bestows a sort of shallow comradery.

"Kirney told me that he had a big problem having to do with the election, with his candidate. I wondered why he was talking politics to me, American politics, yet. In general I dislike politics because they pretty accurately reflect the quality of the citizenry, in short, us. And who wants to have to look and listen to renditions of us all the time, right?

"But this Kirney told me I was in a position to help his candidate. How? You'll like this— with Israeli weapons! He needed Israeli weapons, meaning weapons of American manufacture from our inventories. Of course we have our own, too, goods made right here, but those weren't what Kirney was looking for. His man would lose the election, he said, if the American diplomats who'd been taken hostage by Khomeini's fanatics a year earlier—the people from the Teheran embassy, remember?—were to be released at the wrong moment

"So that was it. This Kirney, banking on the assumption that I, like him, would do anything to throw his candidate's opponent—the weak-on-communism, friendly-to-the-Arabs Democrat president—out of the White House, asked whether I could come up with the goods. Well, of course I could. We talked it over here, among our own people, we weighed the risks, and we decided to go ahead. It meant a lot of money and lots of good-will credits with the Republican once he took the White House. To protect ourselves, we made it look like some big-shot local arms dealer was doing the deal. What Kirney accomplished was simple and to the point: he bribed the Iranians to keep the hostages in Teheran until after the American elections. Kirney had calculated that their untimely release, just before the elections, might put this dangerous Democrat (who, between you and me, was not such a bad fellow) over with the voters. And he knew, you see, that the Iranians were desperate for arms, their military was in a shambles after the Shah's overthrow.

"We surmised from certain facts that Kirney had also made an arrangement with de Bossier of SEDCE, they were friends of the spy sort. He was something, this de Bossier, I doubt we know even now all that he was involved in.

"Well, the deal was as follows: we shipped the goods, from tires for Iran's F-4s to mortar shells, a whole supermarket of goods. And all this, mind you, going to guys who hated our guts, who had vowed that they would one day slaughter us and take Jerusalem back for Islam. God bless them, we're still waiting. They got a bit delayed by that war they fought with Iraq—but that's another story.

"The way Kirney parceled out responsibilities was that we provided and packed the goods and loaded them onto transport planes. Then everything was flown somewhere, we weren't supposed to know where. Except that the transport planes that came for the goods were SEDCE planes and the base they came from and returned to was a SEDCE base in France, so we put our heads together and concluded that the goods were being flown to France and from there to Iran via various widely dispersed locations.

"So who turns up at our base on a SEDCE DC8 to coordinate the shipments but your Gaspar? This good-looking man comes up and shakes my hand and tells me his name is Bruyn. I nearly fell down. I'm not shy, I said, 'You work for that bastard de Bossier?'

"'Not exactly, more like associate with him,' Gaspar said.

"That was close enough, I said. 'You've wandered far afield, my boy.' I mean, when I first met him all he cared about was boats, all he wanted was to be a ship's architect. Sure, people can change their minds, but I didn't like it that he was with de Bossier, no.

"In the end Kirney got his way, his man won the election. The hostages were returned to the U.S. on the very day of the inauguration, can you believe it? Who was it who said truth is stranger than fiction?"

"Find him for me, Paz," she beseeches softly. "Please. We love each other very much. I miss him terribly."

Paz sighs, a sound as laden with sadness as any ram's horn sounding on the High Holidays. He takes her hand, strokes it a few times, releases it. He looks away, up to the not too distant hills, towards Lebanon.

"In the Bible it says: Beware, for from the North shall calamity come." He lifts his arm and points to the hills. "It's like one of those vaporous primordial bogs where living things disappear without a trace."

Sarah weeps.

"Oh, look," he says hurriedly. Shula sticks her head out the door. She gives Paz a scathing look, he waves her back into the house. "I'm not saying I won't try, I will, of course I will. It's just that I don't want you to build up too much hope. People have all kinds of wildly exaggerated ideas about us here, about Mossad. Mossad means the Institute, you know; SEDCE's people called theirs the Firm, CIA is the Company, ours is the Institute. People talk about us like we can part the seas, walk on water. That's nonsense, we make plenty of mistakes. So I don't want you to think that just because I'm going to try means Gaspar is as good as home, but I will do my best, OK? Good, so please stop crying, Shula is looking at me like I'm a murderer. Ah yes, and one more thing: not a word

55

of any of this to the press, not the kidnaping, not any of it. You know how those media people are. Before you know it they'll be doing specials on Gaspar and you. We don't want to make noise, OK? Good, thank you."

As if on cue, Shula emerges with a tray bearing more coffee and pastries as well as some peeled oranges and sliced white peaches. She speaks and Paz translates: Sarah is once again being offered samples of the most splendid baked goods and fruits the Land of Israel is capable of producing.

They sip coffee. Again Sarah admires the beauty of the place. Paz allows that he is most fortunate.

"Everyone lives down near Tel Aviv," he says, "like sardines, all crowded in, each breathes what the other exhales."

There is a pause, then as if on the spur of the moment he says, "Let me ask you something that's been on my mind ever since that whole caper with Kirney. I was left with a puzzle, and hard as I've pondered it I still can't solve it, so maybe you can."

Eagerly she assures him that if it's in her power to help she will.

"When one considers this deal for the hostages that Kirney put together, it's clear that those who helped him or who were involved in it with him benefited, right? We here made lots of money, and made friends with some very powerful people in Washington. Kirney went on to become director of the CIA—what more could a spy ask for? Top of the heap, Langley, a great way to close off a career. Kirney's candidate became president, some people say a great president. Maybe. The Iranians got their weapons—a godsend for them, if I can speak His name in the same breath as I speak of killing machines. So that leaves de Bossier. What did de Bossier get out of it? Surely more than just that curious audience he had with the Republican president-elect. Raised a lot of eyebrows, that meeting did. Our Ambassador to Washington at the time cabled us to say that a meeting between a U.S. president (for all intents and purposes) and a foreign counter-intelligence official, French yet, was unprecedented."

Sarah has to fight to suppress an overwhelming desire to answer Paz's question.

She says, "I just don't know. Perhaps if I give it some thought I may come up with some sort of clue. But the truth is that these things were on the periphery of our life together—mine and Gaspar's—by design. We wanted all that murky stuff behind us. This episode you wonder about, many others for that matter, were just not discussed. Mentioned, yes, but discussed? Not really. We both wanted to get as far away from memories of Bobo de Bossier as we could. Now I fear we haven't gotten far enough away."

From the moment she'd fully grasped Paz's question, she'd seen before her Deadeye's malignant stare in Bobo's parlor at Belle Marais. A stare that had implanted itself in her mind, that could still silence her.

Chapter Eight

Sarah dreams she is strolling in a labyrinth submerged beneath a green sea the color of ancient glass. Far above, she can see the surface. In the distance is the keel of a wooden ship moving in her direction. The keel is sharply curved, like the huge bow of a giant hunter. A Kayiki, she thinks, then realizes that the keel is headed straight for the highest part of the labyrinth and will soon smash against it and sink. Still she is unconcerned.

The telephone rings, waking her. It is nearly eight in the morning and she is in her bed in London. Only a few days have passed since she saw Paz in Israel, two weeks since Gaspar was taken. It is a collect call from Israel.

Paz comes on. "After you left, we passed word around in Beirut to the effect that whoever had information about Gaspar and was willing to pass it on stood to gain by it. In short, we solicited a ransom demand. Last night someone came to one of our stooges there in Beirut and told her they had information for sale."

Happiness effervesces through Sarah. For a brief moment she ceases to be a physical entity, she hovers above her body, a golden glow tinting her mind, the room and everything in it.

"We're not talking about totally reliable people here," Paz warns. "Sometimes they'll make things up to justify their existence. To impress us."

The golden glow begins to fade.

"But look, Sarah, it's better that we heard something. Better than it was before we heard..."

"How do you mean, 'heard,' what sort of a communication?" she demands, her eagerness making her gruff.

"We're being told that Gaspar may be had for a ransom. But we have to be realistic. What we know for certain is that these people—or it could be a single individual—didn't seek us out, didn't ask for money or for anything else. We did all the seeking, all the soliciting. Still, I repeat, it's better than it was before we heard."

"How do you mean, a single individual?" she presses, impatient, at that moment almost despising Paz. "Two people spoke to us at the airport, so it can't be only one person."

"What I mean is that this could be a small-time operation, nothing to do with the larger themes like those behind other hostage takings in Lebanon. You know, religion, politics. For example, several years ago a couple of brothers, Shii fanatics, kidnapped two German businessmen in an effort to free their other brother who was serving time in a prison in Bonn. They were acting strictly on their own, in fact they pissed off the head fanatic in Lebanon with their little escapade. For reasons of his own, he didn't want to upset the German government, but there was nothing he could do about the brothers—they were tough and determined and in the end they got most of what they sought. That's what I mean when I say a single individual."

Sarah crumbles. "What's going on here, Paz?" she whispers, all traces of the surge of relief gone. "Why do I feel you aren't telling me all you know?"

"Look here, Sarah," he says, his tone patient, even tender. "By making inquiries in Beirut I've put people at risk, people we don't want to lose, people who have at times done us good service. I'm only trying to protect them, that's all."

"What you really mean is that you don't trust me."

"I mean that you're human, that you had a life before all this happened. You have friends, a best friend. You will tell him or her the good news about the message from Beirut, swear them to secrecy. And they will keep the secret, except with their mother, who also has a best friend who has a best friend. And I will end up losing a source in Beirut whom I do not wish to lose. So don't personalize my caution, it's not case-specific."

"My best friend was taken from me at Beirut airport," she says. Then hastens to add, lest this become a conversation about anything but the heart of the matter, "Okay, I understand. But I take it you know who has kidnapped Gaspar?"

"Not quite yet, but we're getting warm."

"What happens next?"

"Bravo. Next we ask whoever he is for proof that Gaspar is well."

"You mean that he's still alive."

"Right. I need you to think of something that only you two know, some item or place or phrase."

From the first moments that Sarah and Gaspar had known each other there had existed between them the need for vetting, for checking one another's provenances. Now, as she searches her mind for something suitable to give Paz, she finds herself astonished that they had survived the process.

Approximately five years earlier, before she had known of the existence of SEDCE or of a man named de Bossier or of another named Gaspar Bruyn, Sarah had been a respected, but hardly earthshaking, investigative reporter for The Sentinel in London.

One gray day she retrieved a message from her answering machine— a male voice speaking in a heavy French accent and with a shaky command of English. The caller said he had an important story for her, "the scandal for our time." He asked that she telephone a Paris number, permit the phone to ring twice, hang up, and call again for a single ringing.

She complied, mostly because her home number was unlisted and therefore even if this Frenchman was a crank he was a resourceful one. Cranks were, after all, part of her journalistic experience. At the Sentinel she often received tips from zany would-be contributors to the journalistic process who had uncovered dastardly plots: So-and-so was out to secretly drain the Thames, someone else was scheming to alter the Queen's gender while Her Majesty slept.

But Sarah's return calls to Paris went unanswered.

Late the next evening the Frenchman telephoned again. In a low, urgent voice he instructed that immediately after he hung up she was to alter the outgoing message on her answering machine, then permit his next call ("I will not linger with your time, madame") to ring through so he could hear the new message. By then she was growing annoyed, but she did as the caller asked.

In the end, her patience paid off. The Frenchman's next call, making an appointment to see her, changed her life.

She met with the Frenchman (whose name she would later learn was Chardeau) at a small restaurant near London's Holland Park. He was a tall, gaunt man with sparse black hair and brown eyes that seemed cluttered with the reflections of many speeding thoughts. To her annoyance, he seemed barely to look at her in the way that men unfailingly did and which she had come to anticipate and expect. Chardeau, however, apparently failed to appreciate her large blue eyes, superb nose, exceptionally long torso, endless legs emphasized by rakishly high heels, skin that had stopped aging at twenty. In her youth, that skin had nearly caused her to succumb to the temptation of a model's income. If she'd known then that her skin would last as long as it did, she once told her former husband, she might have reconsidered banking on her brains for a livelihood.

When they took their table, the Frenchman placed himself with his back to the wall, signaling her with a look laden with meaning that he was doing so to protect himself. How dramatic! she thought.

He began to cross-examine her. She had to suppress the urge to say, "Hold off now, friend, I do the asking here." He wanted to know whether she could handle a story with international ramifications. "I have examined your columns, Mrs. Tillinghast. My story is the eclipse of them." He asked whether she trusted her editor.

"Of course not," she said, and immediately realized that her humor was wasted.

Then he asked what she knew about the Gulf War, and something in his voice caused her to sit up and take notice.

"Just what I read in the papers," she said. "I don't do war stories."

He advised her to study up on France's relations with Iraq. Then, to her amazement, he rose to leave. Without thinking, she grasped his hand—a bit too forcefully, causing her long fingernails to dig into his palm. For a moment she thought he would strike her.

"Sit!" she commanded, and he promptly did. "Who the hell are you?" she demanded, "and why should I care a farthing about anything you say? You tell me who you are, friend, and what this is about, or you can piss off."

He told her then that he worked at a secret French government agency and that through his job he had encountered a case of corruption at the highest levels. A case of treason, really, except that this traitor was very powerful, a nobleman who had the ear and affections of the most powerful people in France. "This man is more high than the justice, Mrs. Tillinghast."

She asked why he hadn't gone to the French authorities or to the press, and was awarded a disdainful look. "You teach yourself, please, about such things in France. When the criminal is too important, then he is beyond the hand of the law."

"You mean to say he's untouchable?"

He ignored her. "You know about Bokassa?" he asked, a teacher's question to an idiot student.

She did not.

Once again he rose, this time quickly retracting his hands. She demanded to know when he would call again.

"First you teach yourself about these things, of the press in France, of Bokassa, then I will repeat," he said, and left, his food and drink untouched.

"Ask them to have Gaspar say where the laundry powders are," Sarah instructs Paz, "the location of the laundry powders. If your people in Beirut come back with the correct answer, I will know that Gaspar is well."

Paz waits for her to say more, but she is silent. Finally he laughs, loud enough to force her to move the telephone receiver away from her ear. "Touché," Paz says, "I take your point. You too have secrets to keep, perhaps even people to protect. You are a funny and special woman, Mrs. Bruyn. So where are these laundry detergents to be found?"

"Thank you, Mr. Paz," she replies. "Marseilles. In a Carrefour supermarket in Marseilles."

Chapter Nine

Gaspar is like a man lost in a rain forest, a poor wretch who has taken a dramatic, perhaps fatal, misstep and has learned for himself the frightening truth that in the forest one does not stray from the path for even a second, for in that second the trail will disappear, not to be found again. And as he meanders in the mean thicket, he comes also to know the debilitating pain of regret over that single, oh-so-wrong step. As the sun begins to set, he learns with the speed of the retreating light that the day has to this point been halcyon and gossamer compared to the horrors of the coming night. In the rain forest at night, everything is a threat, every sound, every silence, every step taken, every hesitation. One grows mad with the effort to keep one's mind one's own in the rain forest at night, and the night lasts forever. One yearns for, speculates about, and posts false signs of morning's light when one is a prisoner of the dark. Darkness is master.

Harouni is Gaspar's master of darkness. Everything that happens to Gaspar, from his meals to clearing his bowels—the escorted outings to the grass in back of the shed, gaped at all the while by a young man in running shoes carrying an M16—all are at the time and frequency of Harouni's choosing. Every one of his anxious speculations about Harouni and his men, about Sarah—where is she now?—about his own future, are as and when Harouni wishes. The opening and closing of the shed door, delivery of meals, meals delayed, warmth for the body, its frigid misery, all emanate from Harouni. What is the significance of a meal delayed? Is it in fact late, or has Gaspar lost count of time?

Footsteps on the path. Gaspar listens. He has learned to hear the footsteps from a great distance. Has his hearing improved, he wonders, or is it simply that he has never before in his life had reason to listen so hard? Footsteps at the expected times cause a blend of exhaustion and relief; they promise more of the dreary sameness of the prisoner. Still, sameness is preferable to aberration, that can only mean bad things. Sameness is meals, relieving himself, a resupply of dulled pencils and paper.

These footsteps are now out of the proper time sequence. They are the footsteps of more than one person, something unforeseen, like that visit to Harouni's Phoenician rock, how long ago now?

More than two people. Three? He isn't certain. Fears beset him of the sort that one desperately tries to banish in the rain forest at night. What can it mean? His thoughts gag him.

As Gaspar is shoved through the shed door, Harouni steps up and slaps his face hard. Gaspar falls to the ground. Immediately he stands up again. When he was a boy and had stumbled, staying down was that much closer to never getting up again.

Harouni is saying something. A strange word is imbedded in the midst of his sentence, and it throws Gaspar off.

Harouni says it again: "Why, Mr. Bruyn, my Belgian friend, is Shlomo inquiring after you, sir?"

Gaspar's still-stinging face displays genuine bewilderment. Harouni slaps him once more, equally as hard as the first time. This time Gaspar remains standing. Challenged, Harouni plants a swift and powerful kick on Gaspar's ankle, another on his outer thigh. Gaspar cries out, tears well up, his leg wobbles as if no longer his. Again Harouni moves to kick, winding up like a soccer player about to boot a free kick on the goal. One of his men laughs and says something in Arabic, his words distorted by his own laughter. Harouni also laughs and uncorks his punishing foot.

"Shlomo," he explains to Gaspar. His tone does not in the least reflect the punishment he has just inflicted. He wasn't angry when he slapped and kicked, merely curious. "Shlomo: the Israelis. We call them Shlomo because when they came here in 1982, when they chased out the Palestinian shabab, their fighters, you know, all the Israeli soldiers as far as we could tell were called Shlomo—Solomon in English. So that's my question to you, my friend. Why are the Israelis asking after you?"

Light of a thousand suns rising. Paz. It must be Paz. Sarah has found Paz. Oh, Sarah, Sarah!

"It must be that my wife is trying to find me. She probably got hold of a family friend in Israel."

Harouni says, "She must love you, your wife, if she is willing to pay us to get you back. But she won't get you back. So what? My brother's wife loved him, too."

You fool, Gaspar thinks, she didn't love your brother. She loved Bobo, she despised your brother.

Gaspar catches himself inwardly reciting Bobo's version, Bobo's truth, a silent retort to Harouni. He smiles and Harouni, suspicious, asks why. Sarah, Gaspar replies, he is thinking of Sarah. In actuality, he smiles because again he has caught himself believing Bobo, despite the lies, the thorough and utter deceit. He believes Bobo's version. He does not, however, tell this to Harouni.

Harouni sends his men away. As far as Gaspar can tell, he is not armed. Harouni drops down onto his haunches and motions for Gaspar to

64

do the same.

"I studied at St. Joseph French University in Beirut," Harouni says. "You know it? A fine university. I studied history, also psychology and mathematics, everything. Therefore I know you now hate me for kicking you, but I also know that your hatred will stop. Tomorrow, the day after, you will stop hating me. But if you had kicked me I would never stop hating you, never. Because of my humiliation, I would wait and wait until one day I could do worse to you. I know about humiliation. It is a bad thing to feel, it can make the mind sick. But it can be made better by knowing what the feeling is and by talking about it, right? Well, here in the Middle East, talking about it is nothing, talking about it is shit. Your friend de Bossier humiliated my family. You think talking will make it better for me? One day I shall dig up his bones from his grave and piss on them, that will make me feel better. Because he was your friend, you will die, that will make me feel better. That is how it is here."

Harouni takes a fistful of Gaspar's hair in his hand and yanks it hard enough to make Gaspar yelp. "You tell me now where is the laundry powders, my friend."

After a moment's frenzied reflection, Gaspar's face clears. "In Marseilles," he replies. "In a supermarket in Marseilles."

Later Gaspar writes for Sarah that he dreamed of canoeing with her on a lake on a breezy day. The breeze brought them to the lake's far side and they remained there until the breeze shifted and they were returned back.

Chapter Ten

After that first lunch meeting in London with the skittish Frenchman, Sarah brought herself up to speed on the subjects he had mentioned.

First she read up on France's relations with Iraq and learned that these were indeed good. France had managed to form a special relationship with Iraq's absolute ruler Saddam Hussein, and had become Iraq's second largest arms supplier after the Soviets. Exact figures on the size of the trade between France and Iraq were not available, the information being largely based on deduction and surmise.

London's Institute for Strategic Studies and Stockholm's International Peace Research Institute made available to her data concerning the Gulf War itself, which included mention of France's involvements with Iraq. It was estimated that the combatants were each spending a billion dollars per month on their military. Since the war had been underway since the fall of 1980—six years at that point—it was possible to arrive at a total of sorts, although she'd come across other studies that reported far higher calculations than these. Estimates of quantities and expenditures for the considerable commerce in weapons preceding the war were less available.

From her reading of the materials gathered for her by the <u>Sentinel</u>'s research staff, Sarah constructed a chronology of France's relations with Iraq. She was struck by the realization that ties between the two countries had improved even as Iraq's relations with the West as a whole worsened.

In 1972, Iraq's ruling and sole political party, the Ba'ath (Renascence), nationalized the country's considerable petroleum resources which up to then had been exploited by the West's petroleum producing giants. In short order the English, the Dutch, and the Americans were sent packing. Only Elf, the French national oil company, was permitted to stay on. The reason behind the exception in the case of Elf became clear soon after the nationalization: France began supplying Iraq with arms the others had denied. Far more significantly, France undertook to build for Iraq a nuclear reactor at a place called Almada', not far from Baghdad, a project which became known as Tamuz 17.

Among the documents provided by the <u>Sentinel</u>'s research department was a report from Amnesty International on the practices of Iraq's Mukhabarrat, its secret police and counter-intelligence service. The AI report described a litany of corroborated accusations by political dissi-

66

dents against the Mukhabarrat: illegal detention, torture, disappearances, murder. She came to a paragraph that suddenly drained away her vitality, that made her feel weak and ill. Listlessly, she read it over again. Then she went down to the kitchen, prepared tea, and drank it slowly, taking enough time to gather herself, to rekindle her spirit.

The paragraph consisted of the testimony of several men who told of having been taken into detention along with their families, their wives and children. The complainants testified to AI that in the effort to get them to confess to whatever it was the Mukhabarrat accused them of, their interrogators had gouged out their babies' eyes while they and their wives were forced to look on.

Sarah wondered whether the folks at France's Foreign Ministry on Paris's Quay d'Orsay were aware of this AI document. Then she reprimanded herself for being self-righteous.

The next document she read was about the Central African Republic, once and briefly called the Central African Empire. Chardeau had mentioned Bokassa, former ruler of the C.A.R. during both its incarnations.

Bokassa was an African soldier who had served with France's colonial forces in central Africa. He must have been a good soldier, for he had reached the rank of sergeant and from there risen to become ruler of a nation, the Central African Republic, a country blessed: with diamond deposits.

So all was well for France, except for a large fly in the new ointment: Bokassa himself. The man turned out to be a violent psychotic.

One day Bokassa walked into a schoolroom and clubbed to death several underdressed young people.

Bokassa's action of course proved an embarrassment to his masters in Paris. The media made a fuss and there were other expressions of indignation. Still, the whole unpleasant episode might have blown away had Bokassa not been generous with some members of the family of France's then president, Valéry Giscard d'Estaing, to whom Bokassa had once made a gift of diamonds. Somehow word of his presents got out and a brouhaha ensued.

Then a strange thing happened. The fracas faded away, gradually disappeared until nothing more was said of it.

Sarah telephoned her office and asked that a search be run on the reaction outside of France to the Bokassa affair. It turned out that the story had received wide coverage, but of a secondary nature, more as a curiosity of the sort with which the serious press spices up its readers' day. The exception was a New York Times interview with an unnamed Quay d'Orsay official who plainly stated that in France the press was not permitted to maul the president about the way America's fifth estate regularly did theirs. Democracy and the people's right to know stopped when the issue became the dignity of the man in the Élysée Palace.

What was the point? Sarah wondered when she had finished; what was Chardeau trying to tell her? Most likely that he was on to some high-ranking French politician who was on the take. The components of Chardeau's message to her seemed to indicate that a powerful figure in the French government had in some manner misbehaved in connection with the Gulf War and that in Chardeau's estimation the French press would keep mum even if it became aware of the tale; just look how it behaved in the case of Bokassa.

That was how it usually went, in her experience; names, companies, places might be different, but it was always about lots of illicit money changing hands. Someone lost their head over mammon, dipped their pen in the company ink. This was hardly an earth-shaking story, certainly not worth a newspaper, nothing her editor would permit her to pursue.

Except that her intuition signaled to her like a stuck traffic light, stubbornly glowing red. As she read on, in the back of her mind she schemed of ways to co-opt Colechester, get him to give her the OK and the budget for chasing this story down. She thought of the Official Sercrets Act and of the Belgrado, and all at once she knew how to sell Colechester. Colechester had it in for the Secrets Act in a big way. She would therefore convince him that Chardeau's story could offer an opportunity to snipe at the Act, albeit at one remove, from just across the Channel.

Having accomplished her briefing, Sarah found herself eager to hear again from the Frenchman. As if he had sensed her wish, he telephoned the next day, by which time she had opened a file on his story, an act signifying that she was now on the Chardeau case.

Chardeau asked Sarah to meet him in Marseilles. He telephoned at seven a.m. and told her that the eight-thirty shuttle to Paris would connect her with a flight to Marseilles, "placing you on the earth there at before one o'clock." He gave her an address for their rendezvous, one of the large French chain of Carrefour supermarkets. Before she could protest that he wasn't leaving her enough time to prepare, he had hung up.

Marseilles proved to be a dreadful place, at least the lower part of the city that abutted the harbor, which she skirted on her way to the address he had given her. She met Chardeau at the entrance to the supermarket and assumed that they would go straight in, that he had planned it so that the shoppers would afford them a cover of sorts as they talked.

As soon as he spotted her, however, he came up, clasped her hand, and made her dash with him for a bus that was just taking on the last of a group of passengers. He paid the fare and they walked to the rear and assumed seats across from one another. He gazed past her shoulder.

The bus made its way down the very hills she had traveled up only moments earlier. They got off at the final stop, a large bus depot in which they were virtually the only Europeans among masses of Black Africans and North African Arabs. Although everyone seemed in a great hurry, nearly all glanced curiously their way, so unusual was their presence.

Chardeau became protective of her—protecting her from what? she wondered. "Keep up with my feet and don't be afraid. It is still our country here," he said with a certain vehemence.

"It never occurred to me that it wasn't," she replied quite innocently.

They made their way up narrow, curving alleys, grimy and strewn with debris, Chardeau walking slightly ahead. Occasionally they had to press against one of the blotchy walls to permit passing pedestrians to get by. Passing men. They were all men in the alleys, she realized. At the bus depot there had been women and children, but once Chardeau led her into the maze they encountered only men. Patterns of another culture, she thought.

They arrived at a widening where several small streets converged and there were a couple of hotels with stained facades and some North African restaurants, their names displayed in Arabic letters with smaller Roman letters advertising couscous. Suddenly a group of men came spilling out onto the street, a mass of flailing arms and flying legs, a cacophony of cries and grunts and invectives. Chardeau's hand slipped under his windbreaker and she realized that he was armed.

"Look here," she said to him in an urgent whisper, "what in the hell are you up to? I like the odd spy thriller as much as the next person, but you are taking things a bit too far, aren't you?"

The melee blocked the street, which apparently pleased Chardeau. He took her hand and they hurried past the writhing group and on down to the harbor with its forest of cranes and dozens upon dozens of ships, many of them ferry boats that regularly crossed to Tangiers and other coastal North African cities.

"The spies you will see in the odd spy movie will not kill you and me," Chardeau said, suddenly clear, cogent, and believable. "But my spies here, the ones we are running away from now, they will kill you and me, so you help me run and don't make trouble for me. I don't want to die yet," he said. And she took him at his word.

Sarah spotted a taxi and pointed it out to Chardeau. He gave her an approving glance and flagged it down. They returned to the supermarket.

She pushed a shopping cart down the spanking clean isles, Chardeau walking beside her. Every so often he picked an item off a shelf, examined it, and either replaced it or dropped it into the cart.

"Do you know of La Piscine?" he asked

"The pool?" she said. "That's what it means, right? No, I don't. Which pool?"

"La Piscine is what they call the headquarters building of France's counter-intelligence service in Paris, on the Boulevard Mortier. 'La Piscine' because our press is not free to speak of it, so they speak about the public pools across the way. A euphemism, you see."

She nodded.

"My name is Raoul Chardeau. I work at La Piscine in the Cipher Section of DGSE, our counter-intelligence service. It was called SEDCE when it was run by Count Bertrand de Bossier."

He stepped in front of her cart, rested his arms on it so as to stop her from moving on, and stared at her. This, she deduced, was Chardeau's way of examining her face for signs that de Bossier's name meant something to her. She burst into laughter, which, to judge from his perplexed look, was the one response he had not anticipated.

"He is my scandal," Chardeau whispered. "De Bossier was and is a traitor to the Patrie."

They were standing by then in the section with the detergents and laundry soap powders. Later Sarah would tell Gaspar that the inevitability of their meeting had been set at that moment, amongst the fragrant cleansers and bottles of bleach.

In Sarah's experience, people who approached her with stories were for the most part motivated by personal grievance—antipathy for a superior, anger over having been cheated out of a promotion, something of that sort. The greater the sense of having been wronged, the more cooperative they were likely to prove. She decided to press Chardeau on his motivation for tattling, and asked him to tell her more about his job. His answers were terse, perfunctory, which signaled to her that she was on the right track.

"It must be a very exciting place to work, cloak and dagger and all that," she offered.

"It used to be," he said, so bitterly that she was taken aback. "For some it was."

"Your gun, you know how to use it?" she asked, taking care to smile.

He checked to see whether it showed. Of course he did, he said. His military service had been with the paratroopers, in an elite unit. He glanced at her to make certain she fully appreciated the significance of this information.

Then, she hazarded, Cipher must have left him yearning for more brawny stuff, no?

Yes. She had pressed his button. "I have tried," Chardeau whined, "I have three times asked for a transfer to Action Branch."

It sounded so unlikely she thought at first he had again mangled his words. But he repeated them, saying that this had been SEDCE's military unit and at one time had been under the command of de Bossier's mistress.

And why had he been refused? Because, he said, he had been too reliable at Cipher. They knew they could count on him there, so why should they transfer him?

Why hadn't he resigned, then?

If looks could kill, she would have been lying lifeless on the supermarket's gleaming floor. For all its problems, hissed Chardeau, the Firm—that was what they called it amongst themselves, the Firm—was a place of patriotism, of principle and honor. Ideas of which the civilian world did not even conceive.

Satisfied that Chardeau was a sufficiently complex and embittered man and therefore reliable, she turned her attention to his scandal. She told him that she had brought herself up-to-date about France's relations with Iraq. Also about the timidity, even acquiescence of France's fifth estate when the story led to politicians who wrapped themselves in the flag. She offered to sketch for him what she sensed was the crux of his story. The man de Bossier, she proposed, had malfeased, had abused his office, skimmed some of the cream from the arms trade with Iraq for himself. Wasn't that it?

As if in parody of a movie spy, Chardeau stopped in his tracks and glanced furtively about. At length he turned to her.

"No no, Mrs. Tillinghast. De Bossier is not stealing from Iraq, never, not at all. De Bossier is with Iran; he is selling to Iran."

This she had not expected to hear.

71

Chapter Eleven

Gaspar Bruyn's name first came up as Sarah drove Chardeau from Marseilles to Toulon. In Toulon, Chardeau told her, she would find this Bruyn, an associate of the traitor de Bossier.

What sort of an associate? she wanted to know.

A fancy gentleman, like de Bossier. A Belge, de Bossier's closest friend and a former Honorable Correspondent for SEDCE. He explained about Honorable Correspondents.

How did he know that this Bruyn would be in Toulon?

His workplace was chock full of information about people's doings and whereabouts.

They had rented a car, and since she was driving and was less able to watch his facial expressions, she quickly taught herself to distinguish his emotions by his voice. His emotions ran ugly and rampant, the man was on a journey of fury and loathing.

What did he expect her to do about Bruyn?

"Why do you ask this of me, why?" Chardeau's voice trembled in a vibrato of anger. "You are the journalist, you know what to do with people like Bruyn, no?"

She asked whether Bruyn was in on the scandal.

Indeed he was, Chardeau replied. Bruyn had purchased the ship used to transport weapons to Iran. Chardeau took from his windbreaker pocket a color Polaroid photo and held it out to her. She took it in her hand. It was of a handsome man with dark blond hair, his face serious but open.

"Bruyn, the traitor's partner and friend," Chardeau said.

By the time they reached Toulon, Sarah had come fully to appreciate Chardeau's obsession with de Bossier.

Accepting that Chardeau was right about de Bossier, that the latter had for whatever reasons betrayed France, broken laws, acted against policy he had sworn to uphold, in general been a rat, she was still flabbergasted at the intensity of Chardeau's rancor. There was a primness in his voice as he talked about de Bossier. He was convinced, it seemed, that de Bossier's nobleman's title and treachery were somehow connected, that the upper class as a whole was not to be trusted. And the emphasis in all that he told her was on his own cleverness in having uncovered de Bossier's plot, as if laboring to convince her, himself too, that since de Bossier was clever and since he, Chardeau, had plumbed de Bossier's perfidy, he was by implication the cleverer of the two.

Chardeau's voice tightened into outright prissiness when he described how he had tumbled to the plot in the first place.

"He has a mistress, you see," he said, stealing a furtive look at Sarah.

He was a prig, she decided, and felt better about his indifference to her charms. Sarah had been beautiful all her life and since childhood had learned to search people's eyes for signals of admiration, of resentment and envy, of desire. When she failed to spot them, she grew disturbed. She had berated herself often for this amour-propre, but was unable to put it entirely behind her.

The name of de Bossier's mistress, Chardeau announced accusingly, was Genvieve Greaux. "When de Bossier left SEDCE, so did she. Bruyn also. It was because of Greaux that I first telescoped on de Bossier."

"Zeroed in" he obviously meant, Sarah thought. She'd considered correcting his various goofy misuses but decided against it. She understood him, and besides was reluctant to interrupt. In her business, listening both to what was and was not being said was of first importance.

"Probably she would not have been his mistress at all had he not been a count, and the Director as well. You know how women are about—" Chardeau stopped himself. "And if not for their relationship, she probably would not have been made head of Action Branch. Too bad for him. If he destructs down it will be because of her. I mean, because of you and me, but she first made me curious."

He shifted to face her, so she could better appreciate his gloating. "You see, I work at SEDCE with our most powerful machines, computers. American ones. To do cipher, decoding, we need good machines. And of course my machines talk to other machines at La Piscine. So if my boss at Research Branch (I work for the head of Research Branch but I am also a boss, I have six people to work for me), so if my boss wanted to know, for example, about a communication from St. Barthelemy in the Caribbean—we have a listening station there, we listen to American submarines. I always thought it was a comedy that we use American computers to listen to American submarines. So my boss just looks at the monitor on his desk and sees the communication, he does not have to come down to the basement, where we work. But the truth about such machines is that since they are capable of talking to one another they are also capable of listening to one another. And if you know your way with them, and I do because I work with our best machines, I am a graduate of an École Superieur, you can listen to other machines, ones that have nothing to do with Cipher."

What he had in effect been doing, it seemed, when the Firm had still been SEDCE and de Bossier the Director, was living vicariously in Action Branch by tracking the comings and goings of their operatives.

"Colonel Greaux had her own computer but her assistant worked it for her, Greaux did not know how. One day they posted a requisition for some Farsi language courses—the language of Iran—on tape. I saw this. Aha! I said, we have people in Iran, brave people. So I became alert for more. Any of our people there would have soon communicated with us on the Boulevard Mortier, either directly or indirectly. Sooner or later messages would have passed through my desk. Also, I looked for receipts. Apparently Greaux had sent her assistant to buy these Farsi tapes—I am guessing this—because the assistant posted the purchase and the receipts too, for reimbursement. I printed up a copy. I did this with such things, Action Branch things, to look at in my home. Funny, don't you think? Even our Action Branch daredevils filed receipts for everything, dry cleaning, cabs, that was how I knew what they were doing.

"But when I looked again two days later, the receipts were gone! Expunged! For some reason the assistant had reversed the entry. Why?

"I know how to look in on the machines at Accounting and Requisitions, and I see things. Receipts must always offset purchases, that is procedure. Two tuxedos and two evening gowns are purchased from Balmain? By this I know that Action Branch people are going on a bodyguard detail to some fancy party, and there is a proper receipt. Ten underwater scooters are ordered for the training center in Corsica? The lucky devils there soon will be at work preparing for some special assignment. Often I wished I could be with them in Corsica and on their assignments. But there is also an invoice from the manufacturer, dealer, or the company that fronted for SEDCE on the purchase, you understand?"

At the mention of underwater scooters and Corsica, Sarah thought that Chardeau might break down and weep in frustration for the exciting life his superiors had denied him.

He fell silent for a moment and she reminded him that he had been speaking about Greaux's failure to file the proper receipts.

"Not Greaux, her assistant," he corrected in something of a huff. "Greaux did not know how to manipulate the computer. After some weeks passed and there had not been communication from or about Action Branch, or any one else, in Iran, I began to wonder. I took an extra step, I checked on our intercepts from the Gulf. SEDCE as a matter of course intercepted all radio signals in the Gulf, shipping transmission, military, everything, so as to be aware on Iraq's behalf. Part of SEDCE's cooperation with their Mukhabarrat. And I encountered something unusual. One of the ships irregularly, but not infrequently, sailing the gulf consistently misrepresented its position: we intercepted signals from it that put it in such-and-such position and yet radar reported it consistently south of the reported position.

"Ordinarily this would not have caught my attention. In fact, the people at SEDCE who are meant to look in on such things made nothing of it, it was too small a discrepancy. But then they weren't looking for something unusual. We have stored recordings of ships, their sounds and transmission that lets us identify them—like people's voice prints. I ran those intercepted radio signals through our computer banks and got a match to a large container ship called the Twanee. Further cross-referencing revealed that the Twanee made regular stops at Polish, Yugoslav, Greek, Portugese, Pakistani, and other ports and ostensibly made runs to Baharain in the gulf. That part was true, it did make those stops.

"Then I looked into the Twanee vis-á-vis SEDCE, to see whether it had appeared in our files on previous occasions. It had not, but I was struck by a report on another container ship named the Hydra which matched exactly the specifications of the Twanee. And the reason we had a notation on the Hydra? A report had been filed by one of our paid informants. We pay people around the world for tidbits of information, airport employees, shipping people, brokers and the like. They are unaware that they are being paid by us, they think they are selling information, and not very important information really, to a competitor of their own employer, someone who wishes to keep up on industry doings—I'm sure you are familiar with this practice from your own business, paying for information. The police do it, the press do it, and we do it."

Sarah smiled a noncommital smile.

"In this case," Chardeau went on, "the informant was an Italian ship's broker's assistant from the port of La Spezia. She filed a report to the effect that a Belgian named Gaspar Bruyn had purchased a very large container ship there, near Genoa. Well, I am sure you can speculate about the rest, Mrs. Tillinghast. I ran a check on Bruyn and—what an accident!—the computer turned up his name as being a SEDCE Honorable Correspondent, and arms dealer. And that Bruyn's handler was none other than Vice Admiral de Bossier!"

This depiction of the ease with which Chardeau had been able to slip in and out of SEDCE's computer files concerned Sarah. It sounded, she thought, a bit too made-up. She pressed him on this point and was faced with a bout of extreme indignation and clarifications delivered with a classic display of Gallic pugnacity.

"I am very free," he sputtered, "I mean, I have freedom to all our information, I am a Section Head in Cipher, madame. I am complete with the machines. I found Bruyn by going to HC files. No one can do this except the Director and Research Branch head, and me. And you know what, Mrs. Tillinghast? SEDCE is like Renault or Banque National de Paris, it is a big affair...um, business, right? SEDCE is a big business place, we have many people who work there who are typists and clerks and messengers, not everyone is a spy. These people talk to other people, they say things about the others, about their bosses."

"You mean they gossip?"

"Absolumment!"

"Right. We have it too, at the water cooler." There she lost him, but her point had been made; she understood and believed him.

"That was how I learned that Greaux was de Bossier's mistress and Bruyn his best friend, from the gossip. After that I thought about what I had discovered. All the time I thought about it. I did not know what to do, or if to do anything, but I could not let it go, it was too important. People like de Bossier should not always evade justice, it is wrong, very wrong. But I knew I could not go to people at SEDCE, I would be dead in no time..."

"Really?" she blurted out, incredulous.

"Mrs. Tillinghast," Chardeau said, this time with controlled emphasis, "de Bossier, any Director, had very great power. When de Bossier first took office he discovered that one of his deputies was spying for the Eastern Block. In SEDCE wartime rules always apply because it is always at war. So de Bossier had a secret trial for this man at a SEDCE base not far from Paris. The man was convicted and de Bossier had him shot, right there, and no one ever heard a word about it outside SEDCE. Civilian laws do not matter at the Firm. The person who shot this spy for de Bossier was Colonel Greaux. So what do you think? If I said something inside SEDCE I would turn out like a rabbit on a hook in a butcher shop. That's right. Go to the papers? Bah, never. They would not write a word, SEDCE had friends at many newspapers, some of the best HC's for SEDCE were journalists. From going to the newspapers I would also end up on the hook. So I looked around. We have a good library at SEDCE, we get all the press, and I read the foreign newspapers, so I said, either I go to America and find someone at the New York Times or at the Washington Post, or I go to England. America is too far, I cannot leave my work for so long, so I found you.

She didn't bother asking how he'd gotten her phone number. The answer would have been something like, "Of course, we have someone at British Telecom."

"After de Bossier, Greaux, and Bruyn left SEDCE, they opened a business together, a business of advising those who wish advice on business..."

"Consulting. They started a consulting business together?"

"Yes. They had of course many interested people, especially in the Middle East. The Arabs, they love de Bossier, he knows them very well. The Twanee was still sailing the same as before, only one thing was different. Now it was sending radio messages to someone in Lebanon, someone named Forjieh. I searched his name too and of course I found it. Atrash Forjieh, one of the heads of the Lebanese Maronite Militias. You know about these?"

A bit, she said. They had been in the news over the past few years because of the civil war in Lebanon and because they had slaughtered hundreds of Palestinians at refugee camps near Beirut.

"The file on Forjieh was big. He had been working with, or for, de Bossier ever since 1974 when de Bossier was stationed in Beirut. After de Bossier returned to Paris, Forjieh continued to do all kinds of jobs for him and he was getting paid a lot. Then I understood: de Bossier had been selling to Iran when he was Director of SEDCE. This is a big ship, this Twanee, it has been to Iran many, many times, each time with much material, I am sure..."

"But how can you be certain? Look, I have to ask these questions, better to ask now than to appear foolish, or worse, later. You don't know exactly what was being delivered on the Twanee, is that right?"

"No, I do not know exactly. But I know that if I drive by the Bois de Boulogne in the night and I see a woman and she is opening her coat for me and is only wearing black stockings and nothing else, she is a prostitute. So I know that if there is a war in the Gulf and this ship goes many times to one of the two sides in this war, and this side wants weapons, and de Bossier keeps what he knows about this ship secret, and his friend is a dealer in weapons and his mistress wants to learn Farsi—I know that it is not for Club Med vacations that the Twanee goes there."

She was very tempted to laugh, but resisted.

"He is a dog, de Bossier, a traitor to the Patrie, Mrs. Tillinghast. Yes, he is another Dreyfus..."

"Don't you mean another Esterhazy?"

But Chardeau appeared not to comprehend.

77

Chapter Twelve

Several days go by without word from Paz. Sarah telephones him to ask for more—more words about Gaspar. Details of how Paz and his people are proceeding, the general situation in Lebanon. Anything.

Not much is going on, he tells her. Contacts are being pursued, messages are being passed, responses and rumors checked out. Like that.

She presses him. If only he would tell her <u>something</u>. That communications are underway between his people and those in Lebanon, whoever they are. Surely he knows more about the kidnappers now than he did at first? She is distraught, her nerves have reached the point of inelasticity, capable only of the high-pitched notes of mindless fear.

Paz is sympathetic and wary in roughly equal measure. He cannot say more about the kidnappers, not because he doesn't wish to, "and no, Sarah, not, as you say, because I am congenitally incapable of disclosure. It's OK, I am not offended, I understand your stress. I have unfortunately been witness to too many hostage and kidnaping situations, they are horror shows. Frankly I'm astonished at how well you are holding up. No apologies called for."

He doesn't know more because he and the kidnappers are using intermediaries, people several times removed. In any case, what good will it do her to know exactly how these communications proceed?

She hears the balance shift, wariness gaining on sympathy. She explains hurriedly that knowing more about the situation would help her stave off chaos, help keep at bay the panic that has taken up residence from the moment she realized that Gaspar was taking too long with those men, there at Beirut airport. Panic that is whipping furiously along the parameters of her sanity, searching for a chink to enter and devour her orderly mind, like a hungry weasel scurrying along the fence of a chicken coop. Details would be appreciated, Paz. Details are affirmations of reality, small loops that must be made to add up. The effort of adding them up is the closest she can come to soothing the panic. Can he see that? Good. Great. She is ever so grateful. By fishing boat?

Messages travel by fishing boat from Beirut out to sea, nearly to Cyprus. There a fast Israeli patrol boat—a Dabur class boat, Paz says—stops the fishing boat and a search is conducted. No, this is not unusual, Israeli patrol and missile boats stop and search fishing and other vessels in that area all the time, people have grown to accept this. The sea is the one place where Israel exercises almost complete mastery and because of this virtually no saboteurs now, as they have in the past, enter Israel from the sea.

This particular Dabur's First Officer is a Mossad liaison with the Navy. During the search he will confiscate something from the fishing boat, anything—a can of lubricating grease, a bundle of Lebanese girly magazines. Out at sea, aboard the subject fishing boat, he is omnipotent, his caprice is law. The Lebanese fishermen stare balefully at him, promise him with their eyes that but for his armed back-up, men clutching Galil assault rifles, others manning a large-caliber machine gun, they would surely slit his throat with their razor-sharp fishermen's knives, that this would give them far more pleasure than gutting a snapper or mullet. And yet one of them has deposited a message in the object this First Officer will confiscate, one of them will carry back a message to shore from wherever the First Officer will have deposited it.

Sarah weeps and Paz is startled, upset. What is it? What has he said?

The fishermen's knives. The image of sharp knives gutting fish, slitting throats. Does he think Gaspar is alright? she begs in a voice strangled by tears. Does he think Gaspar is alive?

Yes, he says, his intuition tells him that Gaspar is alive. Because something unusual is underway here. These people, the people holding Gaspar, do not comply with past patterns.

Sarah then drops the last vestiges of a stiff upper lip. She slaps an impatient hand at the table where she is seated and shouts into the phone.

"Pattern, Paz? Intuition? What insanity is this? The kidnaping of a transiting passenger from a fourth-rate airport in a country that when and if it ever straightens out it will become merely schizophrenic may be said to be part of a recognizable pattern, Paz? Who is crazier here: you, me for listening to you, the kidnappers, this festering region itself?"

Paz falls silent and Sarah is certain that she has lost him, for good.

Then he returns, sounding older and speaking slowly. He makes the case for patterns. Back in 1985-6, he recounts for her, he had been in the thick of negotiations with Lebanese kidnappers, Hezbollah boys, fanatics, lovers of a joyless world, adherents of Khomeini's who had assembled a collection of Western hostages, one of them a CIA station head in Beirut. This CIA man Hezbollah first tortured, then executed, and let everyone know what they had done and how. In Gaspar's case, no one appears to have an axe to grind...sorry, poor choice of metaphor. But does she see his point?

Back then the Americans had panicked after their CIA man, who had apparently been a nice, capable chap, was killed. They came running to Paz with yet another barter scheme, nearly identical to the deal Kirney had involved him in six years earlier. Except that this time they sought the opposite outcome: promptness. This time they wanted the Americans not yet slaughtered by Hezbollah released ASAP, fast, like yesterday, Mr. Paz.

Yes, certainly there were political considerations for Mossad and him, just like that other time. Politics always factors into these things, layers of considerations with, at the top, the sine qua non of Western elective politics: that leaders maintain the impression that they are incapable of being shmucks. That unlike the ordinary folks who have elected them they are unencumbered by human foibles, that they do not commit errors. God forbid. Never.

Her panic, by then only somewhat abated, soars. Paz, his people, are certain to make a mess of the effort to extricate Gaspar. No, they have already. Paz is keeping it from her. This self-deprecating talk of fallibilities of leaders, is probably just his way of easing upon her the news that it is over, never really stood a chance. She suddenly despises his chumminess and inability, to form even a single sentence that is free of ethnic flourish, of hollow bravado born of victories against backward foes. And that just beneath the surface insinuations that she, an English Rose, a tea drinker and partaker in other peculiar island customs, must be strung along. For her delicate skin will not protect her against the heartbreaking news, that Gaspar is dead...

Paz grinds on regardless. Impervious to her silent derision. She hears him citing dates, places, events, a spy-salesman offering up past victories to clinch the sale.

He says: back then, there had been narrower, but important, constituencies to appease and reassure. In 1986, for example, the American President, (he who had won office by delaying the release of that previous set of hostages, and by bathing in the glory and gratitude showered upon him by the electorate when the captive, finally, came home--in his good time), came under tremendous self-imposed pressure not to appear weak, foolish. When the Beirut CIA station head met his gruesome fate, the tough talking president had to prove himself equal to the challenge posed by a bunch of bearded Iranian zealots.

"So the Americans came to us, wanting us to sell and deliver goods to Iran, whence emanated Hezbollah's marching orders. We made the deliveries, this time without de Bossier's cargo planes. We flew the goods in ourselves, better goods, too, Hawk anti-craft missiles, top-of-the-line spare parts. We probably kept the Iranians going in their crazy slaughter-house of a war. More, I think these deliveries turned the tide in their favor, fueled their slow push-back of the Iraqis until eventually they conquered goodly chunks of Iraqi territory."

She asks whether de Bossier, Gaspar, knew any of this. She wonders to herself whether Gaspar's kidnappers were motivated by convolutions more serpentine, bloodier, than she had assumed. But Paz, apparently not tuned to her thinking, hastens to reassure her that since he and his people had been competent back then, so they will be once again, this time on her behalf.

No, we didn't even approach de Bossier, he says; we didn't need him and didn't want him involved. We were not great fans of his, you know. He'd made it very cozy for Palestinian terrorists to travel through France, had in fact struck a bargain with them. Decidedly, the Count was not our friend.

Perhaps, yes, certainly, she is wrong. Her tirade was misplaced, a moment of being overwhelmed by the wobbliness. And Paz does not know, she never uttered a word about her collapse of faith. He cannot possibly be making all of this up. Some of it, she now actually recalls, had crossed her journalist's consciousness in the past. She revives, and seizes faith. Paz's lecture actually becomes a comfort, a call to return to their partnership, and she accepts.

"De Bossier, the bastard, did however find out about our deal and although he was long out of office he still had lots of power. He set out to punish us and the Americans, oh yes. He was very much what the Americans call a hardball player. Through his people in Lebanon, he had a Beiruti magazine called Al Shiraa run the arms-for-hostages story, the whole spiel. Where did he get it? I would guess he had a very good source in Teheran. They printed it down to the last detail, the story was picked up by the international press and eventually became the scandal called Irangate. A real mess for us and for the White House.

"'Gey vaiss,' they say in Yiddish. Means 'go know.' I mean, in the beginning of that particular deal we here were unaware of the Contra aspect. That bit—to have us continue to sell to Iran even after the hostages were released—was the bright idea of some White House hot shots. A share of the profits was going to support the anti-communists in Nicaragua, sort of subsidizing a secret foreign policy."

Yes, she knew about that, but not about all the rest.

"Look," he continues in a somewhat apologetic tone, "it was and is true that Israel's survival is a cash-intensive proposition. Not all our busi-

81

ness deals made me proud, but we needed to do them. That's all I'll say about that. But the point of all this is that there was lots of negotiating with hostage-takers going on back then and I was in the midst of it. So again I tell you that my feeling is that so far Gaspar is all right.

"The mess de Bossier made? Oh boy. After the article was published and Israel stopped shipping, there evolved an ongoing scandal in Washington. To this day there are bits of it flying around, cutting up people. Some say the president himself had been behind the deal with Teheran and that it was illegal, immoral, and so on."

Mind you, the French didn't always manage to escape the crap that the Middle East sent flying into the world's air. Did she remember a few years back those nasty explosions in Paris?

She did.

"The shameful truth is, I don't feel sorry for them. I'm not an angel, never claimed to be. Oh, I'm sorry for the innocents who suffered, but not for their government. In a way there was poetic justice in this—how do you say about the dog lying down with fleas? Well, you get my meaning.

"You see, the French did much to aid Palestinian attacks on us in Europe, on Israelis, on Jews, on others who had merely chosen the wrong airline. If not by commission, then by omission. Mind you, I'm not debating about statehood for the Palestinians, but I am telling you the French were full of crap when they claimed they were doing these things for the Palestinians out of sympathy for their plight, because they were stateless. So where was their sympathy when the natives in one of France's Pacific possessions, New Caledonia I think it was, sought a state of their own, eh? Where was their support for self-determination then? I'll tell you where: in the barrels of their guns. They sent their gendarmes to New Caledonia and shot the terrorists dead. When the statehood being sought was at France's expense, the seekers were terrorists, you see. When they were shooting up our busses and schools they were freedom fighters.

"Do I sound indignant? I am! I can't forget that in 1980 there was an attack by Palestinians on a synagogue on the Rue Copernic and a little French Jewish boy was shot dead, along with a couple of non-Jews who simply happened to be in the wrong place at the wrong time. And you know what Raymond Barre, France's Prime Minister, said? Something like, the Palestinians shot at Jews and hit innocent Frenchmen.

"It was after the Rue Copernic attack that de Bossier made his deal with the Palestinians. I mean he'd done things with them before, but this was about keeping peace in France. In return for their promise not to make trouble in France, he agreed to allow them unhindered passage as well as certain logistical privileges. Meaning they could schlep their guns and explosives through French railway stations and airport terminals unmolested so long as they were on their way to other places in Europe. So no, I am not in mourning that the crazies in Teheran exploded some bombs in Paris.

"Now since I called collect, let me hang up on you before you use up all your money on telephone bills and you won't have any left over to buy back Gaspar."

She thanked him and signed off with a plea that he let her know immediately anything further he learned about Gaspar.

Paz's phrase about Israel's survival being a cash-intensive proposition flashed in Sarah's mind with the repetition of a flashing neon restaurant sign. The message bore an eerie similarity to Bobo's. Except that Bobo's had, of course, been about his beloved France.

Chapter Thirteen

"Would you like it if I killed your wife?" The tone of Harouni's question is devoid of malice or guile.

Gaspar has been brought from the shed to Harouni's house, where he has been permitted to bathe. As he lowered himself into the warm tub, his first cleansing since before the airport, he was overtaken by a sensation unlike any he had known. Countless tiny padded probes, each as warm as a lover's breath, each perfectly corresponding to his skin's numberless nerve endings, kneaded, caressed, and teased into a peak of pleasure. Gaspar sat in the warm tub until his fingertips became waterlogged.

He dried off with a thick white towel, prompting another bout of intense pleasure. On a chair near the tub lay fresh underwear, a clean, short-sleeved white shirt, black chino pants, a pair of white cotton socks. He had been permitted his privacy throughout this pleasant and immensely confusing break in his prisoner's pattern. He hadn't the slightest idea why any of it was happening, only assuming it had to do with Sarah's and Paz's efforts to free him.

When he was finished in the bathroom, he was escorted to a parlor by one of Harouni's men. By this time he is able to recognize half a dozen of these young men in their most unmilitary uniforms—jeans, casual shirts, running shoes.

In the parlor, Harouni and a pretty young woman, perhaps seventeen or eighteen years old, sat in chintz-covered chairs, jaunty emerald-green patches of glistening fabric that brightened the room. Their eyes were locked on Gaspar as he approached. It was not until Gaspar had reached a small silk prayer rug, one of several decorating the room, that Harouni posed his startling, frightening question.

Immediately Gaspar wonders whether they are also holding Sarah, whether she was taken when he was. He glances at the young woman's face, oval and smooth with full lips and black candles for eyes, candles that burn with a steady flame that converges on Gaspar's own face and eyes, that deny him any hint of herself.

After Harouni has posed his question he adds, gesturing toward the woman, "She is Mari. She is my love."

"I would not like it," Gaspar answers. "What you asked me. Is my wife all right?"

Harouni laughs happily. "I don't know, you tell me. Is she all right?"

He has made a joke, a sexual double entendre. He looks to the young woman for admiration.

Gaspar is relieved. He believes that Sarah is safe.

"Mr. Harouni," he says, "again I tell you: I had nothing but nothing to do with what happened to your brother and his wife. What Bobo did he did on his own."

Harouni thunders, fury pouring from him, causing him to stumble over his words. "But did you...have you...did you accuse him after you knew? No. So you are the same as him."

A raging indignation overcomes Gaspar, that this Levantine caveman presumes to lecture him on moral imperatives. Would this holier-than-thou Harouni submit an accounting of his own sins? He calculates quickly: Harouni must be in his early thirties. At the time of the carnage at the Sabra and Shatila Palestinian refugee camps in 1982, nine years ago, he would have been in his early twenties. Where were he and his men in running shoes the night the Maronites swooped down on those camps south of Beirut to avenge their freshly assassinated leader? A leader whose death was yet another in a long line in Lebanon, so many that the slaying of Claude and Naama was but a fading memory for most.

The Maronites had entered the camps under the lax, some said winking, eye of the occupying Israeli army and spent a night of frenzied slaughter. Hundreds of men, women, and children were butchered. Did Harouni "accuse" afterwards? Fat chance. Didn't his brother Claude wipe out Forjieh's kin, plug them as if they'd been empty beer cans at a shooting range? Did Harouni "accuse" his older brother afterwards?

Gaspar damps down his indignation; it will do him no good in this house. Harouni is pursuing vengeance, not symmetry. Vengeance is about ridding oneself of torturing nightmares, visualizations of one's kin suffering atrocities, about letting it be known that the family had insurance of sorts, a policy that guaranteed defrayment with the killer's blood.

Gaspar says, "Bobo had a woman too, you know." He leaves unspoken his thoughts; and she is still alive, so why don't you find her, take her in my stead? The implications of what he has said and not said silence him.

Harouni and Mari ignore his statement and regard him with puzzled curiosity.

"Mari is studying at the American University of Beirut," Harouni says. He caresses the woman's face. She kisses the palm of his hand as it brushes her lips. "You tell her about your smart friend de Bossier, about the great things he did, like you told me."

Gaspar looks at the two with a new loathing that comes from being forced to sing for one's supper. His mind runs a prisoner's equation: his time left to live, his time before being set free, over his jailor's lust for his blood, minus Paz's powers. Singing for his supper falls into the equation of his time left to live. He proceeds.

"You remember the Shah of Iran?"

"Sure, I know of him," Harouni assures him.

The woman stares at Gaspar, her beautiful, full lips assuming an expression of patient expectation.

From a nearby room a television blares out an American police drama. Harouni's men are entertaining themselves even as their master is. It is only right.

Someone had rolled a television on casters into the hallway for the Shah's security men to entertain themselves while their master was being examined.

Those four lounged outside the Firm's medical offices on the ground floor of SEDCE's headquarters on the Bvd. Mortier, and another four waited in two cars parked in the yard; they had bracketed the Shah's limousine as it had made its way from his mansion to the Bvd. Mortier, two more in the limousine itself, the driver, and another who sat up front next to the driver. The limousine, a Mercedes, was armored. Genvieve "Deadeye" Greaux and her Action Branch people provided yet additional security along the route. Deadeye was unhappy about the way things had gone up to that point.

When she and her people came to escort the Shah from his Paris home to the Bvd. Mortier, she protested to the Shah's own security person because his Mercedes limousine had been selected for the drive. In Paris, where limousines were Citroëns and aroused interest in any event, a Mercedes was likely to elicit even greater unwelcome curiosity. She suggested that a vehicle from SEDCE's inventory be used, a taxi or delivery van, something that would go unnoticed. The Shah's man replied that when Coco Chanel attended the unveiling of one of her collections in a sweat suit, then the Shah would ride in a taxi. Until then His Highness would be driven in his Mercedes. If it would make her feel better, they would draw the window curtains.

Deadeye was then second in command at Action Branch, the Firm's private military force, its enforcer—a troop of top-of-the-line soldiers, saboteurs, pilots, assassins, burglars, bodyguards, bone breakers. She despised the arrogant moron in charge of the Shah's detail, a man, she intuitively knew, whose thinking was clouded by his testosterone, who could not fathom a woman soldier, a special soldier at that, a commanding officer yet! She fiercely wished she could take the fool into the woods at a Firm training center and put him through the paces. That would chill his roaring Levantine hormones, she thought. Deadeye had, nevertheless, been unfailingly correct with him. She had been given her orders: nothing was to go wrong on this mission, nothing. Deadeye obeyed orders.

She paced the far end of hallway, as the Iranians watched a dumb variety show, the sort that offered up a host in black tie and a sidekick in a tight low-cut dress. The host sang forgettable tunes in a second-rate voice, told crass jokes about cheating wives and unbearable mothers-in-law. The side-kick laughed at his tawdry stuff, and frequently positioned her bosoms for close-up shots. Deadeye heard footsteps approaching, two men; it was night and the building was still, but for the television and for the sound of their shoes. She tossed her cigarette into a wall-mounted ashtray and quietly rounded the corner into an unlit corridor. There she awaited the comers.

"The Black September has woman soldiers, what is the big deal? You ever hear of Layla Khaled? She was a soldier, a very good one, just ask your friends the Jews how good she was," Mari says.

Gaspar remembers the name, Khaled was a Palestinian who, in some way or another, had struck at Israel.

"Well, what I am describing to you happened in 1974, nearly seventeen years ago. Things were still different then, for women I mean," Gaspar assures her.

It was de Bossier, head of Research Branch, and another man, she had seen him before too, leaving de Bossier's office she remembered, then remembered more— that the guy was a friend of de Bossier's, a Belge.

"Good evening Captain, all's well here?" de Bossier asked.

"Sir. Yes sir."

"How long has His Highness been with the doctors?"

She looked at her watch. "Sir, fifty-four minutes, sir."

"This is Mr. Gaspar Bruyn. Gaspar, Captain Greaux."

She began to salute, but, to her embarrassment, Bruyn extended his hand and they exchanged handshakes. Up until then she had been in close proximity to de Bossier on two other occasions, both times in the company of her boss. Both times she had been curious about the count, Vice Admiral de Bossier by military rank, a much-admired man at SEDCE, on the fast track to the director's job. Now she noted to herself that de

Bossier was gazing at her in a rather more personal sort of way. His eyes displayed something between a physical interest in her, which in general she did not welcome, and a need of some sort— perhaps, she thought to herself, the need of a boy for his mother. She thought: de Bossier was, as she recalled from office gossip, unmarried. Also, her intuition told her, his was a solitary nature, like her own.

"Captain, will you please come by my apartment after you have seen His Majesty safely home. Come and have a drink with us; I will be asking you for your impressions of His Majesty's demeanor," de Bossier said. He handed her a card that had an Île St. Louis address on it.

"What did she look like, this dyke Greaux?" Mari demands.

Harouni chortles.

"She was, and is, an attractive woman. She wears her hair short, dark brown hair, light brown eyes, almost golden, small nose, lips on the thin side, good skin, buxom, very limber, like a dancer or an athlete. I can see how you can come away with the impression that Deadeye was mannish. She wasn't, really, she was just very taken with her military role, Action Branch and all that."

"What is that name, Deadeye?" Harouni asks.

"She had been an excellent shot in the military. It means someone who has an excellent eye for shooting."

Deadeye delivered her report. When she arrived at Bobo's she was met at the door by Gaspar, who sensed that she was ill at ease. He assumed that amongst other things Bobo's address, his place, made her self-conscious; as a rule civil servants did not live in twelve-room apartments in one of Paris's most exclusive enclaves. The drive back to the Shah's residence had been uneventful, Deadeye reported. The Shah had at one point said to her, quite unexpectedly and in perfect French, that it was unfair that he, the ruler of so many, could not command his body. To her this sounded, well, sort of fatalistic. But she wasn't an expert at such things. As Bobo was considering this information, a phone call came from the physician who had examined the Shah. Bobo asked Gaspar to show Deadeye the apartment. He took the call only after they left the room.

"Bertrand inherited this place, you know," Gaspar said to her when they stood at a large window looking down onto the Seine.

"Why are you telling me this sir?" she asked.

"Because I do not wish you to labor under misapprehensions about Bobo, Bertrand. Sometimes people resent other's wealth, and Bobo's places have been handed him by his parents, that's all. To be frank with you, mademoiselle, I sensed that you two like one another; I hope this is the case. I wish for Bobo to have a woman friend, I hope I am not embarrassing you, but that is what I wish. I myself am married, and it has done me a world of good; I wish the same for my friend." They heard Bobo's voice calling them to return.

"The Shah has cancer, a leukemia of some kind, and has two or three years to live," Bobo said, his eyes resting on Deadeye as he spoke, and she knew that he meant her to feel that he was placing trust in her. She was grateful and touched.

"We shall make the most of this," Bobo said, this time to Gaspar. His eyes shone brightly as he spoke, and had an altogether peculiar look to them, as if he wasn't seeing Gaspar at all.

"It was a very great coup that the Shah came here for his medical examination," Gaspar confided to Deadeye, "a great achievement for Bobo, you know."

"How?" she asked, and was amazed that she felt as comfortable as she did.

"Bobo had convinced the Shah that it would be wiser to have doctors look him over in France than at the Mayo Clinic or Johns Hopkins or Sloan Kettering in America. At any American hospital, the results of the Shah's examination would lickety split end up on the desk of the CIA director and under the best of circumstances be made known to the American president and no doubt his most trusted advisors. Under the worst, it would be run on the front pages of the New York Times and/or the Washington Post. This, Bobo assured the Shah, would never happen in France."

"The most important factors here were those of timing and exclusivity," Gaspar explains to his audience. The Americans, ostensibly the Shah's great friends and patrons, were kept ignorant of the Shah's condition for another five years, by which time the information was virtually an epitaph. "You can check on this yourself," Gaspar suggests to Mari, the university student, drawing from her another smile.

"What happened to the bastard de Bossier and his Captain Deadeye?" Mari asks. Another thought comes to her, puts a leer onto her lips. "Did they ever do it with each other?" she asks.

"She moved in with him two weeks after the Shah's visit. They remained together until Bobo died," Gaspar says.

"You must be very rich, Mr. Gaspar," Mari says, "because you and your friend made big money in the Gulf, no? Forjieh made big money working with you, everyone in Lebanon knows this, so if he made money being your worker you, the bosses, must have made so much more." She gazes at Harouni as she speaks her piece, wanting to impress him. "I think you can get maybe five million for him, cheri."

"Francs?"

"No, my dove. Dollars, dollars!"

All at once Harouni becomes ruffled, annoyed; because, Gaspar concludes, he's displeased at Mari for discussing these things in front of Gaspar. Mari's pretty lips have said too much.

Gaspar is hustled back to the shed. He lies in the dark and thinks of the house he has just left, of its bright lights and tiled floors, of chairs and tables and lamps. And of Mari. Her greedy thesis about how much of a ransom Gaspar might fetch was the most encouraging message he has heard since Harouni's slap and his explanation of Shlomo's interest.

But Gaspar's optimism is shallow, only a shade above apathy. In truth, he is powerless still, a dried leaf that Harouni's wind is free to toss and jerk, lift and drop at will.

That Mari has permitted him to hear that his life may have a value to them was, in a sense, the antithesis to Harouni's not having bothered to blindfold him when he was first taken. He thinks of Mari, of her pretty lips. Then of Laura, his first wife. She too had beautifully shaped lips. Thoughts of pretty lips, blessed and distancing, transport Gaspar from the ugliness of life in the shed.

They had married when he was barely twenty-three, Laura twenty, a beautiful Italian girl from Sienna. He'd met her at an August Palio while visiting distant banker cousins in that splendid, ancient city. Their love had been made of youthful vigor and lust, a resolute refusal of introspection, and a devotion to bourgeois conformity. They had married because that was what people did after they'd met and experienced exhilaration and possessiveness. Marriage set everyone—parents, friends, even strangers—in an approving mood. Gaspar, for one, had never encountered in his parents' home as much harmony and excitement as he had on the day he returned from Sienna to ask his father's blessing.

With time the momentum of Gaspar's and Laura's beginnings slowed, the reality of who and how they actually were with one another nudged at them and altered their course, like gravity tugging at a spinning top. Laura had a way of minimizing things and Gaspar had a way of letting things be so as not to unleash some great upheaval. On the rare occasion when he brought up an issue between them, Laura accused him of not letting well enough alone.

Her finest rationalizations had been reserved for those few times when Gaspar said something even remotely critical of Bobo. Bobo was her hero. She rooted for him as her countrymen rooted for their favorite soccer clubs. She was thrilled that her husband was on Bobo's team. Bobo could do no wrong.

It fell to Sarah Tillinghast to demonstrate to Gaspar just how much wrong Bobo had done.

Chapter Fourteen

Paz telephones Sarah in London. "You married well, Mrs. Bruyn. They're asking five million so they must believe Gaspar has this kind of money."

"I suppose he may," Sarah says, "I don't really know. You know how Continental men are; they consider their money none of the wife's business."

Paz laughs. He does indeed know.

"We live well," Sarah resumes. I have my own income so his money was never much of an issue. But yes, it's possible he has quite a lot. Probably you know better than I, you were in a similar business."

"I was a civil servant," Paz says. He sounds miffed at the implication. "The dealings I told you about were part of my job. Gaspar dealt in ships—big-ticket items, for his own account."

The first words Sarah ever said to Gaspar had been about ships. She'd telephoned him from a "tabac" near his hotel in Toulon, where Chardeau had dropped her off. "You deal in ships, Mr. Bruyn," she'd stated. "I am a reporter doing an article on shipping to the Persian Gulf war zone."

Gaspar was in Toulon to dine with a high-ranking French naval officer at Mediterranean fleet headquarters. This officer was a useful friend to Bobo and to Boulevard Consultants, frequently helping Boulevard get a jump on competitors. He supplied tips about navy surplus goods and about the navy's selection of particular suppliers—an Alcatel or Breguet product, say, over another manufacturer's—helpful in impressing Boulevard's clients. This beneficial friend was nearing retirement and Bobo had asked Gaspar to meet with him and formally invite him to join Boulevard, an outcome that had been assumed all along.

Gaspar had just showered, dressed, and was brushing his hair before stepping out for a late afternoon espresso when the phone rang in his hotel room. A woman reporter, speaking with obvious self-assurance in an English accent, told him that because he was informed about shipping in the Persian Gulf she would like to interview him. "Off the record, for background only. Merely to help me lull my readers into thinking I know that of which I speak, Mr. Bruyn." She'd tell him how she got his name when they met. Would he please let her buy him a drink? Espresso sounded great.

He considered for a moment that the call was a prank of Bobo's, a teaser premised on Gaspar's propensity for affairs, but the caller's phrasing and determination dissuaded him from that idea. Next, he thought of telephoning Bobo about it, but overruled himself. Too often when things baffled him he took them to Bobo. A telephone call from a reporter ought not to baffle. He felt bemused by the thought that someone had given the English reporter his name. The time left to kill before dinner suddenly took on a new life.

"OK, where are you?"

"Near a "tabac" catty-cornered to your hotel. There's an espresso bar next door. Shall we meet there in ten minutes?"

She turned out to be a dazzler, the proverbial English rose with sex appeal grafted on. He made his way directly to her through the crowded espresso bar. There was no mistaking her identity, she fairly radiated it. He was aware of all eyes in the place fixed on him, the one for whom this beautiful woman had been waiting. People whispered and he knew they were making the sort of disparaging remarks people make when they are feeling envious.

She held out her hand. "I'm Sarah Tillinghast," she said, with a rising intonation that asked whether he recognized her name.

He didn't. He shook her hand, amiable and ever so slightly wary. "Gaspar Bruyn. What's this about?" Amiability with attractive women was his second nature, a practiced pleasantness that permitted women to feel free to seduce him. Seduction, he believed, was a woman's prerogative; men needed only to make themselves available to it.

"I work for a London paper, the Sentinel."

He nodded his recognition of the name. "I'm sorry I'm away from home too often to justify a subscription," he said with a smile.

She didn't smile back, only gazed at him, friendly but distant, interested but noncommittal. "I'm looking into doing a piece about shipping to the war zone. The whys, the hows, the personalities behind what is essentially a risky business. With all these attacks on shipping by both sides, I mean."

Despite himself he felt the warm tingle that flattery induces. He was being buoyed by the attention and deference of this splendid-looking reporter who had come all the way to Toulon to speak with him. He wondered who had led her to him, then considered that she could simply have followed him from Paris, or some employee at Boulevard had tipped her off, or that a reporter who knew of Bobo from the old days had mentioned Gaspar's name—there were any number of possibilities. Boulevard was, after all, not a secret. It had an address and telephone and telex numbers, a receptionist, secretaries. And while its business was private and confidential it was not surreptitious. Arms sales and shipments often required approval by French authorities ranging from Defense Ministry officials to customs clerks. Gaspar was aware that Bobo was acquainted with reporters from his SEDCE days. Some had been honorable corespondents, others knew that Bobo was SEDCE's director, but were obliged by the state to keep it to themselves. On occasion SEDCE planted stories through these reporters, self-serving tales meant either to promote and praise or to scuttle and besmirch, even to ruin a life.

"I'm a ship's architect, Miss Tillinghast," he said. "How on earth, or on the seas, do you expect me to know what goes on in the Persian Gulf? I'm afraid you've been misled."

"First," she countered, "I want to thank you for agreeing to speak with me. Second, I know my business, Mr. Bruyn, just as I'm certain you know yours. I got your name from a credible source and I know you're in the business of shipping arms to the war zone. I know your firm owns at least one container ship, the Twanee—what a good name, by the way. All I ask is that you help me do my job. You have my word the article I'm proposing won't be centered on you. So how about helping a girl out? And before you ask, I won't give my source's name, just as I won't give your name. The ethics of the business, you know."

She watched a collage of responses pass through his eyes—curiosity, wariness, arousal.

He said, "You really don't know why cargo ships go to the Gulf? If I were to guess, I'd say it's the premiums, terrific premiums." His voice took on the tone of a shared confidence. "Best rates in the cargo business anywhere in the world. Not a crime, right? I'd guess that clients are willing to pay premiums to have their goods delivered there. Now, would you like a coffee?"

"Please," she said, and smiled for the first time. An unreserved smile, free of anticipation of the moment certain to arrive when neither of them would be in a smiling mood.

He shouted his order to a waiter behind the counter.

"So that's what this is all about," she said, nodding with an air of enlightenment. "Lucrative shipping fees. Makes sense." She leaned back, happy in her new knowledge. Then a new concern brought a tiny frown to her superb face. "But what about the hows of it? Ships and sailors are expensive, right? Are the premiums worth the risk of putting them in harm's way?"

"So far they have been," he said. He was feeling more comfortable. Her questions and expressions, her gratitude for his help, eased his anxieties and elevated his pleasure at the attention he was getting. His curiosity about her expanded beyond her alluring surface to her intensity, her dedication to absorbing the information he gave. "There are risks," he admitted. "There have been attacks on oil tankers and on some cargo vessels. But if one is careful one gets by all right."

"But what does that mean, 'if one is careful'"? she persisted.

A young man in a tattered leather jacket and white duck slacks walked by their table and cast toward her a lingering look and a smile that said in his company conversation would be the last thing to concern them. She smiled back, at once appreciative and dismissive. The smile vanished so fast Gaspar doubted his own impression of it.

"Isn't it unusual? I mean, that your ships go undisturbed?"

"Oh I don't think so. Many others get through all right; it's a function of proper precautions and skill and luck. Sometimes cargos are unloaded in friendly ports and trucked the rest of the way."

"How do you mean, 'friendly'? Friendly to whom?"

"To Iraq, of course."

"I see. Now what of the sailors: who are they? I mean where do they come from, and do they get paid more than other sailors?"

"They're from all over—Filipinos, Thais, Eastern Europeans, Greeks. English too, I think. And yes, they are paid quite a bit more. Working the Gulf is a sought-after job."

"But what about Iran? You spoke of shipments to Iraq, surely someone ships to Iran."

"China, North Korea, I believe. Neither a mainstream dealer."

"Dealer?"

"Arms dealers."

"Sorry, didn't mean to interrupt."

"I suppose their goods arrive in much the same way as Iraq's."

She nodded to confirm the good sense of his statement.

"I'll apologize in advance for the questions I'm about to ask," she said, "but they pertain to the sorts of things readers want to know, so don't take them personally, okay?"

Their espressos were ready. He collected them at the counter, adding a brioche and a croissant as well. When he returned to their small table they realized they had no sugar, so he fetched that too.

"Okay, shoot," he said.

She wondered how the collage in his eyes would alter when she asked

95

him questions that were not quite accusations, but close enough. With some regret she thought that one prominent message—his desire for her—would probably disappear, that the warmth she experienced from his wanting her (bedroom warmth was her private label) would soon chill. Now she acknowledged to herself the charm that had been enveloping their meeting, making it special, making them amiable with one another. A charm that under the circumstances was an inopportune intruder.

She set out to resist the attraction. This was her work— work occasionally made difficult by encounters with subjects who proved likable and so sapped her willingness to press, to refute, to confront with their lies. Worst were those who provoked desire. The only antidote then was to gird the very loins that were being tempted, to force herself to become focused, ruthless, even at the cost of seeming cold or churlish. Already she knew that with this man she wanted to be neither.

"You were about to be mean to me," he reminded her.

"Right, then." To jar, to provoke, to soften his defenses for the blow to come, she proceeded to climb into the wobbly pulpit of the moralizer. "This horrendous war in the Gulf, Mr. Bruyn, it's in its sixth year now? Adds up to immense casualties, hundreds of thousands dead and wounded. Hundreds of thousands! As my source tells it, you and others in your business have kept this war going, have stoked the horrors. Have you actually considered the sheer, stark numbers, Mr. Bruyn? Not the meaningless sums that flash before us on television newscasts, I mean individuals. One at a time, hundreds of thousands of times."

"Is this still in aid of you becoming informed about shipping in the Gulf? Doesn't sound like it. And no, I haven't actually considered, don't think it's possible to do. Have you?"

She could see his anger, brief but bright.

"And what's this about a source? You make it sound as if I'm some malfeasant American politician. Does that make you Woodward or the other guy?" He stabbed his thumb against his chest. "You have the wrong man, my fetching reporter. I am not who keeps this war going. They are," and his hand swept out to include everyone in the place.

She noted happily that remaining polite and amiable was becoming difficult for him, and pressed on with more of her irritating sermon.

"Mr. Bruyn, what does a dealer typically earn from this war?"

The anger returned and this time remained. Fine with her, at last she had jarred something loose.

Gaspar stared at her. Since he first became an HC he had been banking fires of resentment at the hypocrisy of the citizens whom he, Bobo, and the others at SEDCE had faithfully and tirelessly served. Citizens who willingly accepted the comforts and security delivered them by their governments, but who decried in shock and disbelief the occasional revelations of the methods civil servants had resorted to in order to furnish them with the order and prosperity they had clamored for in the first place.

"I'll answer you," he said, "if you tell me how much money it takes to keep these folks having coffee here contented. And their counterparts in London, or Birmingham, or Bath. If you tell me when was the last time the Sentinel turned down advertisements from armament firms. You've come all the way to Toulon for a story. Have you bothered to chase down Barr & Stroud, or Ferranti, or GEC in jolly old England about their wares that kill ever so many one-at-a-time individuals in the Gulf?"

He leaned towards her, thrusting his face close to hers.

"You're wasting your time on the evil I and some ship named Twanee are committing. That's dull stuff. The exciting story of this endless war in the Gulf is what it's doing for everyone in this place and all the others like it in Europe and elsewhere. A great deal of good, that's what. You want to dazzle your readers? Tell them about the earnings of thirty nations that are purveyors to the Gulf. Why pick on lowly me? What kind of sense does that make, Miss Tillinghast?"

"It's Mrs.," she said. She hadn't flinched when he leaned toward her, but now she pulled slightly away. "But please, Gaspar, call me Sarah. It'll help take the edge off your surliness. So how does a ship's architect come to know this, that thirty nations are involved?"

"Look, obviously I keep informed about Gulf goings-on. And I really am a ship's architect. I read military publications, they're full of Gulf war stories. Not a crime, is it? Ah, you have a great smile. Don't you think it's unfair that one is able to know a woman's marital status from her name, but not a man's?"

She accepted that he deserved a hiatus from her preaching, at the same time doing a hurried post mortem on her waning effort to rattle him. Where had all the rancor gone? she wondered. "I'm divorced. You?"

Perhaps to compensate for his fit of anger he smiled and said, "Not yet, but I will be as soon as you and I admit we should never part again."

A sweet scoundrel! she thought. She kept her gaze on him long enough for a brief, bawdy vision to play in her mind.

"I'm surprised," she said at last. "Thirty? Are you certain? I mean, if it's true why isn't it more widely known?"

He wrenched his mind away from his own vision of the two of them entangled on his bed back at the hotel. He had gotten as far as visualizing his hand on the small of her back and his head at her breasts. "Because, my dear Sarah, this war is a gift horse whose teeth no one wishes to examine too closely. I'm merely telling you things others will not because...well, because others aren't as taken with you as I am. Also, most people don't actively consider such things. Who takes the time to contemplate the gulf war on an ongoing basis except for those who are in some way involved? Perhaps a few odd-balls, journalists and the like. I'm not saying that war is good fun. You haven't encountered a Dr. Strangelove in me, Sarah. Sorry."

He shifted into excruciating reasonableness. "What I'm saying is that people always have made war and probably always will, and that within such a context this war is just what the doctor ordered: therapy for our post-oil embargo anxieties. For one thing, it's being fought in a distant place. Can you point to the Fao Peninsula on the map? Majnoon Island? Of course you can't, and neither could anyone else in this place. Then it's a war free of big power confrontations, threats of nuclear bombs going off and so on. Those casualties you spoke of? You'll think me a jerk for saying it, but the truth is those casualties are people unlike you and me, unlike the folks in this espresso bar or in Birmingham or Bath. People over there are suffused with causes and passions so muddled and archaic that no one here could begin to understand them, so we end up not particularly caring about their suffering. In short, if we must have wars they may as well be like this one. You might call it the perfect war."

"God, you are strange!" she said.

He smiled, uncertain how she meant it, wondering whether it was good or bad for them. Not remembering that they had first met barely an hour earlier.

"So what makes me strange? More importantly, does that mean you've changed your mind?"

"About what?"

"I thought we'd agreed to be together forever."

"Hadn't you better work that out with your wife first, Gaspar? You know, you sound like a cross between General Patton and Bertrand Russell. Very confusing. Why do you use so many American words?"

"Studied there."

"Are you aware of how contradictory you sound? And maybe are?"

"What is it about me that you like?" he said.

"I'm partial to complex, confused men."

"That's good enough for me. I assure you I'm riddled with, overwhelmed by, complexities and confusion, always have been. For me, being merely muddled is clarity itself. I can barely tell whether I'm meant to leave my house or stay in it every morning, chaos is my middle name. Frankly, I'm amazed at being able to construct sensible sentences."

She laughed a long and happy laughter. "Tell me about them," she said, gesturing around the espresso bar. "Tell me about how things are made better for them by the war."

"I am but a ship's architect..."

"Of course you are. Nevertheless, humor me."

"They expect an awful lot of their governments. If one of them loses their job they expect, and receive, as much as ninety percent of their lost income from the government for as long as a year and a half. Governments are expected to provide care, culture, great museums, parks, music in the parks, playgrounds, public theater, before- and after-school programs, playgrounds—I've already said that, see how confused I am? And the plain fact is that tax revenues alone do not remotely defray the costs of all this and that presently the shortfalls are often covered by arms sales to the Gulf. Take Austria, for example. You asked who sells to Iran? Someone whispered to me the other day that Austria does, that they're selling the Iranians artillery pieces. Folks want to attend the Vienna opera, which is government supported, and, truthfully, they couldn't care less how their government pays for it

"You're telling me that governments want the Gulf war to continue so they can put on operas?"

"In so many words, yes. Surely that's not a complete surprise to you."

"No, the idea isn't, but that it's being annunciated by an arms dealer—sorry, I meant ship's architect—is. But you started out telling me that China and North Korea were selling to Iran, now you've added Austria. Who else?"

"I'm sure there are others but I don't know who. People are overwhelmingly on the side of Iraq in this, and for good reasons."

"If that is so, how do the Iranians keep on fighting?"

"They have a substantial numerical advantage. Their population is three times as large as Iraq's. And Khomeini is quite willing to sacrifice huge numbers of men and boys on the battlefield."

"How did you come to conclude that Iraq is in the right? From what I've learned, I am far from convinced of that. Wasn't it Iraq who started the war with a sneak attack?"

"That's like saying that the intended victim of a mugging who turns the tables on his would-be attacker is an aggressor. Khomeini is hardly a

Bertrand Russell. He instigated a series of provocations, including the attempted assassination of a high Iraqi government official and calls for the Shias of Iraq to rise against their government. Saddam acted to protect his country."

"What can you tell me about Saddam?"

"Can you sense that I like you? Why don't we speak of that for a while? I don't know what to say about Saddam, I guess he's a leader like other leaders—good and not so good."

She reached into her bag and fished out the Amnesty report about Saddam's Mukhabbarat, folded to the paragraphs she had found so horrifying. "Not very much good if one is to believe this," she said and handed it to him.

He read what she'd indicated. "This is awful," he said, and meant it.

"You mean you had no idea that this goes on, Gaspar? I assume you've been to Iraq."

"I told you, people over there are not like us, they live in another world," he said in a low voice. "I'm not saying Saddam is a nice guy. Being tough, to him, is inherent to being a leader. But no, I was not aware of what I have just read."

"I believe you," she said, then added casually, "How do you think your partner would react to the AI report?"

"My partner?"

"Please, Gaspar, take me seriously. I promised you that my story, if it gets written, is not about you. Tell me about Count de Bossier. Do you think it would upset him to know what AI's report says?"

"It really would be best if you told me what exactly you are after," he said with immense calm.

"Frankly, I'm not yet certain, that's why I'm here with you. Your ship and your arms deliveries are part of it, but I suspect that these are the least part."

"What then does this partner of mine's reaction have to do with anything?"

"I'm speculating," she said, "scrounging around in my mind for a reason to explain why you two are doing what you're doing. It suddenly occurred to me, especially after I heard the Bertrand Russell in you, to wonder whether you secretly sympathize with Iran, whether you two are sort of Robin Hood arms dealers."

She watched him take a long moment to evaluate this remark, saw him fight back the temptation to speak, consider, debate whether he should get up and leave.

Then she quoted Chardeau to him, word for word, nuance for nuance: Iran, Gaspar. Not Iraq. This was about the Twanee, de Bossier, and Iran. She watched with astonishment, and then with concern and sympathy, a man implode, tumble over the precipice backward into himself, into the hollowness that gaped to receive him.

Sarah sat in Gaspar's room and watched his limp, inebriated, sleeping body. He slept curled up, his face pressed against his upper arm. After he had attempted, and failed, to challenge her assertions, he had consumed drink after drink in a desperate effort to sooth the void she had created in him where his faith in a lifelong friendship had been.

They had left the espresso shop and spent the remainder of the evening at the bar in his hotel. There he talked and reminisced and explained and drank, talked in the way one does of a death in the family, talked for the benefit of his own incomprehension. Then they'd gone to his room.

Chardeau had done well for her, had led her to the right man. There was more to come and she was excited to know what it would be.

She wondered as she watched Gaspar, before she undressed and lay down beside him, how it was that he had not at any point in his misery invoked his wife.

Chapter Fifteen

Gaspar sat up in the bed, attempted to think, and failed. His mind was immobilized, like the mind of a dreamer in a nightmare who is unable to command his limbs to flee a fast-approaching threat. He rose from the bed and realized that he was in a hotel in Toulon. He walked to the bathroom and washed his face. Staring at himself in the mirror, he saw behind him a blond woman watching him from the bed he had just left. She was nude, tall, quite striking, which in his present state made virtually no impact on him. He heard his own name called and realized that it was she—Sarah, the English reporter. Then before his eyes Bobo's name pulsated in vibrant letters, actually not Bobo, but Bertrand de Bossier. He remembered and his heart soured, and he wished he were still asleep.

"Poor Gaspar," Sarah said softly from the bed. "Clean your teeth please and come and make love to me. Then we can sort things out together."

Gaspar's return to Laura in Belgium fell on a weekend. The two of them attended a tennis party at the club where awards were given to the most improved and to the victorious. Laura was prominent in the latter group.

"Selectively silent" was how Gaspar had defined Laura once during an inner polemic about their marriage. Not that she was remotely the quiet type. On the contrary she was lively and loquacious, she laughed often, her manner very much ebullient Italian. Until, that is, the subject became life's shadows, its disappointments and rancor, its failures and heartaches. At these, she fell silent. That silence, her resistence to speaking when he yearned for her words, slowly eroded the affection that had underwritten his love for her.

When on occasion he complained about his work, of the tension and of the less-than-wholesome characters it sometimes sent his way, she refused to speak about it. Later, as he sat in his upstairs office mired in his thoughts, she might come by, and in a clumsy attempt to retrieve him from his darkness observe that he was rather early for male menopause. She meant it as a joke, a way to get them past an uncomfortable moment. At the time he'd made excuses for her reluctance. She was, he reasoned, merely expressing attitudes common to women of their social class. His four years in the United States had made him sensitive to this peculiar mind-set in which wives refused involvement in the part of their husbands' lives not related to home and hearth.

Not that he expected Laura to partake in the minutiae of his trade, but this attitude declared that the husband's business was none of his wife's, and that hers was to make her man happy at home; anything else was his problem. Gaspar knew women who were utterly ignorant of their husband's specific work, knew he was a banker or a lawyer, yes, but couldn't care less what exactly it was that he did at his bank or law office. Once Gaspar brought up the subject with a female member of their golf and tennis club. She candidly told him she thought it wiser not to meddle in her husband's business life. "It's better that way. There is nothing I can gain by prying and there's plenty I can lose."

Maybe it wasn't a fair comparison, but Gaspar could not help remembering on that particular weekend when he came home from Toulon that practically the first thing Sarah had wanted to know from him was his business. For reasons of her own, of course.

Facing Laura after his past escapades had been relatively easy. They followed a script, like a hackneyed vaudeville act: Gaspar steadfastly denied having affairs, Laura steadfastly rejected his denials with light-hearted banter accompanied by a mischievous grin. "It's okay as long as you don't tell me, as long as you don't confess. Confess and you will know my fury," her grin warned. She would tease him, say he was safe so long as he didn't bring back some skin disease and so long as he didn't fall in love.

Before Sarah there had been small loves, inspired by particularly titillating sex, by a passing sense of communion, loves that flowered and withered quickly and painlessly. With Sarah the titillating sex had taken place only after she had, within an hour of meeting him, taken a sledge-hammer to his life. Still, he managed to grin at Laura after Toulon, to issue denials as per usual. It was not yet time to burn this bridge, he told himself. Things were too new, they could change. No use taking drastic steps just yet.

After the weekend at home with Laura, Gaspar took the fast train to Paris, to the office of Boulevard Consultants. Bobo was in Iraq, updating shopping lists with their best client—their only client, Gaspar had believed until Sarah claimed otherwise. Deadeye had gone with Bobo. Were they really in Iraq, Gaspar wondered? Or were they in Teheran with the client he hadn't known about? Whatever it was, Deadeye was in on it, of that he was almost certain.

Everything had changed for Gaspar, everything was discomforting, laden with hidden meanings. Bobo in Iran? Inconceivable, he would have said. Now Sarah's questions had become Gaspar's festering doubts. What business was Boulevard doing that had been kept from him? And why? Why? The word reverberated in his mind until it lost its sense and became a meaningless sound like the cry of some jungle bird. Why had Bobo done it, why had he been carrying on secret commerce with Iran? Why had he lied?

Because by now Gaspar had accepted it as likely that Bobo and Boulevard Consultants were indeed engaged in dealings with Iran. Sarah's description of her source's evidence, her citing of SEDCE's inner workings, of the Twanee's purchase, her familiarity with the relationship between Bobo and Deadeye, had convinced him. But Sarah's stab at the "why"—that Bobo was dealing with Iran out of repugnance for Saddam—was obviously no more than an attempt to elicit a retort from Gaspar, to coax him into refuting her untenable assertion with a more probable answer. Only he didn't have a more probable answer.

After Toulon, Gaspar's store of presumed truths about Bobo took a precipitous plunge. Nothing he had up till then accepted as fact about his friend remained unsuspect–including the certainty that Bobo was his friend.

"Monsieur le Comte and Mademoiselle Greaux" were due back the next day, the secretary informed him.

On the morning of their expected return, Gaspar flew to London.

Sarah had formulated a new working assumption about Bobo's motives. "It is because Bobo became greedy," she explained to Gaspar at her home when he came there seeking shelter from his turmoil. "Because Bobo is land rich and cash poor, as you yourself said. Because he had been for years a well-paid civil servant, but a civil servant nonetheless. What is considered good pay in the world of government employees is a pittance in the world of arms dealing, not even spending money, am I right? So your friend got greedy, that's all."

It happened all the time, she assured him. Many of her past exposés had been about people (men mostly because earning power was male-centric), who had secretly taken to worshiping the Golden Calf, who had at some point given up being good in favor of being well-off. Gaspar himself had been earning a fortune because of Bobo, wasn't that so? Bobo had sent him client after client. That these were clients useful to SEDCE was beside the point; people who succumb to greed accommodate their sin by gearing it down, making it adjust to their inner sense of inequity. Why on earth should so-and-so earn so much, be flush with cash, and not

I? Is so-and-so better, smarter, more dedicated? Will my taking do any important harm? No. Who is victorious and who is slaughtered in the Gulf is not, all said and done, really so important. And that the so-and-so earning so much was Gaspar, that Gaspar was ringing up figures trailed by many noughts right there in plain view, must have made for lots of temptation. That sound of the register ringing could become outright deafening when one's own paycheck emitted merely the prim rustle of a government form.

Then Gaspar told her about the fund, the SEDCE account in Zug into which he had deposited portions of his commission. A secret SEDCE account, definitely not for Bobo's personal use.

She pressed for details.

Yes, Bobo could access the money. But Gaspar received monthly statements on this particular account and could vouch that Bobo had never touched it. Yes, it was a substantial account, tens of millions of dollars. Money for projects and expenses that SEDCE under Bobo wished to keep from its political superiors. What sort of projects? Bribes, payoffs, payrolls to people whose services were necessary, but whom the politicians would not have countenanced. The down payment for the Twanee was made from this fund.

At that Gaspar grew fidgety and balked at saying more.

Sarah was sympathetic, she understood his predicament. Her forbearance intensified his trust in her.

Bobo had always had a high level of distrust of France's political Left, he explained. So, as a matter of fact, did Gaspar. They'd wanted to make certain that France's friends, friends Bobo had made, were not frozen out by the Reds who had come to walk the halls of power in the Élysée and at Matignon.

Talking about Bobo and their business troubled him. He resented this new urge to come clean, resented Sarah for shining a light onto his life that had for all these years been about secrets. And it tweaked at his love for Sarah, brought a chill to the brimming warmth he felt for her.

She read the resentment in his eyes and asked what the matter was. When he attempted to deny that anything was wrong she didn't relent. It was difficult for her too, she too was anxious lest the business that had brought them together should estrange them from one another. Wasn't her position similar to his? After all, what did she really know about him? Only that she had fallen for him.

They both were struggling to keep from falling into a vortex of wariness. What if she was not who she said she was, what if the Twanee and

Bobo and Iran were not at all the story she was pursuing? What if it turned out that these doings were not Bobo's, but Gaspar's? Their only alternative, Sarah pleaded, was to trust in the one fact they had established about themselves for themselves—their love. About all the rest they would simply have to wait and see.

Gaspar began to defend Bobo to Sarah. It was impossible that Bobo would deal with Iran for personal gain, he told her. He had known Bobo a long time, practically all their lives. That Bobo would permit something as crass as sheer greed to taint his life didn't make sense.

All right, Sarah rejoined, Gaspar and Bobo had known each other all their lives, she had no quarrel with the calendar. But during all this time had Gaspar truly known Bobo? Should he not reexamine this assumption?

Perhaps. No. Not possible. Sarah must hear him out, he would describe for her who Bobo is and where he came from. She needs to learn about how Bobo thinks and how he came to think that way.

Chapter Sixteen

"I was six and Bobo seven when my parents brought me to Belle Marais for the first time," Gaspar said. "That's where I met Bobo: Bertrand Charles Guillaum de Bossier. He was born and brought up there in the Loire valley near the tiny village of Cheffes. Belle Marais—"Pretty Swamp"—was the de Bossier's ancestral estate.

"My parents had been to a party in Rennes. There they'd been introduced to the de Bossiers, who had invited them for a subsequent weekend visit. This on the strength of a friendship, discovered during that first meeting, between our relatives and theirs in Africa, where branches of the families had settled a long time ago.

"Belle Marais is the sort of place that very few people in Europe still own. Nowadays estates of that size are likely to be national preserves, or have long since been carved into many smaller plots which even so would be considered sumptuous by many. A small river forms one of its boundaries and there are meadows, a swamp, a bog, and a lake, and a forest that has never been cut, ever."

When he and his parents arrived at the main house on the estate, Gaspar told Sarah, Bobo's parents and their son greeted them. Then Bobo's father, whose name was Yves-André, explained to his son that the Bruyns had people in Africa just as the de Bossiers did, and asked Bobo to speak about Africa. And Bobo did.

"He was as solemn as an undertaker," Gaspar said, "so much so that after a bit I began to giggle. I remember it most vividly. Mother fired me one of her armor-piercing stares. So there stood little Bertrand (I didn't know until later in the day that he was called "Bobo") and declaimed Africa for us—top down, right to left. From Mauritania all the way to the Cape, not leaving out the Seychelles, Madagascar, and Mauritius. After he'd done the countries, he recited its deserts, rivers, lakes, and mountains, then its main tribes and their tongues, then its former French colonies. When he seemed to have finished, his father whispered to him and he rattled off the former Belgian colonies too.

"I was amazed at this smart little boy, so earnest and unsmiling. And, though I didn't know it at the time, so sad. Our parents sent us off to play. Bobo brought me to his treasures—no, not treasures, to his loves. He was in love with places on Belle Marais as sure as I am in love with you now. That was, and is, one of Bobo's problems, that he loves places more than people. Well, one place really. France."

"As do you, Gaspar," Sarah stated in the positive manner that was customary to her. "You love it too, don't you, darling?"

"I do, but it's different for me. I first loved France because my father loved it, I learned from him. It was different for Bobo.

"Tell me what your father taught you."

"To begin with, our family fled France. They were Protestants escaping Catholic persecution. This was hundreds of years ago, of course, and yet my father spoke about it as if it had been a recent event. And his tone was one of forgiveness for the wrongs done us. He spoke of France as some far-off magical place, not the country next door. I think he was a fairly typical expatriate. He longed for and glorified a place in his mind. And I learned from him. Our family had done well in Belgium, we had the shipyard, we belonged. But because of father's attitude, all this seemed a side show. The main event was France.

"So I grew up thinking France, following its trials and tribulations, being proud of its past glories, refusing to find fault, you know? A veritable "Chauvin." It wasn't until I was in my early teens that my outlook became more adult, more politicized, and this was due entirely to Bobo. After that first visit to Belle Marais, you understand, I spent virtually every holiday, every school vacation, there.

"Bobo had views about France, critical, thought-out views. Whereas I saw every public figure of the day as well-meaning, as being a member of the team, Bobo actually questioned what was going on. I didn't make distinctions about political parties, social philosophies—for me they were all French, we were all one big happy French family. But Bobo had strong likes and dislikes. He knew about specific politicians and programs, and he had this obsession about the France of old, its greatness and contributions to civilization. He despised politicians who imported new social theories. As far as he was concerned, they were traitors. What Bobo told me I came to believe.

"I don't mean that I just stood there and grinned like a fool as Bobo made his speeches. I argued with him, but my arguments stood no chance. Beyond their names, for instance, I didn't know who Leon Blum or Michel Debré were, had no idea what they stood for. I couldn't see how they weren't all right so long as they were French. But in time I too evolved views, strong views, much like Bobo's."

Sarah steered him back to that day at Belle Marais when he and Bobo had first met.

"Why?" he wanted to know.

"Because when you were telling me about how you came to love France you said things were different for Bobo. I'm trying to form a picture of him."

"Well, to start with, the household was quite unlike mine. As soon as our parents had settled down to chat, as adults do, Bobo and I went outside. He led me through a forest like no other forest I've ever seen before or since. A forest thick with huge trees that had over the ages acquired their own order and sequence, that had each found for its canopy a place in the sun and was so greedy of it that no light was left to fall onto the trunks and roots. In Belle Marais's forest it was dark at midday.

"When we reached a clearing, Bobo had me help him collect dried twigs and branches and grass. He piled the dry wood and lit it with a cigarette lighter he had in his pocket. When the flame was up, he piled on the grass and a sinuous plume of white smoke rose up. Then he peed on the flame and told me to do the same. It was an ancient ceremony, he said, to keep out witches and warlocks. I was shaken by the idea that such creatures existed at Belle Marais. Indeed they did, Bobo said. His own mother was a witch, and his father a warlock and a liar too.

"Well, I was pretty shocked, what with being in this dark forest and with Bobo having just done his little ceremony and telling me those things about his parents. I'd never heard children say such things about their parents, nor about anyone else's for that matter. He was so earnest about it. I could tell he wasn't saying those things to shock me, that it was simply how he felt and thought about his parents.

"We walked on for quite a while until finally we arrived at a river. Bobo took his shoes off, and I mine. He led the way into the water and onto a sandbar that created a pool of sorts in the river. There he informed me that now we would swim. Didn't ask or suggest, he virtually ordered me. He looked at me with an expression like the one he'd worn when declaiming Africa: solemn, intent, his eyes reflecting only the will that this task be done. I was frightened witless. I barely knew how to swim, certainly I'd never been in a river before. But I did what he commanded. I don't know why, I suppose because his wish had greater mass than my fear. I think such entities within us respond to the laws of physics."

When, Sarah wondered, had he made this observation? Surely not as a boy of six.

True. It was years later, in Baghdad during a business trip. He and Bobo were meeting with Saddam and some of his people.

"Bobo was talking away to Saddam in Arabic. I looked at them and realized that they had in common this property of great personal mass—

greater than most. I knew that Saddam was a determined person, that his ambitions and designs brooked no opposition or interference, and that those around him unfailingly bowed to his will. I sat and watched as he and Bobo spoke together. Saddam spoke only Arabic and was altogether a person of limited exposure to the world. His travels outside Iraq had been to the Soviet Union, India, Cuba, and Yugoslavia. The West and the rest of the world didn't matter to him because, I suppose, they didn't conform with his ideas."

How did he know where Saddam had and had not traveled?

"From a SEDCE briefing. We knew quite a lot about him, from his beginnings. Birth in a village named Ouja, near Tikrit, orphaned early on of his father, raised by a powerful mother and an uncle who was a fierce nationalist—also maybe his mother's lover. Like everyone in the counter-intelligence business, SEDCE compiles dossiers on important people We even knew about Saddam's problems with his lower back, which he'd tried to keep secret."

"How, just out of curiosity, did SEDCE find out about the bad back?"

"From an HC here in London, as a matter of fact. A French woman who attended a dinner party where a Harley Street surgeon's tongue became loosened by drink. In his eagerness to impress this charming HC, he told her about his recent hush-hush visit to Baghdad where he'd been flown to examine a very important man's L5."

"Ah yes, vertebra in the lumbar spine, right? My former husband had a bad back. Least of his failings."

"Right. The surgeon's patient turned out to be Saddam himself. But getting back to my point, Saddam for all his lack of sophistication had managed for years to impose his will on people far more clever, educated, and informed than himself. And I think he succeeded because his will had more mass than theirs."

"But what exactly does that mean, Gaspar? Frankly, it sounds like something out of an American self-improvement course."

"It means that we—well, at least I—am ordinary, and Bobo and Saddam are not. People like me, most people, recognize when we encounter another whose inner boundaries are less confining that ours, whose constraints, conscience, self-control, are on a different plane. When we encounter such people we're attracted to them, their personalities push buttons in our own yearnings. Of course, it's more complex than that because there are accompanying resentments at such people for confronting us with our limitations. Still there's no question in my mind that Bobo had that kind of influence on me from the very first. From the swim in his river and on."

"You've been thinking about this."

"I have," he confirmed with a certain grimness.

"What on earth did Bobo mean when he called his mother a witch and so on?"

"I think she had hurt him deeply. He never explained himself directly, but years later when he and I were on a hike in Switzerland's pre-Alps—beautiful country in German-speaking Switzerland, Appenzell—he said something that seemed to explain his words that day in the forest at Belle Marais. We'd pulled into some tiny village for the night, bushed. The day had been a series of climb-ups and climb-downs and we got mildly lost a couple of times. Bobo drank that night. He only drinks when he can't stand not speaking any longer. He tends to bottle things inside and then they come pouring out."

"This is a general trait? I mean, he does this a lot?"

"Well, no. Only with me, really."

"I see. I interrupted you."

"I'm becoming used to it. Anyway, that night in Appenzell was one of those times. He started musing out loud about the woman who served us our dinner. She was the owner of this tiny inn where we were staying and also the cook. Very good food—hunter's fare, venison, wild boar. Bobo spoke of her simplicity and obvious goodwill, and from there meandered back to his mother, who, he said, was anything but simple and was a stranger to good will. His mother used to betray him, he told me. Yes, those were his words. When he'd confided to her his boy's pranks—he'd borrowed the neighbor's mule for a ride without asking, or he'd messed with the priest's bicycle, things of that sort—his mother bartered his trust for her husband's attention. Old Yves-André, it seemed, was a womanizer, a philanderer who didn't stay home much and didn't pay much attention to his wife when he did. Yet she was crazy about him, did anything she could to capture his attention, including disclosing what Bobo had told her that she had promised to keep to herself. Maybe this was her effort to remind Yves-André of his parental, and, by the by, his husbandly, duties. But the upshot was that Bobo would get a beating."

"Sounds perverse."

"It was sad. Bobo loved his mother, you see, which was too bad for him because after she'd misspent her love on her husband there was precious little left over for Bobo. Madame de Bossier—Berenice was her name—loved this man to distraction while he loved only his lawsuits against other landowners and bedding other women. For Berenice, tattling on her son was just another desperate, losing ploy."

"What a complicated household."

"Aren't most? But yes, it was. I didn't like either of Bobo's parents. Bobo told me once that his father used to praise him to the heavens in front of visitors and deride him when they were alone. And Yves-André didn't permit Bobo to attend ordinary schools, considered them factories for mediocrity. Bobo was educated by tutors. Sort of a throwback, like the de Bossiers as a whole.

"So Bobo never attended university?"

"He did late in life. When he served in the navy they sent him to the Sorbonne for a post-graduate degree. He excelled, naturally. He studied French history, but his knowledge spanned many fields, he dazzled people with his erudition. At MIT we called people like him nerds, except that he was a charming, captivating nerd."

"What happened after the navy?"

"It really happened halfway through his navy time. By then he was already freelancing for SEDCE, doing research. I think his experience at the Sorbonne had a lot to do with his seeking SEDCE out. That was how he got to join. He used family connections to make sure he was recruited, but I think it was the Sorbonne that convinced him SEDCE was the way to go.

"Bobo, of course, was older than his classmates, and the years he attended—1966 to '68—well, I'm sure you remember what happened in '68, France just about fell apart. Labor strikes that were borderline insurrections, virtual warfare between students and police in the streets of Paris. And it all pretty much started right there at the Sorbonne. Bobo's fellow students were the ideologues and in many cases the shock troops of the anti-government forces.

"The experience really shook him up. He used to talk to me about the arrogance of those students who presumed to seek the overthrow of government without have given much thought to how difficult it had been to hold France together to that point. Nor to what would actually replace the order they so despised. Bobo believed that the rioters were mostly unwitting stooges of a Leftist cabal. Their slogans and demands, he said, were crap, nothing to do with what was really going on, namely, a secret agenda of overthrowing French society itself. The very fabric of French society, he said, was the real target, not the government. He pointed out that the Left had been part of the governing process since after World War Two, had even on occasion been elected to lead the nation. But that temporary stewardship of power had not brought them any closer to implementing their true agenda, which was to overturn entrenched social values—family, private ownership of property, the church.

"Bobo said that the secret Left failed in '68 because they'd misread the vast majority of the citizenry. Even though the French voted on occasion for Leftist candidates, they did so out of transitory dissatisfactions, to punish the Right, but never harbored the slightest wish for a truly radical change, alignment with the Soviet Union, for example, or total government control of the economy. That was why the Left's secret agenda was to overthrow the people themselves, so as to remake them. Something like what Pol Pot did in Cambodia. Pol Pot lived and studied in France before he returned to conduct his vast massacres. Bobo always said he got his ideas from the French Left. Bobo formalized this thinking in a paper he submitted early on to his bosses at SEDCE."

"Sounds rather like my time at university," Sarah said. "I mean, it all has the sense of furious Cambridge dons endlessly having at one another, well, except that at Cambridge the clock's chimes to end classes mercifully also put an end to the polemics and fury. For Bobo, the show he ran, no chimes ever sounded, it went on and on." She said a bit dispiritedly. "But never mind, what happened, after Bobo submitted his paper I mean?"

"He was told that SEDCE did not meddle in France's internal politics, that its work was to look after her interests outside her borders, and that he should keep his philosophizing to himself. So once he actually became an employee he set out to prove that he was capable of handling SEDCE's traditional tasks."

"And?"

"Oh, he convinced them in spades. He was posted to Beirut, where he managed to establish a relationship with the Palestine Liberation Organization that situated France in a unique position vis-à-vis contemporary Arab politics. After that success, his rise at SEDCE was meteoric. He was posted to Research Branch, eventually became its head, and from there director. The youngest man ever to hold the job."

"Bright guy."

"The brightest. At Research Branch he authored and implemented the policy that resulted in the Safari Club. I'll tell you about that in a bit."

"What was this analysis, Gaspar?" Sarah wanted to know.

"As Bobo saw it, France had been left in a shambles after World War Two, though it wasn't obviously apparent. On the surface it appeared as if France had recovered from the direct impact of the Nazi occupation and so on, but in fact she was in deep trouble. By 1960 France had forfeited all of her important overseas colonies, the last and the greatest being

Algeria. These colonies were France's critical mass. From them she derived her natural resources, and to them she sold her finished goods. And there was more to it: there was international prestige and influence, French culture had an international foothold and then, it was all gone. France was in decline, lagging fourth in the rankings of the great powers. And even that was an exaggeration. What, for example, did it matter that France had nuclear weapons if Japan and Germany, which did not, dwarfed her economically?

"As this post-war problem became entrenched, politicians seized on it and turned it into a platform for demagoguery, especially the Left—the Socialists and Communists. While the latter were never really serious contenders, the former actually were on a couple of occasions voted into France's highest offices. The Socialists pursued elected office by promoting class strife and by offering programs that were nothing but latter-day bread and circuses, programs so unrealistically generous that they were certain to ruin France financially. This, Bobo believed, was actually their goal, to bring down the old and from its ashes remake France in a new mold. In the late 1960s the country was brought to its knees, with Bobo's fellow students anointing themselves the theoreticians and polemicists of this near-putsch. The experience left Bobo convinced that the nation would not survive another round of the same, that the Left had to be thwarted, and he concluded that SEDCE was the means to accomplish that. SEDCE was a powerful, well-financed institution operating somewhere between the military and civilian sectors. Its mandate to keep France's enemies abroad from harming her afforded it the opportunity to operate internally as well. Bobo decided that he belonged with the Firm, as it was called on the inside."

"How did he propose to thwart the Left? As I understand it, SEDCE was charged with counter-espionage and specifically prohibited from spying on French citizens living within France's borders. Certainly, it wasn't supposed to meddle in domestic politics."

Gaspar appeared not to hear her. He stared at an Italian drawing framed in an ornate gold frame on the opposite wall; hands, drawn in red, gently touching one another. He remembered that the red was called sanguine, red sanguine. That he recalled this trivia from his school days caused him to smile. Sarah looked at quizzically. He refocused.

"The fact was that SEDCE did on occasion do what it wasn't supposed to; that was why it eventually ceased to be SEDCE and became DGSE." Gaspar said. "Bobo's idea was to deny the Left its audience—a discontented population. He felt that while Leftists would sometimes gain office, as long as the nation's economy didn't slow down below a certain level, those office holders would remain powerless to implement their revolutionary schemes. SEDCE's true task, therefore, was to invent temporary prosperities when the need arose, to smooth things over until some future time when the nation's consciousness would have been permanently altered. When the sham equality and false justice proposed by the Left would have been exposed for the frauds they were."

He described for Sarah the Safari Club, the first implementation of Bobo's idea of temporary prosperities. The Safari Club was, in effect, a rehearsal for the relationship with Iraq which brought France a prosperity that pulled her out of the recession she'd been thrown into by the dramatic rise in international petroleum prices.

"Amazing. Very impressive. Can't wait to meet the man," Sarah said. "But all this leaves us with a problem. I mean, if you're right, and I have no reason to doubt you, then I'm wrong. The Twanee is not about stuffing Bobo's pockets. So what is it about?"

"Please don't take this as a slight to your considerable intelligence, my darling," Gaspar said, "but if I know my pal Bobo, whatever he's up to has been planned to perfection. Proofed, made watertight, assembled so as to turn back any conceivable conjectures."

"That only means that I—we—will have to dig and search until we arrive at a point where we can march up to him and punch a hole in his defenses. We need ducks, Gaspar."

"Ducks?"

"So we can line them in a row. As of now we have only two, Chardeau and you. Can you go to Paris and bring back more ducks?"

"I don't want to go back," Gaspar said. "I'm not going back, I'm staying here with you."

"But I'm not staying here, darling, I'm off in the next few days. Another assignment, you know."

"Then I'll come with you."

"Your wife will be very cross, Gaspar, if you don't come home soon."

"Don't you want me along?"

"You're with me now, aren't you?"

"Don't you want me with you more...permanently?"

"I haven't given it a thought. Yes, I have. I don't know yet."

"What do you know?"

"That we're in love. That it's sweet and wonderful. That I haven't felt quite this way before. That I like you."

"That's welcome news! Didn't you like your husband?"

"Certainly not. Nothing to like about him."

"I want us to live together. I'd like it if you'd give it more thought and decide, Sarah."

"My husband was admirable, enviable, but not likable. Took me a while to sort that out."

"Did you hear me?"

"Don't you like your wife? I sense that you do, Gaspar. Anyway, I don't think you should leave her for me; leave because it is your wish to not be with her. Then, in time, perhaps, we can decide to be together."

"How do you come up with this stuff?"

"Useless couples therapy. Tillinghast and I went to couples therapy near the end. Didn't save us but I did pick up a couple of pointers. That was one of them."

"What assignment?"

"Pardon?"

"You said you were off on assignment. Where? How long?"

"Hard to tell how long. Italy, Reggio Calabria, other places."

"While you're away I intend to tell Laura I'm leaving. Because I want to leave. Because I want to be with you." He grinned a prankish grin. "Well, first I want to be on my own. Then, after a suitable period of reflection and contemplation of, say, two or three days we will take up house together."

"That sounds sensible. I think I'd like that, Gaspar. That part about being with me. Oh, and don't forget the duck, dear."

"Frankly, my love, I was very much hoping to forget. And don't push, we're not married. You can't tell me what to do quite yet."

He was feeling the reluctance of a traveler about to depart a warm, hospitable inn for frigid weather and rough roads. Out there wrecks awaited him, crumbling edifices. His marriage, his business, his faith in a life's cause. He didn't want to go out there.

As they lay in bed, Sarah already asleep, he relished the thought of her, the certainty that he wished to be with her. That if he had to face frigid weather and rough roads it was she he wanted by his side.

Chapter Seventeen

Harouni's girl Mari comes to the shed. She is accompanied by one of the men, who clutches his M16 as a peasant would his amulet on passing a dark cemetery.

Mari is barefoot. She is wearing a tee shirt, tiny shorts, and a leer. Harouni is away, she tells Gaspar, visiting with the Jews down south in the place they call their Security Zone, Lebanese land they have seized for themselves—yet another grab at a plot of Arab soil. No matter, she assures him, the Jews will yield it all one day, their greedy tentacles will be severed.

Gaspar wonders what it means that Harouni is talking to the Israelis. Which ones? Probably Paz. Was Sarah with Paz? A shiver travels up his spine. That talks are underway has to be encouraging, they must be bargaining for him. Bargain well, Paz! Think clearly, Sarah!

Mari has Gaspar brought to Harouni's Phoenician altar. She sits cross-legged on the ground, her shorts riding up into her crotch, her leer intact. She has given thought to his story, she tells him, to this tale of the prowess of the imperialist manipulator de Bossier. What had been Gaspar's point, anyway? That Europeans had yet again outwitted Levantines? If so, they should not for much longer, as Saddam's taking of Kuwait, that artifice of Whitehall, has amply demonstrated. Her eyes blaze, the leer replaced by taut lips eagerly dispensing slogans.

What is your point, Mari, Gaspar wonders. Why are you chatting me up in Harouni's absence? Why are you dressed like this? Fear sweeps over him. Mari's youth, her fervent Arab nationalism...is this it? Has she decided that Gaspar will not become yet another European who has cheated the natives? Has Mari decided to strike a blow, albeit a small one, for Arab pride and have him executed here and now?

He searches Mari's eyes for traces of the resolve that had permeated Deadeye's just before she executed Bobo. He is frantic with the effort not to commit an error with Mari of the blazing eyes, not to say the wrong thing.

"I had no point, Mari," he says. "I was asked to speak about Bobo—Bertrand de Bossier—and I did. That is all. I understand how you feel about Europeans. I know Mr. Hussein and I'm certainly familiar with his feelings about how the Arabs have been treated."

She chuckles. "You are afraid of me, aren't you, Gaspar?"

"Yes. I can see that you are angry with me. I hope to make you understand that your anger is misplaced. That I have been a friend to the Arabs."

"Really? What a good man! How have you been a friend?"

"Surely you know that during the war between Iran and Iraq we helped Iraq quite a bit?"

"'We'? What 'we'?"

"Bobo and myself. We supplied Iraq throughout."

"Ah, and you did this for love of the Arabs, Gaspar? How noble!" She leans slowly closer to him until he can smell her freshly washed skin. She tweaks his cheek hard, which makes the guard chuckle. She looks up and laughs with him.

"We benefited, of course," Gaspar allows with submissive candor, "but we treated Iraq fairly. We made certain they received the merchandise they ordered, and on time. This wasn't easy to accomplish during the war. The Iranians had a hell of a time with their suppliers. We heard, for example, that once instead of the shells they ordered they received crates full of dog food."

She laughs again. "So how is it then that you have friends in Israel, Gaspar?" How can a friend of the Arabs have friends in Israel?"

Family friend, he remembers, that's what I told Harouni: Sarah got hold of a family friend in Israel. Whose family? Sarah's, tell her Sarah's family. "My wife's people have friends in Israel. Look, I know how you feel. I've read Aflaq, I know the thinking of the Ba'ath."

She is impressed. He sees the derision in her black eyes, the determination to humiliate him, ebb with his mention of Aflaq. For a brief moment there appears before him a pretty but ordinary young woman, curious, and uninhibited about admitting it. His fear diminishes, permitting him an atavistic visitation of desire for her at which he is, when he catches himself, at once embarrassed and delighted. Conditions in the shed have hardly been conducive to lascivious thoughts, so that this flash of unconscious lust is like rediscovering a skill feared forever lost.

She smiles a smile leagues removed from her customary leer. She pulls up her knees to her chest and embraces them. "How did you come to read Aflaq?" she asks.

"I was a conscientious businessman, that's all. I did business with Iraq, Iraq was ruled by a Ba'athist Party. Saddam used to speak of Aflaq's importance to the progress of the Arabs, so I read up on it and him."

As she continued to regard him with interest, he hurried on, lest the charm should have a chance to dispel. "Aflaq was a schoolteacher in

118

Syria who hated European colonialism. But I think it's fair to say also that he admired some aspects of European life—accomplishments in science, industry, medicine, and so on. Ba'ath means Renaissance, right? And Aflaq said...let's see...that the reality of the present-day Arab was back-wardness, that Arabs were trapped between remembering a glorious past and the reality of a modern world that had passed them by and that they must unify, be and act as one so as to take their rightful place. I always thought that last part was the most difficult. I mean, Saddam is a Ba'athist and so is Syria's President Assad, yet despite being ostensibly dedicated to the same ideology they found a lot to wrangle over. I think it's because they misunderstood the nature of strength. Aflaq's ideas about the Arabs' need to be strong and free of foreign domination were right, but Saddam's and Assad's ideas about what it means to be strong were faulty."

"Would you like some coffee?" she says. "Arab coffee. You know it?"

He does: it is strong, fragrant, sweet. He says he would like it very much.

Mari gives the guard an order. He eyes Gaspar, then her. She speaks again, he hands over his rifle to her, and leaves. When he is gone she releases her knees and rises to her feet. She tugs at her shorts to smooth them and picks up the rifle. Gaspar remains seated on the ground.

"You were speaking of Arabs' faulty ideas of strength," she reminds him. His face is now on a level with her groin. She smiles down at him.

"Yes, well...it's just that from what I know of Saddam I think he con-fuses being ruthless with being strong. I don't think it's possible to run a nation by being ruthless and at the same time expect progress. A certain kind of progress, yes, forcing an infrastructure on a backward population. But the more subtle aspects of progress can't be forced. They're a func-tion of being free, of permitting individuals to pursue self-interest, that sort of thing."

"I heard that English women are cold," she says with an abstracted air, as if the day surrounding them is of far greater interest to her than his answer could possibly be. "Is it true?"

"If you mean my wife, no. She is a very warm person."

"I mean in bed, in lovemaking," she persists. Her leer, having acquired an impetus, returns enriched.

"I can't speak about others, but my wife is wonderful," he says.

She gazes at him for a long, teasing moment—time for his mind and body to sort possibilities and likelihood and choices: between succumb-ing or saying no to himself, to her. Saying, perhaps, the worst wrong words of his life.

"Do you think I am right about Saddam?" he says.

The guard returns with coffee and with another guard. She hands back the M16 and is clearly not pleased. Whether because the man returned at the wrong moment or because he has brought another with him, Gaspar cannot discern.

"It is a question of time, my friend," she announces, the 'my friend' merely a figure of speech, her manner formal, no longer flirtatious. "Sooner or later we will get it right. Sooner or later an Arab man will come along, or perhaps a woman, and we will carry the day. On that day I would not want to be a Jew or a European or American."

For an unconsidered second Gaspar is tempted to refute her, his mind actually composing a retort about diversity, disparity, and religiosity, making it unlikely that her forecast will ever materialize. But he keeps still. The guard pours coffee into tiny cups and passes one to her, one to Gaspar.

"But aren't you Maronite?" Gaspar inquires.

"My mother is Palestinian," she replies.

"I see."

She sips her coffee, peering at him from above her cup's rim. "Do you see, Gaspar?" she challenges.

He chooses not to reply.

"I don't need your comprehension. You seeing is worthless, you are worthless." She spits the words at him, then modifies, "Well, not quite worthless. We will collect a lot for you from your sizzling English wife and her Jew friends."

Once more his imagination is sent hurtling, once more he is aghast lest he has inadvertently provoked the Deadeye in Mari. Deadeye, who had tended to Chardeau, who had trailed Bobo to his river and made his walk to it his very last.

Abruptly Mari turns from Gaspar and strolls away in the direction of the house. Her empty coffee cup dangles and swings from her pinky finger crooked around its handle. One of the men follows her, the other looks after them. Then he motions to Gaspar, who rises and heads for the shed, glad, within this context, to be returning to it.

Back in the shed he thinks of Mari and of Deadeye. The mistake Gaspar, Sarah, and Bobo had each committed about Deadeye had been in assuming that her fierce loyalty to Bobo had been a function of her feelings for him. In fact, her strongest feelings had been about loyalty itself. This they had recognized far too late.

Chapter Eighteen

Laura raged. She called Gaspar every bad name in Italian he had ever heard and some he had not. She accused him of being a professional malcontent, of sparing no effort to seek out unhappiness, of breaking her heart.

He heard her out and repeated what he had already told her: that he had been unhappy for some time, that he wished she would quiet down and hear him out, perhaps hear her own true thoughts. He was glad they had no children. He yearned for Sarah.

Laura had been introduced to him during the Palio in Sienna. His cousins several times removed were residents of that ancient city's Drago Contrada or Dragon Quarter, so he too over the years had become a partisan of the gold-and-purple, fire-breathing dragon that was Drago's. Twice every year for five centuries during the summer months of July and August the Palio had pitted Sienna's sixteen contradas against one another in horseback races. The Palio was a euphemism for war, a horse race not so much run as fought, with guile and cunning and an immense desire by each contrada to vanquish the others. During the race itself, petty violence was not uncommon: jockeys fought jockeys, spectators other spectators. Sometimes spectators fought jockeys.

In the year Gaspar met Laura, the Dragon competed in the August tier.

He first saw her at Drago's feast. Each of the contradas held a huge dinner on the eve of the race, each in its own part of the city—enormous meals served on long tables set for the most part in the city's narrow, winding streets. Drago's dinner was distinguished from the others in that it was held in the cathedral's inner courtyard. Virtually every Drago citizen and multitudes of outside guests attended, while for that festive evening the contrada's young people turned into waiters and wine stewards. Following a raucous parade around the contrada, and after a blessing by the bishop during which Drago's mount and rider received benedictions on the cathedral's steps, the feast commenced.

Because his cousins hailed from a prominent local banking family, Gaspar was seated at the bishop's table. The city's bankers footed the bills for the Palio and helped arrange secret slush funds for bribing opposing contradas' riders and others who might be in a position to influence the outcome, such as the watchmen who guarded the horses from being drugged before the race. For it was at least as important to deny one's great rival victory as it was to attain it for oneself.

Gaspar was struck by the glorious illogic of attempting to bribe riders in a race that was, all said and done, out of the rider's control. Since the race was run on unsaddled horses, chances were considerable that riders would fall off, and the first horse to cross the finish line, riderless or not, was the winner. So why bribe riders when the horses were the controlling variable? he had asked, and been given a pitying look for thinking with the cold logic of a non-Italian.

Laura Bazzini was seated across and down from him. He had only recently returned from studying at MIT, where he'd taken his degree in ship's architecture, and still comported himself more like a Yankee than a European. So when he noticed curious stares from the beautiful girl down the table he assumed his button-down shirt and club tie were the cause— he was virtually the only man in the courtyard wearing a tie on this hot August night. But when he returned her stare, she blushed. Emboldened by the wine he'd been drinking, he kept his eyes on her for longer and longer moments.

Boisterous battle hymns were being continuously bellowed by the diners, in which the girl enthusiastically participated. At the end of one Dra- Dra- Dra- Go-o-o! chant she brought her hands to her throat to indicate she had tired out her voice. On an impulse, Gaspar picked up a wine bottle, climbed onto the table, and walked along it to where she sat. There he chivalrously poured some wine into her glass.

The gesture was well received by the girl, and by the others at the table. Gaspar's cousins were tremendously heartened, for they took his gesture for an indication that some hot blood ran in his veins after all. Even the bishop smiled.

Gaspar's cousin then introduced Laura to him with considerable flourish and in a loud voice: "A fresh flower, Gaspare, the most beautiful in all of Drago. And what an unbelievable figure, cousin. Oof! I have seen her on the beach, you know. Unbelievable! Stupendo! So come to think of it, why am I introducing her to you? Screw you, I want her for myself," and he gave Laura a noisy kiss.

She was indeed very beautiful, of medium height and with a statuesque bearing. Her figure caused men's eyes to linger and some women to regard her critically, as if her voluptuousness were contrived or unseemly. "Hot," had been Bobo's assessment when Gaston first introduced him to Laura. It was apt.

Light brown hair framed her small face, which was marked by prominent features: large eyes the color of a sun-bleached sky; a nose that would have marred her face had it not been so exquisitely proportioned— it absolutely curved, a small arch starting at the level of her lower eyelids and ending well above her upper lip. Her strong figure muted the effect of her large bosom, which in any event she carried with utter confidence.

"I always wondered who gets to sleep with women like Laura," Bobo later said to him. "I wouldn't in a thousand years have guessed someone like you, pal."

Their courtship was delightful. Her temperament and antics melted the overly-correct personality he had come away with from his home and schools.

After their first meeting, he began to visit her often. They took small journeys together, mostly to cities on the Continent. Once in Geneva, after tea in the old town, as they walked down a narrow street she suddenly stopped and kissed him with a glee and vigor that left him lightheaded.

She would wake him from sleep to make love. In Venice she led him to a darkened, dead-end alley just wide enough for two people to walk through and, to the sounds of a nearby canal, undressed first herself, then him. Then she aroused him with her mouth, and when he was erect she smiled and turned her back to him, bent from her waist, and grasped an ancient iron grating to await him.

Of the girls he had been with before, none had been as warm and unrestrained. She became his haven after the long and often lonely crossing from adolescence to his MIT degree—lonely because his parents' home had been a place of hushed reserve, of taciturn correctness rather than warmth and affection.

His mother had never been prominent in his life. A shy, nearly speechless woman, she was primarily concerned with upholding certain aspects of the Bruyn household, aspects she felt had been betrayed by his father's affairs, behavior that was apparently entirely incomprehensible to her. She had early on retreated into her collection of Flemish embroidery. Never a demonstrative woman, her affection for Gaspar, her only child, eventually confined itself to an occasional pat on the back of his hand. She died of an embolism while he was away at MIT.

When he came home for the burial, he accidentally discovered there was much he had not known about his parents. After the funeral there had been a lunch at their home. When it was over, and he was under the impression that all the guests had left, he walked into his father's library

123

to retrieve a book of poetry by Wallace Stevens, then a favorite of his. But as he opened the dark oak door he saw his father in an embrace with a woman who had been a family friend for as long as Gaspar could remember. His father quietly asked him to leave and close the door behind him.

Later, his father told him the woman had been his mistress for thirty years. His father! who had repeatedly admonished him to live by the Good Book.

Laura rescued him from the terrible loneliness into which he had been born. She filled his days with affection and she restored to him warmth, and the will to laugh at little enough simply because laughter was an option as good as any.

But laughter also caused his first doubts about her. Within the sweep of their happiness during their first years together, it seemed a small matter that she responded to everything, but everything, with the same jolly spirit. In time, however, this predilection became impossible to ignore. She refused to acknowledge there might be such things as a dour day or a situation to which sadness was the appropriate response.

She was athletic, and very popular with the aging jocks at their club. He watched her play tennis once, and realized the audience was at least as appreciative of her bosom's movements as she served and volleyed as they were of the quality of her game—which was good.

Once during a long weekend's stay near Portofino, as they were having dinner at their enchanting old-world hotel, he became interested in the couple at the table across from theirs. Laura was gazing out the room's glass wall at the view of spectacular cliffs and the sea below. He nudged her to direct her attention to the other table.

The couple ate in utter silence—not a word during the entire meal. The very way they chewed their food spoke of some pervasive bitterness. In mid-course, and quite without warning, the woman rose and walked away. The man continued eating as if nothing had happened, then, suddenly and with great force, hurled his dinner napkin down onto the table. Then he too left.

What would she guess lay behind the scene? Gaspar wanted to know. She giggled her answer: "Indigestion?"

He felt a lump take hold in his throat. "But don't you see how unhappy they are?" he asked.

"They make themselves unhappy," she said. "How could they be unhappy at a place like this?"

Later he asked whether she was happy with him. She replied that she hadn't thought about it, but that of course she was. When he'd expressed misgivings about his involvement with the Firm, ordinary chafing of the sort anyone could experience at having to work at anything, having to put up with people he didn't particularly like, having to deal with demanding travel schedules, she responded with, "Really, Gaspar, I doubt Bobo wants you to deal with people that horrible. I'm sure you're missing something about this." Afterwards, as he sat in his office, mired in his thoughts, she came by and observed playfully that he was too young for senility to have set in. She meant it in a joking way, to humor him, to get them past an uncomfortable moment.

"I will not have you drag me down, Gaspar, I simply refuse." She hurled the words at him. "We have a wonderful life, a dream. What are you sulking about? I've never known anyone who so relishes discontent."

Their time together since he'd told her he wanted to end the marriage had been episodic; there were moments when they acted out their routine together as if nothing had changed, other moments when they were awkward and sullen with one another.

He went to his study to ponder his complaint, to uphold it: to wit, that he was happy only at the thought of Sarah. To suspect the clarity of this analysis, he tried to pick it apart, to draw comparisons, some of them offputting to himself: Whose body was better to love? Sarah's. Who more beautiful? Laura. What would Laura do? Manage.

On a morning walk to the pond he made it final: "I'm leaving, Laura. I can't stay with you. I don't know what else to say."

She was fury itself. A sort of incomprehension set in which produced a lull. Then she once more raged and wept. He wept too.

"Why didn't you tell me you were unhappy?" she demanded in a choked voice. "Why are you unhappy, anyway, Gaspar, why? What invention! What artifice! Dio!" she said, but when he attempted an answer she cut him off. "I don't want to listen to you. Why should I? You lie, anyway. I can't think of names bad enough to call you." Then she thought up plenty anyway.

What am I to tell you? he queried her inwardly. That Bobo, your hero, is a liar? That he has for some reason been making a fool of me, that he's had me pulling in one direction but not to where he told me we were headed? And what will you say? What you have always said: that Bobo knows, knows what he is doing, where we are headed. That I am imagining, that it is my problem. Let me go in peace, Laura, it'll make both of us happier if I leave.

When some time passed and he said nothing, she asked whether there

125

was someone else. Yes, he said. Yet it became important to him to convince her that he wasn't leaving her to go to another. "I'm leaving because I cannot stay, not because I'm going to her. I give you my word, she doesn't yet know my decision."

"Your word!" she shouted, "Did you think of your word before fucking that slut? Of course she is, she's a slut! And you can take your word to her!" She became distraught and began smashing plates and drinking glasses. Then his shortwave receiver. Then photographs of themselves. She cursed at him in Italian and wept bitterly.

"Laura, listen, listen," he pleaded. "You never gave me a chance to tell you I was unhappy." Finally, he too grew angry. "Where was your voice in all of this?" he demanded. "I suspect you haven't been happy for some time. Why did you never say a word about any of this, Laura, why?" Then he felt foolish and dishonest, retreated into silence. She too appeared spent.

They sat in the kitchen, the quiet between them causing each mundane sound to assume a grandiosity of sorts: the ticking clock on the stove became church bells in a slumbering town, the humming refrigerator an approaching swarm of winged creatures. Inexplicable creaking from the wooden floor seemed to announce the earth itself giving way. Finally, she spoke to say she would go to Sienna.

During the next two days she was calmer. She was to leave on the third. Each day she telephoned her parents and held hushed conversation with them. When he came near she stopped speaking until he was out of hearing range.

When they parted, Laura spoke to him sadly and was self-reproachful. "I wish I'd been clever enough to know. To pause and look. I suppose I'm not very good at that sort of thing. But I'm not a psychiatrist," she said.

126

Chapter Nineteen

"Cobras," Paz says.

"What?" Sarah replies with a start. She has heard his voice through a haze of thoughts superimposed on the passing landscape which forms a blurry backdrop to her scrolling inner gallery of anxious scenes.

They are being driven past what used to be the border with Lebanon in an Israeli military vehicle, a brigade commander's Chevrolet Blazer. For all his worldliness, Paz is possessed of a certain boyish trait that has him cite with relish the names of military hardware and cars. "Blazers," he tells her, are assigned as personal cars to brigade commanders." Then he tells her that "Cobras" are attack helicopters.

They are driving past a mound of earth flattened on top where are perched three sleek helicopters with elongated pods protruding from their front underbellies. The helicopters, tanks, armored personnel carriers, transports, ambulances, water and fuel tankers, boxy vehicles that Paz says are command and control centers on wheels, the brigade commanders's Blazer, all are painted the same dull greenish brown. Paz names every item. Tanks: "Centurion, old but good. British made. Of course, we introduced a lot of upgrades to them." Another brand of tank: "Merkhavas. Means chariot, made in Israel. Good-looking tank, don't you think? One of our great generals designed it." Armored personnel carriers filled with young men, some grinning, some serious, curious about the unlikely occupants of the Blazer: "Zeldas. That's what we call American M113 armored personnel carriers. Never liked them, mobile coffins."

The army is everywhere in this strip of Southern Lebanon that Israel has been holding ever since its 1982 invasion and withdrawal from the rest of Lebanon. The soldiers are young, most not yet twenty, Sarah guesses. Every once in a while an older version of the young faces, an officer, is glimpsed. She notes that there are others, not like the Israelis, wearing slightly different uniforms. They are older, more rumpled, less homogenous.

"SLA, South Lebanon Army," Paz explains. "Local men, Arabs whom we have organized to defend against the terrorist."

"Terrorist" is a word Sarah has heard a lot in connection with South Lebanon. She inquires and learns that the Hebrew equivalent is actually "saboteur," but that it is widely misapplied and mistranslated. At present the terrorists are Hezbollah Islamic fighters; before the 1982 invasion, they were Palestinian fighters who belonged to various factions dedicated to striking at Israel. All had been forced by the Israelis to leave Lebanon.

As someone once said, Sarah thinks, one man's terrorist is another man's freedom fighter. It all comes down to points of view. Even to poor translations.

It is the day after her arrival in Israel. Paz had telephoned to say she should come quickly, that they would be meeting with the people holding Gaspar in a certain place in Southern Lebanon. She took the next flight and went to Paz's home where she was received by his wife, silently sympathetic. Conversation, conducted via Paz, was almost impossible, but they had learned to communicate to a degree with gestures and signals.

Paz told Sarah that he had learned the identity of Gapsar's kidnapper.

"Kidnappers, Paz, there were two," Sarah said.

"They work for Harouni, one of the Harouni brothers," Paz said.

She told him that the name meant nothing to her and was surprised to see doubt fleet through his eyes like a swift-moving cloud's shadow on a sunlit path.

"You don't know about Claude Harouni?"

"Never heard of him. Should I have?"

Paz was perplexed, his goodwill shaken by her claim of ignorance. He fell into a silence. She sensed his turmoil and it increased her own anxiety.

"Please tell me, Paz," she begged, and lied, "I want to know. I'm holding nothing back from you. I can see you think I am, but I'm not. I never heard of the Harouni brothers until this moment." This last was true, but she was still mindful of having deceived him when he'd asked about what Bobo had gotten out of cooperating with the American Kirney.

"Gaspar must have had his reasons for not telling you," Paz allowed. "The story goes back more than twenty years, when de Bossier was SEDCE's man in Lebanon and one of the Harounis, Claude, was head man of the Maronite's militia forces. De Bossier had arranged for this Claude Harouni's assassination. It was a big mess. Harouni was killed in an explosion at his own birthday party. And not alone; his wife and children too."

Sarah gasped. "You can't be serious."

Paz appeared surprised by her response. "Oh yes. Wife, three children, one a toddler. Some of the guests at the party, too. It was a real blood bath, that. Mind you, this Harouni was no angel. He himself had done in a whole family, Forjieh by name. The best part was that Claude's wife was de Bossier's girlfriend."

"But that was the name used by the men who took Gaspar," she said, "the men who came up to us at Beirut airport. They claimed that a Forjieh wanted to speak with Gaspar. A Forjieh also worked for Boulevard— he was their representative for the Middle East— so it made some sort of sense to me, and obviously to Gaspar."

"Right. Makes sense. For de Bossier and Forjieh it was a good, all-around transaction. Wiping out Claude, I mean. Forjieh got to avenge his kin and de Bossier got to do a gun deal with the Palestinians, who back then were a big power in Lebanon. They had money to spend, you know, everyone was quaking in their shoes over them."

"But Gaspar had nothing to do with this terrible thing at the Harounis, he wasn't involved with SEDCE then," Sarah appealed to him, her composure precariously balanced against a fast-expanding dread. "Oh God, what do you mean?" she demanded, doubt swamping her assuredness like a rogue wave.

"Well, he was there—Gaspar—in Beirut, we know that. But we believe he left a few hours before the main event. This can be looked at in two ways: that he was an innocent, had come to visit his pal de Bossier and left without ever knowing about the impending massacre. Or that he was in on the planning and left once everything was set. He never spoke to you about this?"

"No."

"So this also can mean two things: that he was unaware, one, or that he knew how to keep his mouth shut, two."

"Is it possible that he didn't know?"

"Sure. De Bossier was a real pro, and so is Forjieh, and a pro knows that the less said the better. Maybe de Bossier never told Gaspar. Is that possible? I mean, what is your judgement, were there things de Bossier kept from Gaspar?"

"Yes indeed," she said. "A myriad of things."

She had bad dreams that night, half-images of Gaspar speaking wordlessly and all the while words that could have been his were spoken by someone else. By Bobo. She saw Bobo's face and awakened, not returning to sleep until morning, shortly before Paz knocked on her door.

The Blazer stops at a fence.

"We get out here, we walk," Paz says.

The driver gets on the radio. He is a young man in metal-framed sunglasses of the sort favored by Deadeye's men, who had been as ubiquitous to Belle Marais during those closing days as were the soldiers around Paz and Sarah now. The radio hisses and blurts words at once succinct and unintelligible. The driver says something to Paz, then Paz says to her, "Okay, all is clear. Let's go."

As she exits the Blazer, the driver smiles and says in that curt pronunciation of English of the Hebrew speaker, "Good luck, missus."

"Is it safe to be here?" Sarah asks Paz.

"Safe enough. It's daylight, our army is on top of things. No one will try anything now. There." He points at a rusted, barely-upright shambles of a structure on a hillside across from the hill they are descending.

"What is it?"

"Used to be a sheep place, how do you say?"

"A manger?"

"Maybe I mean shack. It's a shack. No sheep there now."

They reach the structure and she sees that it is perforated with bullet holes, holes that attest to hits from all directions. There is a remnant of a fence made of small boulders, and the stump of a tree that points at the sky like the finger of a burned corpse. Paz asks her to sit on the stone fence. He walks along to the side of the shack, to a point where she can see only his back as he faces the shack's far side. "Ahalan wa sahalan," he says to someone on the other side.

"Shalom," someone says in return.

Paz had rehearsed her. He'd sat her in his living room and said, "The money, you will have to speak with them about the money, how much of it. This I will not be able to do on your behalf. I will take care of the rest."

What would the rest consist of? she'd asked.

"Details. Proofs that Gaspar is well, that he is whole, that they really have him. Then how we do it, the exchange. When, where, how many people to be present, who. Don't speak about anything else but the money. Questions may come up, they will insert questions into the conversation, I don't know what questions. No, I'm not upset, it's just my way of speaking."

He acknowledges that it does indeed seem to be the way many Israelis speak, from the El Al ticket agent in London to the security man in Heathrow who wanted to know why she was going to Israel so often. "So how many times can a person see the holy places?" he'd demanded in reply to her stated purpose for going.

From the shack's far side two men come forth, one pale-skinned and nearly handsome, wearing gabardine slacks, a plaid shirt, and topsiders, the other in jeans, a solid green shirt with prominent pockets, and running shoes.

"Hello, Mrs. Bruyn. Gaspar says hello," the nearly handsome one says.

Paz has his back to her and she senses he doesn't want her to reply. The man laughs at her silence. They sit—four people on a broken stone fence at an abandoned shepherd's shack in a land cleansed of all other people by ongoing hatreds. She has been told by Paz that in areas of South Lebanon abandoned by people fleeing the fighting, wildlife has had a resurgence.

They face out, onto neighboring hills, not looking at one another. The conversation commences. Every once in a while Harouni or his man bends forward so as to look at her past Paz, especially when she and Harouni are speaking about money. The money part proves easier than she would have guessed. Harouni flatly says he wants five million dollars for Gaspar. She replies that this is impossible, that the best she can do is two.

This too has been rehearsed with Paz. He has walked her through the negotiation. Why should Gaspar's kidnapper agree to anything less than his demand? she'd asked.

"Because we now know who he is," Paz said, "and that ignites a fire under his feet. He can no longer be sure that we will not at some point lose patience and pay him a visit. He knows better than to doubt our resolve, our people have successfully looked after our interests in Lebanon when the need has arisen. He cannot afford to gamble on us not coming after him. I don't think he wants to keep Gaspar any longer than he has to at this point. I think if you give him a figure he can live with, he will deal. So you have to convince him that you and not Gaspar are paying for this and that it was difficult for you to raise the money. Maybe you won't convince him, but maybe you will leave him feeling that it will take longer to collect the amount he's after, and as I said, I think he'll be interested now in making things move faster. So you have to put up his time against your money."

"Your husband is very rich, Mrs. Bruyn," Harouni says.

"Then you know more than I about him," she says. "I will have to mortgage my house and my next twenty years of earnings to pay you. Two million dollars, or British pound equivalent, is all I can raise. That is a huge amount of money," she says grimly.

A helicopter flies low over the hill they had descended to reach the shack. Harouni looks up at it, squints, picks up a pebble, and tosses it away. It sails in a lazy arc.

"Your people are nervous about you, my friend?" Harouni says to Paz. Paz is silent.

The helicopter sinks out of sight, but just as Sarah's attention reverts to Harouni, the air is filled with a most unsettling, entirely unclassifiable sound, as if nearby, just hidden from sight, a legion of old people simultaneously and with uncanny rapidity, uniformity, and duration, were clearing their collective throats.

Harouni, his man, and Paz respond to the sound with a uniformity of their own: their necks spring upwards, attaining a stretch that would do a dancer proud; their heads now lofty and alert. They look like a troop of prairie dogs who have just sensed a coyote, their eyes trained in the direction of the strange sound. Sarah's eyes are trained on them.

"Maybe my people are nervous about your friends," Paz says to Harouni, who appears slighted.

"What's going on?" Sarah demands of anyone.

"The Cobra is firing at someone, there, beyond that hill," Harouni says.

It is Sarah's turn to laugh derisively. "It appears, gentlemen, that I am the only one in this group ignorant of the classifications and identifying traits of the local wildlife," she says.

"Perhaps you are better at the varieties which proliferate in Belfast and along the border between the Republic and the province of Ireland," an equally derisive Paz softly replies.

"Three million," Harouni says. "Take it or not."

Hard-edged, she thinks, such people. Bobo, Paz, Deadeye, Harouni. In ordinary life grinding heart-wrenching difficulties come up; but, all said and done, they are the grinds and heartaches of normalcy. This was not. This was take-it-or-not or you, or someone, will die. In their hard-edged lives quandaries—seeing both sides of an issue—are not acceptable. Bobo used to cite von Moltke, Bismark's boss, to the effect that those people are fortunate who see merely one side of an issue, the others being condemned to meander around it until exhausted, in search of its best side.

"This is appalling, Mr. Harouni," Sarah says. "What you are doing is appalling, brutish, and altogether uncivilized behavior."

Paz stares in the direction whence the helicopter's grotesque emanations were last heard. His lips are pursed and his open hands press together in a tight and disapproving gesture.

"Is this woman majnoon?" Harouni says past Sarah to Paz. To Sarah he says, "Vouz etes fous, crazy English. Did you tell her, Mr. Paz, what her husband did to my family? Did you tell her my brother and his children were collected into black garbage bags when her husband and his friend the Count were finished being civilized with them? Then I too shall be like them, like her husband and his friend, civilized, not appalling. I shall send your husband back to you in a black garbage bag, then we will all be the same."

"Two million is a good price, my friend," Paz says. "You think about it, please, talk it over with Mari, and let me know in two days. Two million in used bills. Cash. When you decide, we can talk about where and when and how."

"Forgive me, Mr. Harouni, I have hardly been myself lately," Sarah says.

As Harouni stares at Paz, she see in his eyes hatred colored by fear.

Harouni rises and begins to walk to the back of the shack, to the side opposite from the Security Zone. His man follows. Paz does not stir.

Harouni swivels back and faces them. "In two days," he says.

Chapter Twenty

"You will not have to be there the second time. I'll handle it alone," Paz says.

They are back in his home. Sarah is disheveled, distraught.

"You are being too hard on yourself," Paz comforts her. "If you're laboring under the impression that this Harouni brought away from our meeting that you lost your head, you're way off. It doesn't work like that, Harouni doesn't care that you got mad. What he took away with him from the shack is figures. Big numbers, millions, five million, three, seven, four. Big, big numbers."

"I couldn't help it," she explains despite having just been told that no explanation is necessary. "I became so incensed with that lout."

Mrs. Paz places a basket of fruit and a pitcher filled with a purplish, semi-translucent liquid in which are floating slices of lemon and chunks of ice on the coffee table at which Paz and Sarah are sitting. She gives her husband a decidedly dirty look.

"Do me a favor," Paz pleads. "Smile at Shula, or I'm dead around here."

Sarah decides that as soon as Gaspar is back with her she will tell Paz everything. He has asked about Bobo and Kirney, he deserves an answer.

"Why are you doing this, Paz?" she asks.

"What?"

"Helping us, Gaspar and me."

He looks her over as if the answer is printed somewhere on her person.

"Why do you think?"

"I think it is true about Jews."

"What?"

"That you answer questions with a question."

"I am doing it for the memory of Gaspar's father."

"Really?"

"Yes. Look, if I speak to you about the ten obscure righteous people, will that mean something to you?"

"You're doing it again."

"What?"

"Answering a question with a question."

"And you are becoming a nudnik, a pest. I doubt they mean some-

134

thing to you, so I will tell you about them. I am not observant, not, I mean, a ritualistic Jew. I enjoy knowing the little I know about my religion, I go to synagogues once in a while. I apply phrases like 'God forbid' and 'God willing.' I like it that I am a Jew. Well, in Judaism there is a belief—I don't know whether it's from the Talmud, the Mishna, the Gemmarah, or what—it goes something like this: God the Almighty suffers every generation on earth in its time because in its midst live ten righteous, but obscure people. I mean, they are visible to everyone. Indeed they're just like everyone else, you can't tell by looking at them, that only they are truly righteous. We don't have saints in Judaism, but if we had, these particular people would easily qualify. They do only good deeds and they worship the Almighty in the manner that pleases Him. Most everyone else does not, you see, but because these people do we all are permitted to survive.

"The story has its origins in the biblical tale of Sodom and Gomorrah. The part about every generation grew out of it. You remember, don't you? When God wished to destroy those sinful cities He sent down His angel to warn His servant Lot to flee and Lot began to bargain with Him. Lot said, 'Lord, you cannot destroy the righteous with the wicked, it isn't right.' So the Lord said, all right, if you can come up with one hundred righteous people amongst the sinners I will spare everyone. Lot searched and couldn't find a hundred, but he refused to give up. He bargained on down with God until finally he arrived at ten. But he couldn't even find ten righteous people, so God destroyed the cities. So as to spare humanity since that time God provides that there be ten, I think it is ten, such good guys in our midst. The part I like best about this tale is its implied call for a certain attitude of respect towards all. Since we owe our survival to these ten, and since we don't know who exactly they are, we have to be beholden to everyone, treat everyone with a little respect, lest the one we disdain should be a tenth of the entire reason we are still on earth."

"Great story," Sarah says. "Do you mean to tell me I have to treat Harouni with respect?"

"Harouni I'm not so sure about. But I will say this about him—I'm sure someone sees him as a terrific guy. Even the worst murderer is liked, even loved, by someone. When Dr. Mengele, the Nazi monster who conducted perverted experiments on live human beings in the concentration camps, was briefly imprisoned by the Allies after World War Two, he received mail from women the world over proposing marriage because he was a handsome man. Never mind that he personally sent thousands upon thousands of young women to their deaths."

135

"Who is Mari?" Sarah wants to know.

"Harouni's girlfriend."

"Why did you bring her up?"

"To let him know I know where he sleeps and with whom."

"Ah. Eons ago you began to tell me about Gaspar's father."

"Yes. For me, he was a righteous man. He helped us when we really needed help and I never got to properly repay him. I'm getting old and I'm interested in accumulating as many good credits on my ledger as I can, to offset other things."

"You mean you've done bad things?"

"Some would say so. I figure if I help get your Gaspar back it will count as if I did something for his old man, too."

"That's amazingly nice, Paz. I hope I'll be able to find a good deed with which to repay you. What happens next?"

"In two days I'll return to that shepherd's shack, I'll hear out Harouni. I assume that if I have to go five or ten percent above three million it will be okay?"

"Yes. The <u>Sentinel</u> will arrange for me to get the money. Naturally, I've agreed to do a book and articles. And Gaspar will repay the money once he's back."

"Personally, I'm sure that the minute Gaspar is back he'll gladly repay whoever it is who got him away from that Maronite pirate."

Something occurs to her. "Weren't you and the Maronites once friendly? If I recall correctly, Israel and the Maronite militias were allied at one point."

"Allied is a strong word, but we had good relations with some of them. In this part of the world, now and since time immemorial, the idea prevails that the enemy of one's enemy is one's friend. Over the years the Maronites have been in a tough spot, and so have we. For that matter so have other religious and ethnic minorities in the region. Alawites, Druse, Copts, Bahais..."

"Goodness, who can keep track of them all?"

"When you're in the thick of it you find yourself keeping track minute-to-minute, day-to-day. There are others—Nestorites, Circassi, Abyssinians, Kurds. The Maronites are among the few Christians in a sea of Muslims and they have had to navigate an unerring course to stay afloat. Within that context they've at one time or another allied them-selves with France, the Vatican, Syria, and with us."

"Why the Vatican?"

"Because the Maronites are essentially Catholic and most Christians in the region are in one way or another Orthodox—the Eastern Church, Greek, Russian, Bulgarian, and so on. With us it went as follows. We had a defense minister, a very capable soldier, but a volatile fellow."

"Sharon?"

"Right. Ariel Sharon, Arik. In 1982 Sharon finagled the government into expanding an ostensibly limited invasion of South Lebanon for the purpose of removing the Palestinian military forces from the area. But Sharon never intended to keep to the south. Anyway, Israel's interests at the time coincided with those of some, I would say even most, Maronites. They despised the Palestinians because the PLO had severely infringed on the Maronite militias' turf and upset the delicate, lopsided status quo in Lebanon.

"So the Maronites got together with Sharon, with us, and we ganged up on the PLO and we broke its back. Only Sharon's promised limited operation turned out to be a full-fledged war. The Syrians became involved. They'd long since considered Lebanon their protectorate, still do, so we had to take them on too. This, in turn, pulled the Soviets into the equation. You see, the Syrians deployed their finest systems against us, meaning the Soviets' finest. Against this we put up the best of the West—U.S.-made weapons. We trounced their stuff.

"All of this didn't go unnoticed in the Pentagon and Kremlin. And after all the excuses had been made about the Syrians' ineptitude and so on, the Kremlin and those on their side were left badly shaken. I think that it was then that the notion took hold that in a conventional war the Soviets would be the losers, and who wants to win a nuclear war? Mind you, we ourselves didn't come out so well, at least in a political or public relations sense. As we fought the PLO in the streets of Beirut, the world seized the opportunity to portray us as latter-day Visigoth; bloodthirsty, wild-eyed Jewish beasts indiscriminately killing innocents. But the long and the short of it was that the PLO lost. They had to withdraw from Lebanon altogether, and fled to Tunis. The Maronites loved it, but the glory, for them, was short lived. Their leader was soon afterwards blown up—yes, just like Claude Harouni; large explosions were definitely a favorite expression of disapproval in Lebanon. Then Sabra and Shatilla happened, such horrors! People here became very frightened. We were not supposed to be involved in such things, not even at arms' length. So we pulled back, all the way to that shack you and I visited today, leaving the Maronites fissured along pro-Syrian and anti-Syrian lines. There's more, of course, but that's roughly it."

"Is that how you know so much about Harouni? Because you still

137

have sympathizers there?"

"Are you interviewing me?"

"Asking questions is my second nature. I really don't mean to make you uncomfortable, Paz, I hope you know that."

"It's okay. My second nature is to be wary. Look, there's no magic to what we do, our counter-intelligence services, I mean. First and foremost, it's imperative that we stay informed and we're willing to go to great lengths to obtain information. Most of the time this means we pay for it, but there are other means. We apply pressure, do whatever it takes. In the end, counter-intelligence is not a complicated business. Secretive, yes, surreptitious, sneaky and at times violent, although it's best to avoid strong-arm stuff as much as possible—too messy, too many unforeseen consequences. Also, we're hardly infallible. We make mistakes, overlook things, go after the wrong people, make faulty analyses, and so on. On balance, however, we do a good job. Our people are dedicated, we have at our disposal excellent technologies. And we're fortunate in that the other side is rife with conflicts and factions and is relatively backward. Makes our job easier."

"Does Mari work for you, then?"

Paz smiles. "If I answer, do I have your word that it goes no further?"

"Absolutely."

"No, she does not." And he smiled, as if he had just made a joke.

Sarah lies in bed unable to sleep. She is weary, but the day has laced her blood with too many stimulants, Morpheus is staved off. She hears again the Blazer's radio, its driver's stilted farewell, the helicopter gunship berserk racket. She envisions bodies being collected into black garbage bags. Why black, she wonders, why not green or grey? Night noises filter in through the barred windows of her small room. Someone upstairs coughs. Paz? Mrs. Paz? The night's fragrances too arrive at her bed. She wonders where Gaspar is at this moment, what he hears and smells. She thinks of Sharon and Bobo, people who out of anxiety and love for their country take it upon themselves to make history. At last she falls asleep.

She has two days to kill before Paz's meeting with Harouni. Paz proposes to her an itinerary for a brief tour of Israel. She takes a bus for a two-hour ride to Tel Aviv.

Along the way a man strikes up a conversation with her. Abruptly, without warning or introduction, he makes a series of declaratory statements interspaced with a single inquiry, posed seemingly either to her or to himself: Is she American or Australian? he demands, and comes down

138

on the side of Australia. He announces that were he to have a choice in the matter he would leave Israel in a moment, that it is a place rife with political corruption, that the pursuit of wealth has replaced pioneering values.

Before long several of the other passengers wade in to refute him. A free-for-all ensues that makes the question period of London's Parliament look like a dainty tea at the home of a Sussex dowager. Sarah is astonished by the vehemence and lack of restraint. One passenger advises the detractor that for all that is wrong with Israel it still offers universal medical coverage and that he'd best avail himself of its psychiatric program. The faces of the quarrelsome are racially and ethnically varied, some light-skinned, some swarthy. Sarah muses to herself that this bus would present a eugenics advocate with a large headache.

In Tel Aviv she visits an antiquities museum with a superb collection of ancient glass: flasks, bottles, and vases, plates and bowls and trinkets made of greenish, nearly opaque glass, its color and consistency evocative of seawater that had somehow been crystalized. Some of the items on display have acquired over the millennia a brilliant, multi-colored patina, a glaze of rainbows and peacock feathers.

She takes lunch at a harbor side restaurant in Jaffa whence, according to her guide book, Jonah sailed on his fateful voyage, and where Prometheus was bound by the vengeful Gods.

After lunch she takes a cab to Jerusalem, a forty-five-minute drive up from the coast, the road winding through high hills covered in pines. She arrives at the King David hotel and is given a room overlooking the Old City, the vista a tapestry of ancient and wizened stones. Waking from an afternoon nap as replenishing as a lazy weekend, she walks in the direction of the Old City and finds her way to the Western Wall, remnant of the Jews' temple, and to the splendid mosque situated above it. She walks the Via Dolorosa, Christ's last walk on earth, and comes to his putative sepulcher.

The Old City is grim. An anxious wariness hangs in the air, as in a marriage rife with bad blood. The merchants who stand at the doorways of their shops are tense. Young Arab men walk past her and eye her with a hard-eyed curiosity. The walls along the narrow alleys are covered with political graffiti that declare the hard feelings of the wronged and the vengeful. The walls bear messages of the Intifada, the Palestinians' ongoing violent rage at having been relegated to a lesser place by the Israelis, by the world. She recalls Gaspar's description of graffiti on the walls outside Chardeau's home. Other walls, other rage.

139

She takes her dinner in her room, along with a bottle of decent local Chardonnay. She falls asleep in tears.

The next morning she visits the display of memorabilia from European Jewry's demise at the hands of the Nazis and their minions. Again she weeps, this time out of an ache at the bitter fate of so many, and at the sense that such mass horrors are, finally, small horrors that mushroomed, that grew from small inflammations to one gigantic opportunistic infection.

Afterwards she walks the streets of the new city, a bustling, thriving burg, a locus of ongoing life. She takes a taxi back to Paz's, telling the driver to take the road that runs along the nadir of the Syrian/African fault, that deepest chink in the earth's surface that at its lowest point passes through Israel. Paz has recommended this route of return. This fault, he suggests, is a seminal feature in the history of humankind, running as it does north from Kenya, a place where some of the oldest bones of mankind's forefathers have been discovered, up to and through the Red Sea, then through Israel. Along its path lie the Dead Sea, farther below sea level than any other spot on earth, site of Sodom and Gomorrah, and the Jordan River, a paltry stream that conducts far more lore and legend than it does water. It passes also the Sea of Galilee, a lake dwarfed in dimension by many of Europe's lesser lakes, but which, nevertheless, in many hearts outshines all others.

She arrives at Paz's house in the early evening. Mrs. Paz greets her with a warm smile and with gestures that beckon her out to the terrace, where the jar of purplish refreshment again awaits her. Paz himself arrives a short while later. He apologizes for not having been home to greet her. He was attending a meeting of the area's civil guard, in which he and nearly all other men of an age beyond military reserve duty participate.

In the morning, Paz is driven to, and past, the very border that on the previous night had been the subject of his and his fellow aging warriors' discussion. He makes his way to the perforated shack, accompanied by his driver, the same who had driven to the previous meeting. Harouni is there with his man.

After brief bargaining, tension-free, each willing to let the other take some advantage, each happy to let the other know they are being taken advantage of, they reach agreement: three million dollars for Gaspar's freedom. Paz takes care not to equate the money with Gaspar's life. It is merely the cost of his release, his return; a simple transaction, not the elixir that will ensure continued breath for Gaspar. Three million in five days, the time needed to accommodate the logistics, to bring the money from Europe. Three million in five days, the exchange to take place where they now stand.

Next, they discuss the number of people to be present at the exchange. They agree on up to three for each side. Gaspar will remain in Harouni's car until the money is examined. Denominations are of no consequence. Harouni smiles at this stipulation, as does Paz. Both know that, in this case, denominations and serial numbers hardly matter; Swiss banks gladly accept Lebanese deposits. Both are aware of a recent case in which a Lebanese drug dealer was making deposits of such magnitude that the bank in question, one of the majors, was obliged to send trucks to the airport to transport the notes to its vaults.

They then discuss the trivia inherent to the exchange. Is Gaspar to walk ahead of or behind Harouni's person? What will Gaspar wear?

What of Gaspar's papers? Harouni asks.

What papers? Paz demands to know.

Letters, lots of letters. Gaspar has been writing copiously. Probably he will wish to take these away with him.

Fine, what else?

Nothing. Gaspar will be wearing new clothing, things he has been given while Harouni's...guest. Is this all right? The old things may have been tossed out.

What are the new clothes like?

Harouni describes them, and that too is acceptable to Paz.

"Perhaps I shall see you in Beirut some day," Harouni says. "Maybe you will bring Mrs. Bruyn with you. She is a good-looking woman."

"I don't think I will be in Beirut anytime soon," Paz replies. "And I have the feeling that Mrs. Bruyn also will wait a bit before she next visits that city."

Chapter Twenty-one

As he traveled on the fast train from Brussels to Paris, Gaspar thought about his visit some years ago to a royal albatross colony on the high cliffs of Duneeden, New Zealand. He'd gone there following a business trip to Auckland Harbor to look over a couple of destroyers for sale by New Zealand's navy. The ships had proved to be of museum quality, no longer fit for anyone's fleet. While he went over the ships and photographed them, he also studied and photographed the harbor, which had been his SEDCE assignment. He good-naturedly assured his hosts that he would do his utmost to seek out a collector who might want the ships.

His photographs of the harbor went into SEDCE files and were inherited by DGSE. Eventually, they were used by the two Action Branch people who were sent to that very harbor to blow up an environmentalist's ship that had been harassing French vessels instrumental to France's nuclear experimentation in the South Pacific. A man had been killed in the explosion of the ship—the Rainbow Warrior—and the Action Branch people apprehended. Still, Gaspar had done his job.

Now he remembered the albatrosses of Duneeden, remembered the loneliness that nature had imposed on them. While fledglings, he was told by an attendant at the sanctuary, the birds were tended to with great care by their parents, stuffed with bits of fish until they could barely waddle. Then, all at once and without warning, the compact ceased and the parents utterly ignored their young, essentially leaving them to starve. Eventually, out of desperation the famished young leapt off the high cliff and flew, without ever having been taught to use their wings. Once aloft, the novice flyers didn't set foot on solid ground again for weeks on end, but flew in search of fish that could be plucked from the sea.

Gaspar thought of strong connections suddenly severed: Laura, and next, Bobo. That had become inevitable.

Sarah picked up and went. In that period between Toulon and London, after he left Laura, it never occurred to Gaspar that Sarah would leave his side. He'd become certain in some unreasoning place in his mind that ever since she'd disclosed to him what Chardeau had revealed to her, ever since they had fallen in love, there was room only for the effort to uncover Bobo's plot, for their love and for their bed. It turned out, however, that Sarah intended to live her life and pursue her work. The search for new topics was continuous, and so off she went on assignment to Italy's deep south.

"I'm helpless to do more about Bobo at the moment," she told Gaspar when he expressed his dismay. "It's up to you now, darling. I can't and don't want to loll about while you un-puzzle Bobo. I'll jump back in once we know more, but it's up to you to take matters to a point where I can be of value again. Right now you and I are at precisely the same place of ignorance: we have our suspicions but no more. Anyway, an Italian friend has asked me for assistance and I have to give it."

What sort of assistance? Her assistance was needed right here. Blast the Italian friend. Who was he anyway?

"I like it that you are stupidly jealous, I really do," she comforted him. "I like it that you need me."

She was off to Calabria, where poor farmers who had sought to save a few lira by purchasing discounted cooking oil had died of it. At least the fortunate ones did. The bargain cooking oil was actually engine oil which killed twenty of the penny-pinchers and left about sixty paralyzed or otherwise deathly ill. A Neapolitan newspaper reporter friend wanted Sarah to accompany him as he chased down the story, much of which he already knew. He needed her for his security, both as he gathered the last of the story and later when it would be published. The Italian reporter reasoned that the Ndrangheta, the Calabrese mob, one of whose protected merchants had peddled the poison oil, would be less eager to shoot him if he was in the company of an Englishwoman investigative journalist, whose death was far more likely to provoke scrutiny than his. They struck an agreement: she would run the story first in the Sentinel and he would follow in his paper with a reprint from the eminently respectable English journal. That way he would be able to claim it was her story, that he was merely reporting on her report.

"I'm coming with you, Sarah. I'm not leaving you to run around romantic Italy for days on end with some hot-blooded Neapolitan," Gaspar pleaded.

"He's sixty-four, darling, and a homosexual. And I'm not yet ready to cheat on you, Gaspar, not for a couple of years anyway. Now shall we go over what has to be done while I'm gone?"

Everything to do with Bobo and Iran had to be dredged up, reexamined, rethought. Whatever Bobo's reason for supplying Teheran, the answer lay in his past ties to the country.

"Consider these ties, Gaspar," Sarah urged. "Lay them out like good tableware for a festive meal, until they're all in their proper place, until your eye tells you that every detail is just right. Then you'll spot the piece that is missing."

Bobo was flabbergasted, as shaken as Gaspar had ever seen him. "But why? What in God's good name has come over you, Gaspar? You'll never find another Laura. You fool, Gaspar! I can't think of another couple as good together as you two."

"Be honest, Bobo," Gaspar said. "What in the hell do you know about good couples?"

Gaspar hadn't brought up the subject of Laura until the end of a meeting during which he, Bobo, and Deadeye went over a shopping list that those brought back with them from Baghdad. He examined his copy: parts for Panhard armored vehicles, replacements for products of Giat and Alcatel. Nothing, he thought, that would be of use to Iran's arsenal.

They conducted the meeting as they always had: the list was broken down into those items they were most likely to obtain for Saddam. Bobo had a separate list of items having to do with Iraq's nuclear research. These were his responsibility, calling for special handling and purchase through dummy companies, often abroad, for which his expertise and contacts made him most suitable. Deadeye handled shooting weapons, rifles, grenade launchers, side arms, telescopes, night vision equipment, goodies for Iraq's commandos. Gaspar's areas were electronics, radar, communication equipment, and consulting.

They discussed items by likelihood of attainability. One reason they had lasted with Saddam as long as they had was that they quickly let him know what they could and could not offer him. Other dealers sought to delay, to string Saddam along for as long as possible, hoping to somehow come up with goods in the intervening period. Boulevard delivered what it promised on time. They set deadlines by which to come up with those items they had each undertaken to locate.

Then Gaspar told them: Laura and he were to be divorced. She had gone to Sienna to be with her parents. Also, in the coming days he would not be able to carry his load because...well, because of certain demands on his time, what with divorce lawyers and all.

Deadeye glanced at him, at Bobo, then at him again in anticipation of an elaboration, an explanation. Bobo brought his hands held in a loose fist to his mouth and gazed at Gaspar. He gestured for Deadeye to leave.

"What happened, Gaspar? What went wrong?" he demanded.

"I was unhappy, have been for a long time. I was in Toulon about to have dinner with our friend—I never did, by the way, but I've since talked to him on the phone. He'll gladly join us. Anyway, there I was, shaving, getting ready to meet with the guy, and suddenly I felt as unhappy as I've ever imagined possible. You don't understand, Bobo. You assume about us—Laura and me—that because she's beautiful and smiles a lot and is always happy to see you that everything is all right. Well it isn't. Wasn't. I'm not in the mood to say more now. We'll talk later. I'll be staying at the apartment for a while. Do we have anyone coming?"

The apartment belonged to Boulevard. It was a small but elegant place on the Avenue de Friendland that they kept for special guests, for guests they wanted to feel special.

"No, it's clear, all yours. Listen, Gaspar, I hate to bring this up, but Saddam asked me, twice, to find out about his Italian order. Can you please look in on it?"

"Nothing to look in on, Bobo. They want payment and they won't release the vessels until they see some money."

"Make the call, Gaspar, please, so I can tell him I did as he asked and not be a liar."

"Since when do you care whether or not you lie to Saddam?"

Bobo cast a quizzical look his way and laughed. "It's just that I don't do small lies," he said.

"So he has serious money problems?" Gaspar mused out loud.

"Yes. Still, he pays us on time. Probably because of you. He likes and trusts you."

Early on in the war Saddam had placed an order worth nearly three billion dollars with Fincantieri, an Italian shipyard which was to construct for Iraq a floating dock, a supply ship, four frigates, and six corvettes. After he'd placed the order, Saddam had hired Gaspar to make certain that Fincantieri was giving him his money's worth, much to the Italian's chagrin. For his trouble Gaspar and Boulevard collected one percent of the outlay, nearly thirty million dollars. As the war dragged on, Saddam began to experience difficulties in making payments to Fincantieri and the majority of the completed vessels were embargoed by the Italian authorities. Yet Boulevard's bills were paid.

"What's going to happen now?" Gaspar asked.

"About what?"

"About his not being able to pay. He owes France, what—fifteen, twenty billion francs?"

"Twenty-five," Bobo said. "And Dassault wants another five billion in credit extended him; so do Matra, SENCMA, and a gaggle of subcontractors. Dassault is salivating over the Alpha Jet and Mirage 2000 order.

Naturally enough, the air force is pushing hard for the export credit people to see things Dassault's way. They want production lines to remain active, but the guys in charge at the ministry are balking."

"What do you think will happen?"

"Oh, they'll okay it in the end, they have no choice. They may view the credits they issue as liabilities, but Dassault and the others carry them on the asset side of their balance sheets, and Dassault contributes a lot more money to political campaigns than the civil servants at the ministry."

Gaspar slept in Boulevard's apartment two nights, then moved into a hotel in the Seventh, the Relais Christine. He'd been dialing Sarah's number in Calabria when he realized that he couldn't risk speaking with her from the apartment. It was, after all, Bobo's apartment too and very possibly it too had a secret purpose. At any rate, it now had doubts attached to it, and Gaspar removed himself.

He told Bobo that he would be spending time in Brussels and in any event didn't want to keep the place from serving its intended purpose. Bobo seemed concerned, disturbed that Gaspar's life was all at once in such a shambles. He asked for Laura's telephone number in Sienna and spoke with her. She sounded well, he told Gaspar. After this he became almost jovial, as if relieved by the conversation. He proposed that Gaspar and he take some time off and go on a trek together, perhaps to the Pyrenees.

Gaspar declined. "I need time to myself," he said. "I'll be all right. I'll phone you in a few days."

Once Bobo and Gaspar had been on their way to a meeting in Bobo's car when suddenly he'd told his driver to pull over. Bobo had just been made head of Research Branch, and Gaspar's admiration of his friend was as a warming, and blinding, sun.

"Look," Bobo said, pointing to two men dressed in well-cut, conservative suits, white shirts, sedate ties, black shoes—clearly businessmen, perhaps lawyers, who were arguing in the street. One was doing most of the talking, his words punctuated with forceful hand motions and rapid body tilts. "What do you think's going on there?"

"I've no idea," Gaspar said. "At a guess? Looks like the one guy messed up and the other one is letting him have it. What do you think?"

"I think the guy doing all the talking is the one who messed up. I think his anger is really fear. I think he feels the other has let him down, permitted him to mess up with a superior or an important client."

They looked on a while longer, until the one who had been carrying on suddenly stopped, turned away, and covered his face with both hands."

"The point is," Bobo explained, "that you went along with the guy doing the talking when you made your assumption. Since he seemed to be the angry one you identified with him, gave him your sympathy. I, on the other hand, was struck by the one on the receiving end, by his patience, by the fact that he took it all so calmly. You see, for a correct analysis of a situation you must first and foremost doubt what seems obvious, then search out that which is not."

Gaspar's small suite in the Relais Christine looked out onto an enclosed space, one of Paris's secret gardens, places of privilege that in the past were hidden by their owners behind high walls. At that time, in the late eighteenth century, privilege was a crime. More, it was a mortal sin punishable by swift and final judgement at the rigid edge of citizen Guillotine's invention.

Gaspar stared out at this small garden with its neat shrubs and two trees stunted by their confining circumstances into mere allusions to their full-grown possibilities, and attempted to consider the facts along the lines of Bobo's admonition to doubt the obvious. Compulsively, he sifted through his recollections of Bobo and Iran, from Bobo's friendship with General Assiri, to the Shah's medical exam in Paris, to Khomeini's forced exile in a Paris suburb.

Assiri had in his time headed Savak, the Shah's pervasive and merciless secret police cum counter-intelligence service. Assiri had been a signatory to the Safari Club treaties and a great fan and professional collaborator of Bobo's. Despite, or perhaps due to, U.S. dominance of Iran, Assiri disliked and derided Americans. He used to speak of their uncouth, blunt ways, mocking them for their arrogance. "These CIA hicks from the Midwest in their polyester shirts who have never heard of Scipio Africanus," Assiri once chortled to Bobo and Gaspar, referring to the Roman general who, on finally defeating Rome's nemesis, Carthage, was said to have observed that it was the fate of every great power eventually to meet ruination.

"They have deep religion, those boys," Assiri sneered. "They believe in Christ, in baseball, and in their Constitution, a document barely two hundred years old! They think the world didn't exist before they came along."

Assiri was not enamored of religious people. Savak's foremost domestic foe was orthodox Islam, Iran's pious Shia clerics who despised the Shah for his Western ways. Alas, Americans also built F-4 Phantom and F-14 Tomcat fighter jets complete with Sidewinder and Phoenix missiles, unexcelled weapon systems that the Shah, convinced that he was meant to possess the finest, had acquired. For that reason, and for considerations that were elaborations of that reason, Assiri had been forced to suffer the men in polyester shirts. But he didn't have to like them.

Bobo's Safari Club had been a soothing balm for Assiri, an opportunity to stand up to Washington and at the same time please his megalomaniacal master. For this he was grateful to Bobo and generous in showing his gratitude.

"The things that man knows—and tells me!" Bobo once remarked to Gaspar. At the time, Gaspar had not bothered about what things. Now, in his room at the Relais Christine, he worked at reconstructing knowledge from his substantial, but irregular, store of recollections.

When Khomeini overthrew the Shah, Assiri was put to death by firing squad. Apparently, he had been brave in his exit, too, as reported to Bobo by a key operative of Assiri's who had taken refuge in Paris. Khomeini himself had once been a refugee in Paris—in a suburb, to be precise. (Gaspar labored strenuously during these hours at imposing precision upon himself.) It had been from this suburb, as a matter of fact, that Khomeini had returned to rule Iran. Bobo and Gaspar had watched, literally sat in a parked car and observed, as the frail old man arrived at his temporary home, then again barely a year later when he left to assume power in Iran.

Khomeini in Paris—how had that come to pass? It happened because even the greatest of chess players occasionally fails to foresee the consequences of a certain move. The match in question had been the negotiations between the American Secretary of State Henry Kissinger on one side of the board, and the Shah and Saddam Hussein on the other. The Shah and Saddam had been quarreling over territories, some islands in the Gulf, some land up along their border. Kissinger sought to broker a deal between the two, and he succeeded. The land disputes were settled, the Shah dropped his support for rebellious Kurds who had been a thorn in Saddam's side, and, in return and in a gesture of good will, Saddam expelled from Iraq a certain Shia religious figure who had taken refuge from the Shah's secret police there. What Kissinger failed to foresee was that once out of Iraq, Khomeini, this man of God in question, would also be free of Saddam's own secret police, who had watched his every nap and sneeze. Khomeini went to Paris, where he was yet again placed under observation by the authorities, but in Paris he was free to move about, to communicate, freedoms he used to set in motion subsequent events.

So what, Gaspar puzzled, was obvious in all of this and therefore to be disregarded, and what was not? Why had Bobo brought him to watch Khomeini and his entourage move in, and later move out? At the time it had seemed simply a function of their friendship—who else to share mementoes of the trade but Gaspar?

True enough, Bobo did speak of the reasons for having offered Khomeini shelter. There in the car he'd explained that he'd suggested France as a solution when it turned out that no one—literally no relevant Muslim country—was willing to harbor Khomeini because he was potential trouble. The memory filtered back to Gaspar as does flavor to the palate from an airborne scent of cooking. Bobo had stepped in and suggested to the concerned parties that Khomeini come to France. He'd pointed out that France had a tradition of sheltering, and keeping on ice, controversial leaders who had lost their audience, men of influence and prominence whose influence was no longer desired, whose prominence had become a pain.

The solution, everyone agreed, was inspired. Khomeini in Paris would be Khomeini out of sight and out of mind. Perfect. And so Bobo had driven Gaspar to sit with him in the car and watch as the bearded old man in white made his way to his exile home. Khomeini's eyes had seemed puzzled by nearly everything, from the sidewalk onto which he was gently guided by his adoring helpers, to the helpers themselves, bearded acolytes who offered to help smooth his way past the temporal nuisances of this world, and whom he regarded with a mixture of puzzlement and misapprehension.

Bobo had smiled and shaken his head in admiration. He admired Khomeini, he said, because "he was someone to believe in, someone who could be neither flattered nor bribed nor made a fool for love of another's flesh."

Gaspar had observed that Khomeini's people, a troop of earnest young men intensely attentive to their master, had the eyes of avenging angels.

"Fortunately for us, at least one among them is flesh and blood," Bobo had replied with a smug smile.

But why admire him? Gaspar had demanded. Why approve of this old man who refused the future, who abided others' love of God only as he loved Him, his way or no way, worship as he worshiped or die? Who implied that the Almighty Creator was dependent on man's pedantic adherence to ritual for upholding His honor?

Laughingly, Bobo assured Gaspar that he admired Khomeini as one would a work of art. That his admiration ceased where his and France's purposes began.

Khomeini wore black when he departed Paris after the Shah had fled Iran, after jubilant throngs of Iranians had choked the streets of Teheran to demonstrate their preference for a man to believe in over a man who had believed foremost in himself. Bobo observed that among the actors of history who had lost their stardom and come to live out their days in France hardly any had ever regained the stage. Khomeini, he said, was therefore likely to give a most captivating performance which Bobo, for one, intended fully to enjoy.

Sarah had left a message including her telephone number on his Brussels answering machine. He called her back that evening. Their conversation was lengthy.

Gaspar related his recollections of Bobo and Iran. When he was done they agreed that it was grist, but hardly flour, certainly not yet bread. Perhaps another tack was in order.

She suggested he try tossing things around, the variables, what he had recalled, what he knew, and see what came up.

He said that he would and asked how her work was going.

"Well," she said, "if one may say well about such a grim tale of greed and callousness. Such nice people, these folks down here, so much grief inflicted on them."

He pointed out that the grief had been inflicted by their own.

Then, as if her own process of digesting what he had told her about Bobo had lagged and was only now up to speed, she began to ask questions. She sifted through his recollections once more, item by item. It was clear, she observed, that Bobo had been very well-informed about Iran under the Shah, could even be said to have had influence there. He'd probably recruited one of Khomeini's people when the cleric had taken refuge in Paris. Not in itself unusual; Bobo had been in the business of being informed. She observed that from what she'd learned about Bobo it appeared that he operated on what she termed a macro scale, that he addressed large pictures and devised solutions and operations of magnitude and great finesse. That he combined statecraft with spycraft. She asked Gaspar about that aspect of Bobo's tenure at SEDCE, whether his way of operating didn't rankle France's foreign policy establishment on the Quay d'Orsay.

It did indeed, Gaspar confirmed, but there was nothing they could do about it. The way Bobo had set things up and how he conducted himself left them only two choices: to resent or to admire him. Some opted for both. When, for example, Bobo had been assembling the Safari Club, he took care to deal only with counter-intelligence types in Egypt, Iran, Saudi Arabia, and Morocco, keeping scrupulously away from the foreign policy people. But the reality was that in those places the people who ran counter-intelligence were only a step removed from their respective heads of state, while the people who ostensibly ran foreign policy were secondary players. Since the nations in question were all ruled by autocrats, and autocrats prize above all intelligence about their opponents, real and imagined, they necessarily came to rely on their secret police, which in most cases doubled as a counter-intelligence service.

In France the counter-intelligence service answered to the political leadership, elected or appointed, Bobo's turn at the helm being the exception. The political leadership defined the national interest, SEDCE and other relevant agencies executed it. In the case of the Safari Club, however, Bobo essentially made foreign policy. He authored treaties between France and several nations and left the political leadership with no choice but to accept his brainchild, which was, after all, in France's national interest. About that, everyone agreed.

"The truth is," Sarah said finally, "that at this point the investigation is still all up to you, you alone can bring us further along. Also, darling, permit me to restate the obvious: that you and I are pursuing this tale for different reasons. So please, do this only if you wish it for yourself, for your own reasons. I don't want us to find ourselves regretting all of this some day."

"I need to know why he has lied to me," Gaspar said.

She sighed. "Very well, then. We're still no closer to the Twanee than we were."

And then it came to him. He was amazed that he hadn't thought of it before, that it hadn't occurred to him that the ship itself would be as good a source of information as any. If he wanted to know whether the ship was carrying secret cargoes, why not go aboard and take a look?

"Splendid idea, superb," Sarah said. She added that she could hardly wait to see him, and that she was concerned that their love was too dependent on physical attraction.

151

Chapter Twenty-two

There had been a negotiating session with the Chadian driver of the Paris taxi, when Gaspar explained that he might need to wait in the cab for some time once they arrived at their destination. Waiting time was not nearly so profitable as driving time, the Chadian explained with a happy grin. Gaspar offered to pay three times the meter amount, which made the Chadian so happy that he several times slapped his huge hand on the cab's padded steering wheel.

They sat and watched as Boulevard's management and employees left for the day. Gaspar sat well back in his seat, while the driver glanced repeatedly in the rearview mirror trying to fathom what his generous client was after.

Bobo and Deadeye were the first to leave, accompanied by one Paul Georges, a former air force general they used as a consultant. Bobo was having an animated discussion with Georges. Deadeye walked alongside Bobo, her head tilted downward as if she expected to encounter obstacles on the sidewalk. Then, in sequence, came the receptionists and office manager, then the secretaries, arriving at the building's entrance together like a flock of doves and like doves at the sound of a hunter's gun scattering in different directions. Then there were no more.

Gaspar paid the driver, who smiled broadly, wrote down his car telephone number, and urged that Gaspar use him often in the future.

Gaspar went directly into Bobo's office and opened the safe, to which they both had access although Gaspar hadn't opened it once since they'd moved into these offices. He had assumed that the Twanee's time sheet, the schedule of its voyages and stops, would be in the safe. It was not. The safe held cash—thirty-five thousand U.S. dollars in hundred-dollar bills—Bobo's Rolodex from SEDCE, in-house telephone directories of half the world's relevant counter-intelligence agencies and other bodies that had been connected to Bobo's work at SEDCE (M16, CIA, the various Mukhabbarats of the Arab world, the two Germanies, the KGB, GRU, the Élysée Palace, the Socialist Party headquarters, the Defense and Foreign ministries, Matingnon—the Prime Minister's office—and others). Also, a list of Iraqi airbases, their commanders, head mechanics, numbers and types of aircraft. A list of companies that manufactured or distributed what Gaspar recognized as instruments and parts useful to Saddam's reactor project. A list of the names of French citizens officially connected with the reactor. A typed page of numbers, apparently phone numbers, but without accompanying names. And an envelope on which the sealing gum had dried and was no longer effective. This last contained photographic negatives, which Gaspar held up against the desk lamp. They were of lovers in the act, clear shots all from the same angle of two men copulating. One was bearded and dark, one fair. They appeared to be enjoying themselves immensely. Gaspar knew with certainty that the bearded man was the one Bobo had alluded to when they'd been watching Khomeini and his entourage move into the cleric's temporary home near Paris. He replaced the negatives and the papers, peeled off three thousand dollars from the money stack, and closed the safe.

It took him nearly an hour of searching to find what he was looking for. The schedule was lying on top of the posting clerk's desk, a photocopy of a calender page with penned-in notations indicating that on that very day the Twanee was in Pireus and scheduled to remain there for another day. He left the offices and from the street telephoned both Air France and Olympic. He found the former's schedule more suitable, and booked a seat to Athens for the next morning.

The Twance was commanded by a Greek named Charalambos Pandiakis. He was an unusual Greek, quiet, not given to the rough, boisterous talk affected by most Greek men. He had never given Boulevard cause to complain, nor they him.

When Gaspar arrived at the Twance's berth, he found the gangplank guarded by a Polish crewman and had a difficult time convincing the man to fetch his captain, whom the Pole obviously held in some fear. Pandiakis looked down from high on the ship for a long moment, but when he finally recognized Gaspar he hurried down and greeted him warmly. It had been Gaspar who had hired him. Pandiakis did not presume to question why he hadn't been given warning that Gaspar intended to visit.

It was nearly lunch time, and Pandiakis suggested they take it together. They went by taxi up the road a way from Pireus to the yacht port called Zea and a restaurant that looked down on the slick gold-and-blue Soviet-built hydrofoils that offered high-speed connections to nearby islands and points on the Peloponnese coast to well-off Athenians and tourists. Gaspar deferred to Pandiakis for the ordering and was rewarded with excellent grilled octopus, a tangy eggplant salad, crisp Greek salad, and a platter of fried barbouni, a small Mediterranean fish. As they ate, Gaspar inquired about the ship: was it running well? were there problems he ought to be aware of? did its crew perform to Pandiakis's satisfaction?

All was shipshape, he was told; the ship performed very well, the crew was reliable and loved the hazard pay they received for working the Gulf.

And how was it going with Forjieh?

"Forjieh is a gentleman," Pandiakis assured him. "He looks after the ship's stops, and when we have unscheduled cargoes everything goes like clockwork. He makes sure that things run smoothly once the ship is in the Gulf itself. He's a good man."

"That's good to know," Gaspar said, and made a joke about Forjieh, not only being a gentleman, but also dressing like one. He asked Pandiakis whether he had unscheduled cargo on this trip, adding with a wink that he hoped this was the case. After all, unscheduled cargoes helped profitability, right?"

O yes, Pandiakis assured him, they were in Pireus to pick up three containers that had not been originally scheduled. "But they may as well have been. As you know Mr. Bruyn, the Pireus pickups are all the time, like a normal stop."

"Good, great." Gaspar beamed. After lunch, he said, he intended to do a spot check on the contents of the three new containers. That, indeed, was why he had come to Pireus. Boulevard wished to make certain that their client would be receiving exactly what he ordered, that nothing went amiss between loading and unloading. There had been complaints from the Gulf—not about the <u>Twanee</u>, of course—that what arrived was not always what had been ordered, so better safe than sorry.

As far as Pandiakis knew there had never been complaints on the receiving end, but then he was not there for the actual unloading. The man Forjieh had arranged for, the Gulf professor—

Gulf professor?

Ah yes, that was what they had taken to calling the local pilot because he knew the Gulf so very well.

Right, Gaspar said, and allowed that he didn't even know the pilot's name.

Neither, it seemed, did Pandiakis. But surely Forjieh knew. This local guy, from Baharain, came on board just past the Straits of Hormuz and took the wheel. Brought a skeleton crew along too, a procedure about which Pandiakis confessed he at first had reservations. As the captain, he felt he should stay with his ship, but he has since come around to seeing the wisdom of this procedure. The Gulf was best handled by a local who appeared to know its ins and outs. Witness the fact that the <u>Twanee</u> had gone unscathed all this time.

Gaspar agreed that it was an unconventional but practical solution to sailing the hazardous waters of a war zone.

After lunch they boarded the <u>Twanee</u> and Pandiakis arranged for the three containers in question to be opened. Before entering the first container, Gaspar removed from his briefcase a calculator and writing pad. Pandiakis and the two crewmen who had unlocked the giant metal crate discreetly withdrew as soon as the gate had swung open.

In the plentiful light of the afternoon sun, Gaspar stood and gazed at the wooden crates that filled the container—dozens and dozens of them. Through their slats it was possible to see metal tubes, each a bit under three feet long. The <u>Twanee</u>'s unscheduled cargo was artillery shells for hundred-and-fifty-five-millimeter howitzer long-range guns. Not Iraqi howitzers, because Iraq got its shells directly from Luchair; Boulevard did not supply shells to its client in Baghdad. These shells were bound for someone else's howitzers.

A hard lump formed in Gaspar's throat. He stood there for long minutes to permit his surprise and anger to dissipate. Then he walked into the next container, then into the last.

"All's in order, thank you," he said to Pandiakis. "Not that we had any doubts, but it's good to check every once in a while, don't you think?"

Pandiakis agreed.

Gaspar wished him good sailing.

"There was nothing outwardly strange about it," Gaspar told Sarah when she joined him at the Relais Christine after his return from Athens. "It's a large ship. We ship large items, but there's plenty of cargo space left over, so we arrange to take on additional cargoes. I don't check on what goes aboard, not part of my duties. Anyway, some of what we purchase on Iraq's behalf gets loaded along the way—Portugal, Italy, Yugoslavia. So it was easy for Bobo and whoever else to add cargo without my ever knowing about it. Forjieh's arrangements took care of the unloading, and that was that."

"At least we now know for certain that something is under way, that Chardeau had it right. You still think this isn't about money, Gaspar? Certainly sounds to me like lots of money is involved."

"It may be about money to someone, but not to Bobo. On that I'd stake my life."

"What about this company, Luchair? Do you know anything about it, know any of the people?"

"Naturally I know about it, they're a household name in the arms business. But I don't know anyone in it, really. Over the years I must have run into someone or other who works there but I've had no cause to develop a relationship. We don't do ammunition shells, you see. I may, however, know another dealer who can fill me in."

"Don't waste time, get hold of him."

He telephoned the man and arranged to meet the next day.

Sarah visited the Musée d'Orsay while Gaspar and his munitions-dealing acquaintance walked along the Seine's left bank and chatted about artillery shells. Gaspar learned that rumors had circulated for some time within the munitions industry that as long ago as 1982 a diligent Defense Ministry accountant had discovered that Luchair was manufacturing many more artillery shells than it was reporting. Also, that when shipments were monitored it was indeed discovered that extra shells were going to an unnamed arms dealer who, in turn, proved exceedingly vague about whom he had sold to, but some suspected that the shells were making their way to Iran. It was said that Luchair's top managers claimed ignorance, that they fired some people and promised the Defense Ministry and Élysée Palace that stringent controls would be introduced, and that was the end of it. So why was Gaspar asking?

Precisely because, Gaspar confessed gratefully, some clients of his were concerned about the very story he'd just been told. These clients were a precarious regime which desired a non-controversial source of shells for their shipboard four-inch guns. When Gaspar had proposed Luchair, the clients had brought up the Iran rumor and stressed that they didn't want to depend on a firm that could find itself in trouble with the French authorities. Gaspar was therefore protecting himself, exercising due diligence, and much appreciated the help he was now getting. What he had just learned, he confided, had caused him to altogether reconsider this deal—not his line of work, really. They shook hands, promised to keep in touch, and went their ways.

Gaspar sat across from Sarah at a table in a small restaurant on the Rue de Rennes, a place where fabrics draped just so and candles placed just there transported one from the city to a splendid tent pitched in a magical oasis in a nameless desert. He was amazed at himself for feeling so calm.

"On the one hand I feel an utter fool," he said. "All these things of which I was unaware going on around me—it's as if my alarm clock has failed to go off for the last four or five years and I've missed all the impor-

156

tant morning office meetings. On the other hand I can see how this happened. Bobo is a master. I've always know that, and therefore I excuse myself."

"I do too, darling," she said. "A masterly choice of restaurant, by the by. But how do you excuse yourself?"

She had a way of inquiring, he thought, that was at once irritating—the substance of her question, its provocative bent—and yet endearing for the smile on her lips, the affection in her eyes.

"There was no reason for me to know, none. These things were simply beyond my ken. My business is ships, electronics, things that go on the water or that see through it. I advised Saddam, who rarely listened, and got paid for it. I trusted Bobo, lived far away in Brussels, and that was that."

"And you spied."

"Right."

"Sort of the spy who was kept in the dark."

"Now you're mocking me."

"No I'm not, sweetie. It's only that keeping a sense of humor is important. Speaking of humor, I'll contact Chardeau and advise him that his story checks out, that it's on. All right with you?"

"I suppose so."

"I'll be asking him to supply me with something tangible— computer printouts, something to back up his assertions about how he got onto Bobo."

"Why? I should think he'd be putting himself at a good deal of risk getting them."

"To have handy for when I confront Bobo. To convince him that this story will be told with or without his cooperation. I should think it will make him more likely to see things my way."

"You're too clever, Sarah. How did Tillinghast ever let you go?"

"I let him go, Gaspar. He was just too bloody perfect for me, God's right-hand man on earth, utterly free of flaws, blameless, knew everything and worked relentlessly at lifting me to his level. Wouldn't let me buy a light bulb without lecturing me on filaments. Knew absolutely the way to slice open a melon, the way to drink water straight from the bottle when we traveled so as to spare us from touching our lips to unsanitary glasses. Had the formula down for me to have the best orgasms, even if he said so himself. Was incapable of not dominating a dinner conversation. I finally figured he deserved much more than merely me: he deserved himself."

"Very picky on your part, Sarah."

"You're teasing me, right? Because I was being bossy back there. I didn't want to be perfect, Gaspar. Shall I call you the great Gaspy? Guess not. Can't be perfect, didn't want to have perfection forced upon me."

"Then you've come to the right man. But didn't you see that in him right away?"

"Falling in love is like having a great big gaping need suddenly tended to. At first one is imbued with a powerful gratitude for having been lifted above the mundane, for feeling happy for days on end, so one suspends one's critical faculties. Then one discovers the rest. But between inertia, fear of being thought a failure, and hoping against hope, time passes."

"Will that happen to us?"

"I can't predict, darling. But I'm satisfied that you are a good man, terribly sweet and kind. You yearn for more than the status quo, you want to be better. I love that about you. You'd be surprised at how many people never consider admitting to being in the wrong, or that they've been had. And how few really want to change."

"Thank you, my love. But please keep all these nice things about me to yourself. I'd hate for the word to get out."

"Promise. Now what do we do about Bobo?"

"Whatever happens, Sarah, somewhere in me I know that fundamentally Bobo is not a bad guy."

"Be prepared to change your mind, darling. Bad guys don't necessarily go around with marks of Cain on their foreheads."

"You think I should be the one to confront him?"

"I don't know. But whichever one of us, the time isn't right yet. I should meet him, get to know him. Can you work on that? I mean, break it to him that you're involved with someone and that you'd like him to meet her? And Gaspar, don't give him my real name. Use Corrine Blaine, she's a friend of mine."

Chapter Twenty-three

"I haven't been honest with you," Gaspar said.

Bobo put down the proposal he'd been scrutinizing and peered at Gaspar with some anticipation.

"And I don't feel right about it," Gaspar went on. "I mean, we've always been straight with one another, right?"

Bobo nodded a confirmation.

They were killing time in Bobo's office, waiting for Deadeye to bring by a Dutch manufacturer of night vision equipment, her contribution toward filling the latest shopping list from Baghdad.

"Don't feel right about what?" Bobo said, then answered his own question. "About the money, am I right?"

"What money?"

"Oh-oh, now you've got me worried," Bobo said. "I thought you were going to tell me about the money you took from the safe."

"Hell, the three thousand? I forgot about that, sorry. I needed cash, the banks were closed. Speaking of the office safe, those are some racy negatives you keep there, didn't know you went in for that stuff. Wouldn't have let you sleep so close to me on our hikes had I known."

Bobo smirked. "Oh, those," he said dismissively. "Actually you've seen one of the guys before, you just don't remember."

"Bet I do. He was with Khomeini's people, right? That night when the old man moved into the house in Paris."

"Good for you, Gaspar."

"I assume the other one was one of yours? Right. So what's this smut doing in our safe, Bobo? How are we using them?"

Bobo's face took on a sly grin. "What makes you think we're using them?"

"Why else would you keep them in the safe?"

"Why indeed?"

"Come on, Bobo," Gaspar protested, "the days of keeping me in the dark for my own good are long gone, don't you think? I do. No good reason left for me not to know."

"If you say so, Gaspar. We used them to blackmail the Iranian, of course. Quite a yield, too. I'll bet none of my competitors had anyone in place so close to Khomeini. So...if not about the money, then what did you lie to me about?"

"Oh...about Laura. About leaving her. It was more than just being unhappy with her. There's someone else."

"What a surprise, Gaspar! Don't tell me the law of chance has finally caught up with my layabout friend, and one of your snacks turned out to be a full meal. Who is she?"

"A wonderful, amazing, beautiful Englishwoman named Corrine Blaine. I can't wait for you to meet her. In fact, I'd love to bring her to Belle Marais next weekend."

"I should have known," Bobo said. "My philandering boy, you took one too many sips of stolen wine. You were bound to stumble across a vintage you liked better than the one in your own cellar. So what did it? Was she stupefying in bed, or what? Next weekend is a good idea. Where did you meet her?"

"In Toulon."

"When you were supposed to have dinner with our friend? Well that explains much better why you stood him up—better than that melodramatic crap you gave me about being unhappy."

"What I told you was true, only there was more to it. I don't think I'd have fallen for another woman had things been otherwise with Laura." Gaspar paused because he thought he'd heard the elevator door shutting. He listened for a moment, but heard nothing more.

"Let me ask you something, Bobo. How is it for you with Deadeye? I mean, you two don't give the impression that you really thrill each other."

"She's all right. I'm not with her for thrills, I get all the thrills I want from my work."

"Then why do you stay with her?"

"She's loyal, she does what I tell her, she pleases me in bed. I don't fancy being alone. To me she's like an adjutant I sleep with, you know?"

"Really, that's it?"

"You doubt me?"

"It's just that you two don't give the impression of being fulfilled. You were always flirting with Laura, Deadeye is off to herself a lot. I never know what's really going on with her, you know? Frankly, you two simply don't give the impression of being a couple."

"Gaspar, Gaspar! You can't blame me for flirting with Laura! I mean, Laura! I'd have to be a Sphinx not to. She's some woman!"

"Looks aren't everything."

"Did you just tell me that your Englishwoman is homely?"

"No, but..."

160

"Somehow I'm not surprised. What does she do?"

"Lectures at university. Politics."

"What did you tell her about your business? I'm just curious. How did you put it?"

"I gave her the truth, of course. I told her I was a merchant of death, an impresario of mass violence, and that my partner was a cold-blooded schemer out to rule the world."

"Great," Bobo said, "well put."

"I told her I was in the military boat business, a ship's broker. That way I was able to carry on a normal conversation with her."

"What did she say?"

"That I was bullshitting her. That I was obviously a merchant of death, an impresario of mass violence."

"Sounds like you two get along well."

"We do. So let me ask you, Bobo, what about you and Deadeye? Don't you yearn to be with someone you're crazy about?"

"My mother was crazy about my father, and a lot of good it did her. No thanks. Anyway, in life a person can be crazy about many things. I don't know what you're getting at, but Deadeye is just fine by me."

"Not getting at anything, Bobo, just wondering. You think you'll ever have kids? I think I will, but I'm glad Laura and I waited. The separation would have been a lot harder with children."

"How is Laura taking it?"

"Okay, I guess. I called her yesterday about giving me the divorce. She wants to think about it, I suspect she's hoping I'll change my mind. Why don't you give her another call? I'm sure she'd love to hear from you."

"Sounds like you're trying to relieve yourself of guilt, Gaspar. But I'll do it, I'll do it. Anything for friendship. In the end, divorce is about money, don't you think?"

"Do you believe everything is about money, Bobo?"

"Listen, pal," Bobo said with a sudden spurt of annoyance, "it isn't like you've turned down money. Money in the service of a good cause is all right, let me tell you."

"Sorry, Bobo. I'm going through a rough time. I guess I was also thinking about Saddam and money—that talk we had the other day about him not paying people. What if he begins to do the same with us?"

"Deadeye and I were wondering about that. What do you think?"

"I guess we could do a couple of things. Try to set things up so that he has to pay the principal for whatever he buys through us directly to manufacturers, for one. We broker the goods, collect our commissions from him and from the manufacturers, and let them work out payments among themselves. That would tend to reduce our leverage with both, but at least we'd get paid. Or we could demand cash up front—no cash, no merchandise—and see what happens. Or we could bow out altogether. It's been a long time, going on seven years. Don't you think we've accomplished what we set out to accomplish?"

"How's that?" Bobo said. His question had an absentminded quality, as if to say, "Remind me, what exactly did we set out to do?"

"Look around you, Bobo. France is as prosperous as it's been since the end of World War Two. That socialist in the Élysée Palace you so feared has been tamed. You've won, Bobo. He's behaving like a regular person—stopped nationalizing things, doesn't hassle people for being wealthy, hasn't dropped the Arabs or the PLO in favor of Israel, is doing all sorts of business with Iraq. Your strategy has proven out. So maybe it's time to quit, take our stash and go away. I'm not telling you to stop caring, stop helping your friends, only that it may be the right time to slow down. What do you think?"

"Could be you're right. I'm not as certain as you appear to be about our pinko friends, I mean there's prosperity now, but what happens when the economy turns down, as it inevitably will? He and his cabal will still be there, and I for one do not for a moment believe that their agenda has altered one iota. They've merely postponed acting because things are going too well now. They know it's no use trying to foment trouble when conditions aren't right. From that point of view, I shouldn't quit, I should take as much advantage of our strengths as possible."

Gaspar rose and walked over to the large window in Bobo's office, looking down onto the boulevard below. It was nearly eight in the evening, but mid-June's sunlight still bathed the outside world. He wished he was out there, strolling the street with Sarah, as carefree as others appeared to be.

At last he said, "Speaking for myself, that's what I intend to do, Bobo. I'll be moving on as soon as I'm divorced. I've never pressed you for details; I always figured you knew best. I haven't asked how you distributed the money in Zug, how you worked things with suppliers, whom you favored and why, all that. I had no reason to. I understood what you theorized about France, I agreed with you, I tried to be helpful. Listening to you now, though, it strikes me that you speak as if it all rests on your shoulders, as if without you the nation would collapse, the devil would take over. I wonder whether you're aware that this is what you sound like.

162

erhaps it's true, perhaps you are that titan on whose shoulders France ests, has rested these past years. If that's so, then I wish you would tell me just how it works."

To Gaspar's surprise, Bobo hesitated a long moment, during which it appeared that he might actually respond. In the end he apparently decided against it.

"Not just yet, Gaspar. I hear the elevator. I think Deadeye is here with her Dutchman."

Chapter Twenty-four

"I spoke with Chardeau," Sarah said. "Asked him to bring me some printouts from his office. He spat fire, raged, said it was much too risky, that his word ought to suffice, but I insisted. At the very least I want to see Agatha's original report about the purchase of the <u>Twanee</u>. Hope you enjoyed her, Gaspar."

He checked an impulse to assure her that he had.

"Chardeau claims that DGSE has updated SEDCE's computer programs and he suspects they may have introduced certain safety measures—triggers to alert them to any tampering. He says as yet he's unfamiliar with these. I reckon he was just making excuses, I'm sure he'll come through. He really hates your pal de Bossier—envy more than anything else, I think."

Sarah was driving as she spoke. She and Gaspar had rendezvoused at Charles de Gaulle airport, rented a car there, then driven on. They were now just past Angre on their way to Belle Marais.

It was a lovely Friday morning, early enough in the day to avoid the weekend traffic. They were happy. Though it was left unsaid, they had become a couple, easy with one another, anticipative of each other's thoughts and moods.

"How do you intend to go about bringing it all up with Bobo?" Gaspar said.

"It's inevitable that we will talk politics—I supposedly teach the subject, after all. I'll steer the conversation in the direction of the Gulf War, France's involvement, and so on. We'll see how things go. Sooner or later, of course, I'll have to tell him who I really am, can't run the story otherwise. Not if I intend to quote him, or even allude to him by name. Unless you come up with the goods, in which case I can quote you. Ah, but I promised you I wouldn't do that. And there's Deadeye. We know nothing about her role, if any, or what her response to possible exposure might be. My guess is that it will all come down to facing Bobo with Chardeau's evidence. That will probably decide the issue."

As they approached the tiny village of Cheffes, Gaspar warned her to slow down. The road, he explained, ran through the village center and people tended to use it as if it was their back yard. "Not a lot of traffic comes through, you see. Cheffes is the sort of place that used to make me wonder about the people in it—what on earth do they do? How do they live in this one-street place where nothing ever happens, where you can't remove a plate from the cupboard without your neighbor knowing it? It used to belong to the de Bossiers, you know, the whole village. They still treat Bobo somewhat like the lord of the manor."

At the turn-off to Belle Marais they drove up a long, unpaved driveway. When finally they were in sight of the house, Sarah involuntarily exclaimed, "But the place is absolutely sublime, Gaspar!"

As Sarah pulled in between an old Peugeot and an older Rover, Bobo and Deadeye emerged from the house. Gaspar felt a spasm of anxiety. It suddenly occurred to him that Bobo would plumb out everything upon first setting eyes on Sarah.

Sarah put her hand briefly and lightly on his knee, then opened her door. She stepped up to Deadeye and introduced herself, shook her hand and said, "How very lucky you are! What an absolutely smashing place!" She turned to Bobo. "Count de Bossier, Gaspar has told me so much about you. I'm so very pleased to meet you."

"And I you," Bobo replied. "But Gaspar ought to have told you that you must call me Bobo. Certainly not 'Count.' Things being how they are these days in France, I may be in jeopardy for having inherited an ancient, silly title."

Gaspar emerged from the car and was greeted by Deadeye and Bobo. Deadeye offered them a drink, which they declined. She and Gaspar briefly discussed the room they would be staying in. Lunch, she said, would be in half an hour. "I took the liberty of putting you in a room together," she said to Sarah rather solemnly. Then, she smiled a shy, and, as it turned out, the only, smile of their acquaintance. She cupped a hand about Sarah's elbow and guided her to the house.

"Please call me Corrine," Gaspar heard Sarah say, and yet another pang of anxiety shot through him.

Bobo came up and gave him a large, theatrical wink. "My boy, I don't know how you do it, but you obviously have the knack. She is...well, perfection, Gaspar. Quite perfect."

"I'm glad you like her," Gaspar mumbled.

Over lunch, Bobo carried on about Belle Marais, the region, the house. This house, he explained, had once upon a time been a sort of hideaway. The de Bossiers had owned another place, a château, not far away, but in the nineteenth century the château had been sold. He then began describing his and Gaspar's days together at Belle Marais. Although he glanced frequently at Gaspar, looking to him for confirmation of one or another recollection, Sarah had the distinct impression that he was speaking for his own benefit. She wondered whether he sensed that things between him and his old friend were about to change.

After lunch Deadeye suggested that Sarah accompany her on a small hunt to help stock the larder. "For supper and tomorrow's lunch," she explained. "Pheasant, perhaps." Since Bobo stifled yawns and spoke in praise of an afternoon's nap and Gaspar agreed that napping was a good idea, Sarah accepted. If nothing else, she would get to know Deadeye better. She declined, however, Deadeye's offer to fit her with a gun. "I'll assist, carry the birds and all that," she countered.

"Let's cut through the forest to the meadow. You never know, we might come across a wild turkey," Deadeye suggested.

They walked into the thick woods, crowded trees that had long since sorted out among themselves which owned what parcel of the rich, dark forest floor and how much of the sky and sun. The allocations left precious little sunlight and only fragments of sky visible through the ancient trees' canopies. What light there was fell onto absorbent ground made pliant by a matting of long-decayed leaves and branches.

Deadeye walked at a good pace, surefooted in the opulent gloom. Silent, too, as she deftly avoided stepping on anything that would broadcast her presence—twigs, branches, acorns. Sarah trailed along, trying as best she could to emulate her guide. She noticed that Deadeye did not carry her rifle as English hunters did, cradled in the arms with the barrel pointing downwards and away. Rather she held it out and slightly ahead of her, tilted at an upward angle, almost as one might hold a fishing pole. If nothing else, such a carrying style, Sarah thought, required a powerful wrist.

Something stirred up ahead, then thrashed and lifted off the ground with powerful beatings of large wings. As Sarah watched the blur of colors from the fast-moving feathers and the commotion, movement, and suddenness of it all whirled in her mind, she saw Deadeye's gun snap downward, Deadeye's free arm fly forward to meet and steady the barrel support, which came into her hand with the assurance and fit of two halves of a clamshell snapping shut. The bird flew towards a meager opening in the umbrella above, away from danger, towards the clear sky and life, but in vain. The rifle fired once, not very loudly, and the bird's flight was forever stilled. A small dusting of under feathers followed it down, confetti for its own funeral.

"My God! Remind me never to make you cross with me," Sarah whispered. "Deadeye, indeed! Where on earth did you learn to do that?"

166

"I grew up in a small place in the Pyrénéés. There we either caught dinner or went without. At least that was the case with my family." Deadeye's words were matter-of-fact, devoid of pathos or self-pity.

"Is that why you're called Deadeye?"

"No. When I served in the army the boys were jealous of my shooting. Someone started calling me that, so they all did. Comes from a character in some German novelist's stories."

"Karl May," Sarah said. "He wrote about the wild west, mostly while he was in debtor's prison. Happens he was Hitler's favorite writer. Would you like me to call you by your given name?"

"No, I'm used to it by now. Shall we go on? I could try for one more."

"Anything you say, chére Deadeye, anything at all."

The next victim, glorious tail feathers and all, tried to hide in the tall grass as they approached. To Sarah it appeared that the pretty pheasant had made it to safety, which pleased her. Deadeye, however, was not to be denied.

They had left the forest and had been walking for five minutes or so along a barely discernable trail. "What gorgeous country," Sarah whispered, "how spectacular!"

It was at that moment that the pheasant made its dash for safety. Deadeye slapped her rifle into position and began tracking the bird as it scampered for shelter, following the now unseen quarry to the spot where its rate and direction would have placed it. She fired into the grass, lowered her rifle, walked into the shelter that wasn't, and emerged with the pheasant. It had been shot nearly at its center.

"Bad shot," she said.

Sarah ejaculated a brief burst of laughter at the discrepancy between Deadeye's judgment of herself and the facts, to which Deadeye returned an uncomprehending look. She handed the bird to Sarah by its still-warm legs, and they turned to walk back to the house.

"Do you like what you do now?" Sarah asked.

"How do you mean?"

"Your work with Gaspar and Bobo must be far less exciting than the army."

"Oh. Couldn't stay in forever. One must move on in life. What do you do?"

"Teach at university. Politics, contemporary politics."

"Is that fun?" The question proved to be rhetorical as Deadeye continued, "I doubt that I could put up with all that theoretical stuff, all that crap flying around. I mean, when do you get to actually do things?"

167

She wasn't out deliberately to insult or belittle, Sarah reflected, it wa only that she had a rough streak that she didn't bother to hide.

"How did you happen to meet Gaspar, then?" Deadeye said.

"I was working on a paper about the Gulf war and I went to Toulon to educate myself about shipping in the Gulf. He picked me up at a bar, or maybe I picked him up. Who knows?"

"Why Toulon?"

"I had someone who was willing to talk to me on the subject and that's where he works, so I went."

"Someone in the French navy?"

"Why do you ask?"

"I just assumed, Toulon being a navy town. What you call home base for our Mediterranean fleet."

"No, he wasn't, actually. Not even French. Just happened to be there and willing to speak with me. I was lucky to meet Gaspar, turned out he's informed on the subject too. But you must know that."

"But how did it happen? I mean, that you actually spoke to Gaspar?"

"This person and I were sitting at a bar, Gaspar heard us talking and joined in, one thing led to another. You know how it is."

"Must have been out to get laid, it's a big thing with him," Deadeye observed matter-of-factly.

"Yes, I know," Sarah said.

"I'm not used to talking about it—the business—because people don't like us to talk about the stuff they're buying or selling. By now it's second nature to me not to discuss."

"Makes sense," Sarah said. "I assume, however, that Bobo and you discuss the business. I mean, it takes up so much of your time together I should think it would be unavoidable."

"Bobo doesn't talk with me much about most things," Deadeye said.

She sounded, thought Sarah, neither complaining nor unhappy. She was merely stating a fact.

"These are goals, hoped-for behavior, certainly not etched in stone. Nothing about human conduct is, don't you agree?" Bobo said.

They were having supper in a room that was a blend of library and dining room. Its dark, heavy furniture and leather and cloth book spines were offset by trinkets from the levant: Bedu headdresses, an ornate wedding gown from Yemen, thick strands of silver beads, a hat rack covered with fezzes, bowls brimming with worry beads. Following the main course, washed down with two excellent wines poured out of oversized, dusty, and unlabeled bottles, they had become enmeshed in a discussion that rapidly strayed from its origin—a compliment of sorts by Gaspar to Deadeye. "This bird gave its life for a great cause," he'd said with an admiration and sentimentality heavily influenced by the nameless vintage.

Sarah, in a mock-teacherly manner, placed a question on the table. "Is there," she asked, "such a thing as a cause worth dying for? Or killing for?"

The expected answers poured forth: yes, in order to save lives, one's own life, other people's.

And beyond these?

Beyond these matters grew vague, more difficult to define. But yes, other situations existed that called for the ultimate judgement or sacrifice.

"What causes supersede the sanctity of life?" Sarah demanded.

"All sorts," Bobo said. "Surely you have taken up with your pupils the English general in India who shot down hundreds of unarmed protesting natives. And that other Englishman who set up concentration camps in South Africa during the Boer War."

"How did this become a British/French thing?" Sarah protested.

"French, English, whatever," Bobo said. "When one's interest is sufficiently threatened, one is willing to act forcefully. Didn't someone set out to prove—Game Theory, wasn't that it?—that altruism, too, is finally self-interest."

Sarah confessed that she regularly posed questions of this sort in her lectures because one or two students took them up and so kept the others awake.

"But what is your interest in the Gulf?" Bobo said. "Deadeye told me of your project."

"Contemporary history. One of my subjects, you know. But I'm glad you brought it up. Push that gorgeous bottle down here, would you, Bobo? Thanks."

And had she drawn any conclusions yet about the war?

Indeed. That it was beastly, unusually cruel, and for many people a topic of utter indifference. Also that she wasn't happy with Europe's posture in it.

Gaspar drew Deadeye into a side conversation about her old Rover, as much to spare himself spasms of nervousness at Sarah's evolving game as clear the stage for her. The car, Deadeye confessed, was dear to her—solid and heavy and impossible to miss in a parking lot among all the Peugeots and Citroens and Fiats. She'd bought it for a song from a neigh-

169

bor. Bobo teased her about it, called her unpatriotic for owning a foreign car. Gaspar said that Bobo had a point, and Deadeye took a long second to conclude that she was again being teased.

At the other end of the table, Bobo said, "What is Europe's posture as you see it?"

"Self-serving indifference," Sarah replied.

"And why should people take an interest?"

"Surely you were taught ethics at school, Bobo. They do teach ethics in French schools, don't they, darling? Gaspar?"

Gaspar stopped chatting up Deadeye long enough to remind her that a significant part of his education had been acquired in Boston.

"What I mean is that we're in bed with a regime whose ends unfailingly justify the most heinous means. How would you explain that?" Sarah demanded of a smiling Bobo. "If you read the recent Stockholm Institute for International Peace report it's impossible not to conclude that we Europeans are enjoying this war, that we're stuffing our bank accounts as never before with mounds of loot earned from Iraq. Iraq, the aggressor. How do you justify that, Bobo?"

"I'll let my partner answer that one. How do we justify this, Gaspar?"

Gamely, Gaspar played along. "We believe that Saddam is on the side of right in this, that he's the lesser of evils, that we live in an imperfect world." He did not look at either Sarah or Bobo.

"Bravo!" Deadeye exclaimed.

Sarah frowned. "I don't buy it. Do you deny that Iraq struck first? Of course not. Then shouldn't someone help the victim? Why aren't we at least balancing things by selling weapons to Iran so they can defend themselves? What about it, Bobo? Will you noble characters at Alleyway or Side street or whatever your enterprise is called do at least that much to mitigate your sins?"

"A good idea!" Bobo said. "Wish I'd thought of it. Why don't you abandon academia and come to work with us at Boulevard? Our enterprise is called Boulevard, my dear Corrine."

"Only if you can find a way for me to leave my conscience at home, Bobo," she said.

"You two better get married soon so that we can all feel safe," Deadeye observed.

"By implication you must be feeling quite insecure with me, Genvieve," Bobo said to Deadeye.

Deadeye turned to Sarah. "He is no more capable of marrying than I am of writing poetry," she said.

"Oh sure, marriage can be a pain," Sarah admitted. "But seriously, what do I say to my bright, innocent students about all this? What, for example do I say when they ask how Iran has managed to fight on?"

Bobo leaned forward. "Khomeini's Iran is extremely unpopular with almost everyone, surely with your students too. In the Middle East only Syria and Israel—now there's an odd couple—are helping Iran, and not out of love. They both despise Iraq, and Israel is making lots of money from sales to Iran. Khomeini is just too scary. He's making the Arabs very nervous because he's Persian and because his brand of Islam is far too threatening for even the conservative regimes of the region. As to how Iran manages...well, its back is against the wall. Having one's back against the wall prompts all sorts of tenacity and inventiveness."

Sarah contemplated this for a moment. "Now hold on," she said, "someone somewhere has to be supplying Iran. Back against the wall or not, Israel aside, surely they need many things. Where are they getting them?" She tapped her finger on the back of Bobo's hand resting on the table top. "I have a theory. I'll bet that some in the West, perhaps the very ones selling arms to Iraq, are surreptitiously also supplying Iran. Think about it, Bobo, who among your competitors would...ah, but you don't even admit you're in the business. When we first met, Gaspar refused likewise. But I'll bet some are, what do you think?"

"Yes, I think someone is selling to Iran, but I don't think it's Europeans. More likely the Chinese, North Koreans, the odd dealer here and there in South America. And of course the Israelis. I've heard that from reliable people, and if true then it can mean quite a lot. I mean, they both use American-made weapons. Dessert, anyone?"

To Gaspar's enormous relief, Sarah rose to help clear away the dinner plates.

"Anyway, Corrine," Deadeye said as she brought a large porcelain bowl filled with fruit salad to the table, "I don't think your theory can work. Such things are not easily accomplished. One would have to circumvent formidable laws and stringent controls in order to supply Iran...ah, shit!" She had lowered the serving spoon into the bowl with too much force and sent bits of fruit flying onto the table. "You can't just load stuff onto a train or ship and send it to Teheran. Someone is sure to notice among all the eyes trained on comings and goings in the Gulf."

Gaspar had risen to collect the spilt fruit. Now he went off in search of a bottle of dessert wine.

"Still, I'd wager that it's being done," Sarah said.

"Do you ride horseback?" Bobo asked Sarah.

171

"It's been a while. Still, I can probably manage," she replied.

It was early Saturday morning. Sarah had awakened and decided to let Gaspar sleep. She went down to the kitchen where she searched for and found some tea. She set the kettle on the huge old-fashioned stove, then sat and waited for it to boil, basking in the quiet. She poured the water, waited for the tea to steep, poured herself a large cup and took it outside into the brilliant morning light. She was sitting on a rough-hewn bench that encircled the trunk of a huge oak near the house when she heard horses.

Bobo came around the tree's far side. In one hand he casually held the reins of two beautiful horses. As he stopped to speak to Sarah, the horses stepped slowly sideways until they had once more put themselves behind him.

"Good morning my dear. Sleep well?" Bobo spoke languidly, the animation of the dinner table altogether missing. He wore a white, quite shabby sweater, dark green riding pants, and boots that were decidedly not the riding sort.

She squinted and looked up at him. This was a man, she thought, who had an innate appeal but who preferred not to be desired.

"Deadeye went for the papers," Bobo said. "Rather a distance to go around these parts, she'll be a while. Gaspar snoring? Want to ride?"

Once they'd mounted their horses, silence made peace with the muted sounds of the hoofs, then prevailed once again. When they reached the forest the horses walked in tandem on the narrow path, and picked up to a light trot when they came to the grass where Deadeye had bagged the pheasant. Every now and then Bobo glanced back at Sarah and smiled.

Beyond the point at which she and Deadeye had turned back, the ground began to slope down to a distant line of trees planted in the linear arrangement that bespoke a river's bank. On reaching the river they dismounted and Bobo led the way to the high bank, where they walked slowly along.

"Their names are Aysha and Assad. They were given to me by an Arab associate—a birthday gift. I get to ride all too little. In fact, I get to relax all too little."

"Why don't you take more time for yourself?"

"Duty calls."

"Is that how you think of your business? Duty?"

"Actually, it was duty that put me in business. I wanted to do something that would benefit France in some concrete fashion and Boulevard

172

grew out of that desire. You see that place there? Beautiful, isn't it?"

He pointed to a sandbar that sectioned the river, creating a small, slow-moving flow to one side and a wide and swift current to the other. In places the lesser and greater waters touched and mingled.

"This is where I brought Gaspar when he first came to Belle Marais thirty-two, thirty-three years ago. Poor guy, I made him swim right there. He was pretty scared, but swim he did, overcame his fright and went on. You have a good man there, Corrine."

"I think so too."

"Does he know who you really are?"

She answered easily because this conversation, or some version of it, had played in her mind ever since Chardeau had first told her of the Count de Bossier, ever since she'd known she fancied Gaspar. It was her mind's way to grasp the variables and protagonists of a story and tumble them around so that a number of courses and outcomes resulted, as well as contingencies for situations like the present one.

"He does indeed, Bobo. Please don't take this badly, but I'm not so certain that he knows who you really are. I certainly don't. Just to sate my curiosity, how did you find out?"

"Corrine Blaine answered her telephone in London not two hours ago when Deadeye called to check." Bobo sat at the edge of the break, where the ground fell steeply down to the water. Sarah dropped down beside him.

"My name is Sarah Tillinghast and I'm a reporter for a London newspaper called the <u>Sentinel</u>. I have a credible source who says that you are secretly shipping arms to Iran and have been for quite some time, even when you ran SEDCE. Yes, I know about that, too. My question—and Gaspar's too, but we ask for different reasons, I'll let him speak for himself—is why? Why do you do this, Bobo? Contravene official policy, break your oath, make your president a liar, deceive your best friend. Gaspar says that whatever your reason it wasn't money, that you're not in this to enrich yourself. Now that we've met, I tend to agree with him. So why? Is it what I guessed at last night? That you want to prolong the war because French firms are earning huge sums from Iraq?"

"How do you mean, 'a credible source?'" Bobo said. "Frankly I can't see how you can have such a source. No one but I knows my business."

"Just as I know mine. I'll make a deal with you, Bobo, it will save us lots of time if you accept. I'll present you with hard evidence, docu-

173

ments, that will force the conclusion that you have been and are conducting this covert trade with Iran; you'll give me your word as a patriot that after examining my evidence you'll tell me your side of the story. Is it a deal?"

Bobo gazed thoughtfully at the water, then nodded his head. "I'll go along, for Gaspar's sake. My God, I hope I haven't hurt him too much," he said.

Chapter Twenty-five

Over the years, Paz has encountered numerous versions of these particular young men: fit, handsome under their neat military haircuts, faces earnest as they listened to their commanding officer, eyes free of guile, filled with anticipation and eagerness for their marching orders, for action. In a couple of years most would have finished their service and returned to civilian life to attend university, take jobs. They would look back on this day with pride and amazement that they had actually done all those blood-curdling things. Those, that is, who had not died, or made the army their life's work, as had their commanding officer.

"This uncle here needs help," says their commander. "He has a delicate operation to accomplish, so naturally he came to us, because we are the finest. Except for Yenukka."

The young men grin and look to Yenukka, who remains impassive at the affectionate slight.

"I am here because you are the finest of the Sayyarot," Paz says.

The Sayyarot are Israel's elite, a few small units each attached to a regional command headquarters and to a branch of the service commanders who could call on their Sayyeret when special difficulties arose. Or, as one regional commander put it, when the trouble at hand was beyond the capability of the ordinary superior soldiers. Paz is speaking with Sayyeret Matkal, the unit attached to the Chief of Staff.

At Paz's words, the one called Yenukka turns to his neighbor and addresses him as if they were alone in the room. "This is going to be the ballbuster of all times," he advises, "something really special."

"Like what?" the friend demands, part cautious, part excited.

"Oh...maybe go to some date palm orchard in Syria and bring back dates for some big shot's party. Something important like that."

"Tomer, is it possible to know who this uncle is?" Yenukka's friend asks the commanding officer.

"Certainly," Tomer says, "He's the person we will now hear out so that we can do exactly as he asks."

"Thank you," Paz says. "It's like this. In a few days there will be a hostage release, a single individual. It will take place here." He points to a spot on the map. "This hostage is a man to whose family the State of Israel has long owed a debt of gratitude, so we mean to defray it. Problem is that the kidnapper holding our friend is a bad gentleman and I'm pretty sure he finds himself greatly tempted not to keep his bargain with me, so I need you with me just in case. I can't very well show up at the meeting place with the whole army, can't make a big fuss, can't afford to make this bad gentleman uneasy, because if we do we won't get our friend back. So you have to figure out how to be there and not be seen, how to give me fire power if and when I need it. That is the story. Thank you."

"Uncle, just out of curiosity, what did your friend's family do for the State?" one of the young men asks, his voice not without a hint of sarcasm.

This Israeli Army policy of informality, Paz muses, of encouraging soldiers to question assertions and assumptions, can be carried to an irritating extreme. Still, the doubting whippersnapper will be putting his ass on the line. I'd better say something.

"Our friend's father helped rescue lots of Jewish refugees. At a time when others did not give us the time of day he gave us ships with which to haul survivors to this land of milk and honey. To save a single soul is as if to save the entire world, our sages said. By that standard, our friend's father helped save a couple of galaxies. Here, have a look." He takes several photos from an envelope. "This one is the bad gentleman, this one is the bad gentleman's girlfriend. This one is the hostage, this one is his wife. She will be standing to my left as the exchange goes down."

Several pairs of hands reach out to grab the photos of Mari and Sarah.

Chapter Twenty-six

At Belle Marais, Sarah had returned to the house alone from the morning's ride. Bobo had stayed down by the river. She found Gaspar in the kitchen, drinking coffee from a huge mug adorned with yellow and blue bees.

"My old mug," he said, lifting it for her to see. "From when I used to stay here. Want some coffee? Want a good-morning kiss?"

When she told him of her conversation with Bobo, he put down his cup. "Is he all right?"

She stared at him, baffled by his sense of priorities. "He is. Are you?"

She asked him to get dressed, they had to drive to the village to telephone Chardeau. She didn't want to use Bobo's phone.

At the cafe they bought a telephone card and used it in a booth just outside the door.

Chardeau's voice quaked with consternation, but Sarah was adamant. "I can't come, it's impossible. You know the man I'm sending you—well, you know of him. You sent me to him, in Toulon. Now he is my trusted associate. Give him the blasted papers and that will be that. You're far too deep in this to make demands now, Chardeau."

Gaspar, listening, was taken aback by the ferocity of her resolve.

She scribbled down an address and emerged from the phone booth. Speed was of the essence, she said, the sooner Gaspar got back to Belle Marais with the papers, the better.

Gaspar drove off and was in Paris in under three hours, then consumed nearly another hour making his way from the Peripheric road encircling the city to the Fourteenth, to Chardeau's bucolic street. He drove along, reading house numbers until he found the number thirty-one painted on a wall. Three young men were spraying a nearby wall with "France To The French" and "Foreigners Out" messages, from which Gaspar deduced that Chardeau's neighborhood had recently become mixed and that some took exception to the new blend.

He parked the car and walked to a locked iron gate in the wall. He rang the bell and was buzzed in. The path from the gate to the front door was concrete imbedded with fragments of colored tiles. Plants lined either side of the path. They glistened with water drops and beneath them the dark brown earth was wet. Chardeau had made use of his day off to water his small garden.

Gaspar rang the doorbell. Chardeau opened the door a crack. He looked Gaspar over. Recognition leapt in his eyes, then astonishment. "You?!" he said, and pressed two fingertips to his forehead, as if to keep his amazement from spilling over.

"I come from Mrs. Tillinghast," Gaspar said. "We are working together in this."

As if to see better, Chardeau opened the door another inch. Through the enlarged opening his arm shot out holding a pistol pointed at Gaspar's chest. He opened the door wider and walked backwards into his house, beckoning Gaspar to follow. Once inside, he motioned for Gaspar to sit on the floor with his back against a wall. "What's going on, why are you here?" he hissed.

"I'm working with Mrs. Tillinghast. I wish I'd known you would be this upset. I'm with you in this, Chardeau, not with Bobo—M. de Bossier. Please, don't do anything rash."

"You have an accent," Chardeau noted. "Of course—you are a foreigner. What in the hell is going on here? Are you alone? Where are the others? You son of a bitch, he sent you, you came to kill me."

"Frankly, I didn't think I had an accent," Gaspar said.

Chardeau raised the pistol and cuffed Gaspar's cheek with it. "Do you know what this is all about?" he said.

"No, not yet. That's why I'm here. De Bossier lied to me too, you see."

"Your Mrs. Tillinghast is going to get me killed is what this is about. You tell your crazy Englishwoman, who doesn't have the least idea...she thinks de Bossier and you and the others are like cricket players, that you will politely accept her victory. Well they are not. She has put me in great danger. I hope she appreciates that, you tell her that."

"I will."

"Like hell you will, I'm going to shoot you, you bastard—you and your de Bossier, all traitors, bastards. You see this?" He whipped an envelope from the back pocket of his trousers and waved it a safe distance from Gaspar's face. "I'll be sending this to Radio Luxembourg, they'll read it over the air. That should cook your fancy asses. I should never have called that English cunt. Can you believe her? I send her to capture the thieves and she ends up falling for one of them. That's what happened, right? I can see it on your face. My God, that English fool! Sit! There on the couch."

Gaspar did as he was told. Chardeau shoved the envelope back into his pocket and picked up a cushion. With his free hand he clamped it around the pistol. With the crude silencer in place, he pointed the muzzle at Gaspar.

There was a splintering sound, like kindling being split for a fire. The front door shattered and the three young men who had been spraying racist messages burst into the house. One held a pistol to Chardeau's forehead, the other to Gaspar's. Both pistols were fixed with real silencers. The third figure stood beside the doorway. He looked back out to the yard, then again into the room. He nodded, and the one who had his pistol against Chardeau's forehead fired two rapid shots.

Chardeau flew backwards with all the conviction of a high-diver embarking on a back somersault. By the time his body came to rest on the couch the cushions were already soaked in his blood.

His killer attempted to retrieve the envelope, but Chardeau's back pocket was not easily reachable. The figure at the door sniggered at his friend's troubles. Finally, the killer managed to wrench the envelope away. He tucked it under his arm and all three turned to leave.

A moment later they had reached the outside gate and tucked their pistols away. The door guardian now had his hand on the gate, pushed down on the handle, and cracked the gate open, but immediately kicked it shut again in a movement that appeared to Gaspar frenzied, even desperate. Suddenly, he was crumpling backward, his arm reaching out to the wall in a struggle to remain upright. Bright red blood pumped in great spurts from his chest. It spilled onto his clothing and from there onto the gaudy mosaic path.

The two other gunmen's hands flew to their pistols. They hurried toward the gate, then stepped back, as if to gain space to prepare themselves. The gate was now fully open, and whoever they now perceived standing beyond it made them turn and run back toward the house. Halfway down the path, one man turned abruptly and stared at his fallen partner, his palms turned up as if in supplication.

From the other side of the gate, a blur wearing something blue with a black streak running through it rolled onto the concrete like a gymnast dismounting the parallel bars. The blur unwound and defined itself as a slight body wearing oversized mechanic's overalls. A black ski mask covered the face. The acrobatic mechanic held out a pistol; it popped twice, like caps coming off bottles of soda, and the two remaining graffiti artists sank onto Chardeau's doorstep.

One of them, though, apparently having anticipated the shot, emitted a Gallic "bah!" of disapproval and chagrin and made for the newcomer. He did this with remarkable flair, running the short distance between himself and the killer mechanic in truncated, irregular steps so as to offer the least constant target. All for naught. The mechanic dropped into a crouch, a precise plunge like a piston slipping into its shaft, and fired twice. The target, in a wild muddle of his evasive dance, took a sideways step that faltered in mid-motion, sending him headfirst onto the front yard. Then he too lay still.

Gaspar and the mechanic were now alone. Gaspar winced but did not stir. The figure in blue and black walked with small steps to the dead graffiti artist in the doorway and, eyes firmly trained on Gaspar, began tugging at the envelope. A brief struggle ensued between the live killer's greed for the envelope and the dead man's refusal to surrender it. The mechanic placed a foot on the dead man's chest and used the leverage to wrest the envelope away.

"Bobo said that I wasn't to harm you," Deadeye said. "I probably wouldn't have anyway, Gaspar, I like you. Maybe more than I like him."

They were on their way back to Belle Marais. Deadeye was still in her mechanic's costume, Chardeau's envelope tucked into one of its pockets.

"Bobo said that we couldn't afford to wait for you to return, that we had to get Chardeau's evidence before you could mail copies away—he couldn't be certain you didn't intend to send it somewhere. I don't know who the others were or what they were doing there. I'll ask Bobo, maybe he knows. He knows so many things he doesn't tell me. Same for you I guess, right, Gaspar?"

He nodded. They drove on in silence. The adrenalin that had flooded his system slowly retreated, leaving his limbs in something close to an anti-gravity mode. His mouth was dry and tasted foul. Flashes from a day filled with violent death appeared before him like fragments in a hellish kaleidoscope.

The car phone rang. For some reason the sound jolted Deadeye so much that her quick move to retrieve it from its cradle caused the car to slip into the next lane, much to the chagrin of a prior occupant. She held the receiver to her ear and listened, then glanced at Gaspar as if to see whether he was able to hear the caller's voice. He wasn't. What's more it did not in the least matter to him.

"I'll be there, asshole," she said, and threw the phone down onto the car's floor.

Chapter Twenty-seven

They sat on the large, rough-hewn bench that encircled the oak tree outside the kitchen door, Gaspar next to Sarah, Deadeye with Bobo. Each was turned slightly from the other, a function of the tree's girth and the straight angles of the bench.

Bobo heard Deadeye out as she recounted the events at Chardeau's house. When she'd finished, she handed him Chardeau's envelope as Sarah looked on silently. To Gaspar it felt as if with each word of Deadeye's dispassionate prose Sarah slipped a little more away from him.

Bobo expressed regrets to Deadeye for her ordeal. No, he had no idea who those men were.

At that, Deadeye's expression became grim. She sat bent at the waist, elbows propped on her knees, hands supporting her head at her cheek-bones. She stared ahead, chin and lips tight.

At that moment, Gaspar pitied her. In the end, she was just a simple soldier, a no-jokes order-taker who happened to be pretty and exception-ally skilled at her work. He sensed her turmoil, knew she was thinking that something about the episode at Chardeau's was terribly off, although she didn't yet know what. He remembered the phone call that had come on the way back from Paris. Sooner or later, he assumed, she would get to the truth, and he wouldn't want to be in Bobo's shoes when she did. Bobo had never extended himself toward her as he had to Gaspar. Her reservoir of goodwill for him was, therefore, probably not deep.

Sarah stirred. "We had a deal, Bobo," she said softly. She was scared. Chardeau's death, the risk to which Gaspar had been exposed, questions of what would have happened had she gone to pick up the papers instead of Gaspar, astonishment at how matter-of-factly Bobo and Deadeye dis-cussed the killings, swirled in her mind.

"So we had," he confirmed. "Go ahead and ask now, why don't you?"

"First, I want to know something," Gaspar said abruptly.

"Certainly, Gaspar," Bobo said.

"What were the explosions in Paris about? Not for the reasons you suggested at the time, but you knew why they happened, didn't you?"

"I did know. In fact, they happened indirectly because of you, Gaspar."

"Try to talk truth with me–and do it in a straightforward fashion for once, Bobo."

"On the whole I have told you the truth, Gaspar. That is, I haven't kept my true purposes from you. You remember the walk you took with your informative friend along the Seine, after you'd been to Pireus to check on the Twanee?"

"You knew about that?"

"Of course. When you returned I had you tailed, and also had a talk with your man after you did. So I knew what you had learned. Because of that walk I had to call off the shipments to Bushehr–that's a navy port in Iran presumed to be out of commission, but in fact, still operating. They took it badly there, they're desperate for goods. But I couldn't risk it any longer so I had the Twanee skip that particular delivery and keep to her overt course. This upset some of the people in Teheran. They viewed it as a breach of contract, so they sent some maniacs to plant bombs in Paris. The Twanee has since made deliveries to Bushehr and the zealots have been sated, but who knows for how long?

"What can I say about that poor woman at the Gallerie Lafayette, Gaspar? You must know that her fate was the very last thing on earth I wished for. The most I can say in my defense is that when you hear me out you may come to feel that her death was part of something that has made life for very many French women and men immeasurably better."

"What crap, Bobo, what convoluted crap! Because I set out to discover why my best friend has been bullshitting me, bombs go off in Paris? Because that woman died, life will be better for others? What in hell are you spinning here?"

"Actually, if you let Sarah ask her questions we'll get the answer to yours. I want to put all this behind us. I have the feeling, perhaps a premonition, that this is a good moment to square things between us, Gaspar."

"Nothing you can say will square things with me, Bobo, nothing."

"I hope you're wrong."

Sarah put a calming hand on Gaspar's knee. "Let me start with what brought me to you in the first place, Bobo. The Twanee. What was that about? Why were you shipping arms to Iran?"

"I was repaying a debt. And I was making sure that my business kept going, remained relevant."

"What business did you have back then?"

"Then, as now, my business was to keep France financially solvent. That was the rightful job description for SEDCE, until the Reds took over and subverted its mission. Money alone would keep her from falling apart, from becoming yet another property in the portfolio of international people's democracies, from becoming yet another dictatorship of the envious and the chronically under- productive. SEDCE was about keeping France in business, keeping her solvent."

"I am under the impression that spy craft was your domain; the economy is the Ministry of Finance's business."

"Bobo believes it is all his domain," Gaspar said. Bobo shook his head as if to protest the increasingly strident attitude from Gaspar.

Sarah stayed her course. "Your debt, Bobo, how did you incur it?" she asked.

"Let me take you back in time a bit," Bobo said. "It is important that you come to understand where France had been and where it was headed. Only then will you see, as I had seen, what needed to be done, no matter the cost."

"OK Bobo, then help me to see it your way," Sarah said.

"France was stumbling from one failure to the next, from one catastrophe to another. Oh, it may not have appeared that way, what with our City of Lights, panache, and all those other good things that have no substance, and lots of style. Supposedly, we ended up on the winning side in both world wars. But of course we lost them. No other way of putting it. Germany signed surrender papers, but she came away a winner, as her economy improved, then soared, within a few short years after the war's ending. And we? We were victorious and we came away with labor unions of the Left that owned and ran the country, shut it down any time they wished it, dictated terms that no economy could sustain. The wars had cost us our colonies, our sources of raw material, and of that most valuable of intangible assets: prestige. We were reduced to using tricks of state, shameful manipulations, like getting the Americans to uphold us in Southeast Asia, a ploy that finally failed at Dien Bien Phu. Then we went on to pretend that we could project military power when we teamed up with the Brits and the Israelis to try and take the Suez Canal away from the Egyptians in 1956, only to have the Americans send us to our room without supper for our bad behavior. But you see, these failures were precisely what some in France, and I am loath to call them Frenchmen, wished for, and welcomed. For with the crumbling of the French establishment, of the order and families that upheld then, these louts of the Left sought to introduce a new order, one that relied on a forced and unnatural equality. And requisite for attaining their new order was, first and foremost, disorder, discontent born of mass dissatisfaction of the populace, lead by the middle class. I realized then that there existed but a single antidote available to me with which to ward off this impending ultimate disaster for France: prosperity. And this brings me back to my debt to my man in Teheran. The weapons ferried on the Twanee bought him credibility, kept him going, and kept me going too. I was helping France onto that road to prosperity, you see?"

"Who was that Bobo, your man?" Gapsar asked.

"He had been a translator in the American embassy in Teheran. You never knew of him, Gaspar. There was no need. It was better that way, believe me."

Gaspar laughed bitterly.

"This man, his code name was Hafez–after a Persian poet of old–was in place under the Shah, spied for SAVAK, the shah's secret police."

"Spied on the Americans?" Sarah asked.

"Yes. When the shah fled Hafez was handed down to me, a parting gift from my old pal Assiri who had run the shah's counter-intelligence service. Poor Assiri did not know, of course, that it was I, we, who permitted Khomeini to depart Paris for Teheran when the Shah left."

"You permitted him, Bobo? I hope this does not upset you, but you sound a bit grandiose," Sarah observed.

"Yes my dear. I can see how you would think me grandiose. At this point in the game, however, grandiosity is the farthest thing from my mind. Indeed, I am feeling quite mortal, in a terminal sort of way. No. I am being precise: it was all in my hands." Bobo said. And Gaspar nodded his disapproving confirmation.

"Khomeini lived here, you see, in a suburb of Paris, after he was thrown out by the Iraqis and no one else would have him," Gaspar said.

"It was a favor to me, you see, that the Iraqis sent away the old cleric. Look, this is intricate, multi-layered, took me years to put together and all my wit and energy to manage. It would be unreasonable to expect that you can make sense of it from the bits and pieces we are tossing about here."

"So make sense of it for me, for us, Bobo. Please." Sarah appeared overwhelmed.

"Yes. Yes. I will," Bobo said.

"It went as follows." Bobo spoke in a measured, deliberate, pace.

"One day I learned from the shah's sister, she was a friend to me…"

"You mean you were screwing her?" Deadeye interrupted.

"I was her sometime lover, Deadeye. You are about to screw me for good. Do you see the difference?" Bobo asked.

"Never mind. Please, please go on Bobo," Sarah said exasperatedly.

"I learned that the shah was ill, something serious but she did not know then just what it was. In time I convinced her to have him come to Paris, to our headquarters on the Rue Mortier, for a medical examination. This unto itself was a coup. He could have gone to a big-name hospital in America–certainly his patrons in Washington would have expected and preferred it. But I explained to him that with us his privacy and secrecy were guaranteed, while in the U.S. his visit and illness would have been on the front pages in no time. Well, our doctors told me after they saw him that he had three years to live. As it turned out he lived five. So there I was, in possession of an enormously significant piece of information: the shah, lynchpin of America's Near East policy, keeper of Iran's vast petroleum wealth, the dominant military power in the Persian Gulf, was a short-timer. I wondered what to do with this. I took a long time to think it out–I did it alone, no one helped, no one else knew of my thoughts. It was chess, appropriate for a Persian master plan. I reasoned and calculated move after move, numerous, complicated, farsighted."

"No one ever said you were stupid, Bobo," Deadeye said.

"So how did it go, Bobo? What was your chess game?" Sarah asked.

Bobo smiled. "I will tell you Sarah my dear, but I will bet you a year's worth of Belle Marais' finest grapes that you will not get to publish it in your paper."

"Never mind. I will tend to that part of things. Just tell me, please."

"Across the Gulf from Iran there ruled a man whose megalomaniacal visions put the shah's to shame. This man, Iraq's Saddam Hussein, controlled a huge military, sat on enormous oil reserves, hated Iran, as well as a good many other nations. The most important fact about him was, however, that he was a big spender. Saddam spent billions of dollars annually on arms. At the time his largesse went mostly to the Soviets. I decided to take some of that business away from Moscow, to find a way to divert arms sales to French companies."

"Bobo, forgive me, I don't mean to doubt you, but you are one man. How could you possibly have hoped to single-handedly change Saddam's foreign policies?"

"He invented the Safari Club single-handed, Sarah. With it Bobo wrested influence and positioning away from powers far greater than France. And to remind you, in the time period Bobo is describing he was not yet running SEDCE," Gaspar said.

Bobo smiled, as if relieved to at long last hear his old friend's old voice.

"I had help, mind you. France went ahead and sold Iraq a nuclear reactor; that made for a good entree. Now, Saddam too was not yet officially at the top–he was vice president. In fact, however, he ran the place. Look, I don't wish to sound self- aggrandizing, but I stood out, you see. I spoke Arabic, I knew their ways. Gaining favor, getting noticed, is an art; making use of having been noticed is a science. Saddam took notice, liked to tease me in his own crude way, you know, jokes about frogs eating oversexed Frenchmen. I laughed uproariously at them all. The Iraqis were fighting their indigenous Kurds back then, and having a hell of a time of it, too. Iraq's Kurds did not go down in defeat lightly. Then it was time. Saddam moved up, became head man. I learned of the shah's illness. I had made my plan, and I began to execute it. I went to see Saddam one day and told him about the shah's illness. 'So what?' he said. Note, Mr. President, I said to him, that I just told you something no one else knows. There will be more where that came from, I said, and one day some of it will prove of much use to you. 'Why' he asked, 'are you doing this?' 'Because France needs rich friends,' I said—'and to make such friends we are willing to go to greater length than would others—and we have more to offer than is, at first, obviously apparent.' Then, in a light-hearted manner, as when two friends wager, I said, 'Mr. President, how would it be if I got the shah to actually ask you for a favor?' Saddam laughed heartily at this. The shah and he despised one another, so it seemed unlikely that the shah would render himself a supplicant. I pressed him: 'May I proceed then sir, with your permission?' He gestured magnanimously. 'Go ahead,' he said. So I got to move another piece forward on the chessboard; a powerful piece at that. You see, I was merely piggy-backing on what another grand manipulator–the American Kissinger–had arranged. From my friends Assiri, the shah's counterintelligence chief, and from the princess, the shah's sister, I learned that as part of a deal to cut the shah's support for Iraq's Kurds Saddam will be asked to throw out old Khomeini. I merely got Saddam to believe that it was I who had gotten the shah to make the request. There was no way Saddam could find out the true sequence of events. Saddam then expelled from Iraq this Iranian religious leader who had taken refuge there–one Ruhollah Khomeini.

"You are kidding," Sarah said.

"No. And there is more, much more," Bobo said.

Deadeye rose to her feet and took to pacing to and fro. "To remind you, Admiral de Bossier," she suddenly said, her voice taut, harsh, "Sarah Tillinghast is a foreign national, and you are divulging sensitive information."

"Your concerns are noted, Captain. Now sit down or leave," Bobo said. Deadeye stared at him for a brief moment, as hard and searing a stare as she had even seen, Sarah thought. Deadeye resumed her seat.

"Khomeini left Iran in the first place under pressure from the Savak secret police, went to a city named Najf, a holy place to the Shii Muslims, among whom Khomeini mattered a great deal.

"We contacted Khomeini's people, a certain aide de camp in particular, and extended their leader an invitation to come live in France. Ours was a credible invitation, we have done it in the past, given refuge to controversial personalities."

"Why do it?" Sarah asked.

"Little downside. They cannot do much while we have them under watch in France, and you never know when the wheel will turn and they will emerge on top in their homelands, in which case we have gained an influential friend."

"Smart."

"We have to be. So there it was, Saddam was my pal, Khomeini my guest, and the shah on his way to checking out. I was in business."

"What business was that, Bobo?" Sarah asked.

"The business of authoring history."

"There you go again being grandiose."

"But that is exactly what I did. I was not a mere participant, I was the creator, originator, of events."

"Events?"

"The shah's health failed, and as it did I made it more and more possible for Khomeini to take what steps he needed so as to take over Iran when the shah died, or left. As it was, he left. You see, don't you? I knew exactly what the shah's every move was, and I made Khomeini's every move possible, I made the next ruler of Iran possible. And all the while I kept my pal Saddam apprized. Not the American, or the Brits, or the Russians, but us— SEDCE, France."

"But wait a minute, Bobo. I can see how you interacted with Khomeini while he lived in Paris, but from what we now know of this man, surely he did not give you the time of day once he was back in Iran."

"You remember Khomeini's aide de camp, the chap we dealt with when making arrangements for the old man's move to Paris? Well, he gave me the time of day, and lots more, any time I demanded it of him."

"But why?"

"This guy was ruled by certain penchants of the flesh, desires that placed him on the very wrong side of strict Islam," Gaspar said.

"He liked boys. Blond-haired, blue-eyed boys." Bobo said. "We helped him enjoy what he liked, and we kept visual and audio records of what he did when he got what he liked. So he was very helpful to me. And there was more, I had other help."

"What?"

"Assiri, my friend the shah's intelligence guy, actually stayed on, and died a mean death at the hands of Khomeini's people, but not before he bequeathed Hafez to me, the operative whom he had long ago placed in the American embassy as a translator. Hafez got to keep his job after the shah left, and I ran him."

"You mean that Savak which was a creature of the Americans, their wholly owned subsidiary, spied on them? But why am I not surprised? And what did that do for you Bobo, having Hafez, I mean?" Sarah asked.

"Once Khomeini took over in Iran, a devil's dance erupted: wholesale arrests, liquidations of entire classes of people— anyone connected with the shah, anyone of wealth or power, all senior bureaucrats and military people. The revolution was busy dismantling a superbly well-equipped military, and that was very, very significant."

"To whom?"

"Why, to my friend and client Saddam, of course."

"Right. What next?"

"Next, I informed Khomeini, through our friend on his staff, that the American Embassy's safe held contingency plans to shelter the shah, who was dying but still shuttling about the planet in search of a shelter. He went to Egypt, Panama, then a hospital in the United States, at which point it was useful to get Khomeini and his people to believe that the Americans were plotting to restore the shah to his throne–something they had done before."

"You mean the attack on the American Embassy in Teheran, the hostages— you?"

"Indeed."

Deadeye smashed a clenched fist into her knee. She rose abruptly and left. Bobo smiled a wry smile. "She is back on the job, my sharpshooter girlfriend," he said.

"I told Saddam what was about to happen at the embassy, and I got Hafez out of Iran—didn't want him to fall into the hands of the revolutionaries and have them learn about his connection to me. He lives in Paris to this day, owns a spice shop."

"Why, Bobo? The American Embassy: what did the take over, the hostages, accomplish?"

"What do you think Deadeye is up to Bobo?" Gaspar asked, sounding concerned.

"I think it is off between Deadeye and me, don't you Gaspar? I think she is shopping for another boyfriend, one whose longevity prospects are better than mine."

"What is he talking about, Gaspar?" Sarah asked.

"No matter, Sarah. This will play itself out in accordance with SEDCE rules. According to SEDCE rules I am, even as we speak here, failing to comply with secrecy protocols. Deadeye is undoubtedly seeking a ruling on the matter. It is important to me now that we, you and I, Gaspar and I, get this done. You need to know."

"What is it that I need to know, Bobo?" Gaspar asked.

"I am getting to it. Let's return to the embassy in Teheran. You see, at that point in time the Americans had been opposed to Saddam. His ruthless conduct with his domestic opposition, his human rights violations, his ties to the Russians, his threatening ambitions in the Gulf, his bellicosity toward Israel, all these placed him on Washington's black list. But the embassy takeover changed all that. Suddenly, Saddam became a potential counterweight to Khomeini's Iran—America's new enemy. For us, for France, Washington's altered view of the situation made life easier. Before they came around, the Americans endlessly lectured, harassed, and generally annoyed us about our relationship with Saddam. They could not do anything outright to stop our ties to him, but they could, and did, let us know that they did not like certain things, and that the next time we needed rescuing they may think twice about it."

"OK. So now the Americans were pro Saddam. So what?"

"So that enabled me to upgrade Saddam's client status from a B minus to an A plus."

"Come again?"

"I will lay it out for you. It was 1980, a great year for France. Great. By late spring, early summer of 1980, relations had become tense between Iran and Iraq. Khomeini had long despised Saddam for the shabby treatment he'd received when he lived in Najf and he had taken to exhorting Iraq's sizable Shia minority to rise against him. For his part, Saddam cracked down hard on the Shia, had a major Iraqi Shia cleric and his sister murdered, made mass arrests. In short, Saddam was being himself. A beast. A fool. But increasingly, my beast, my fool."

"On this we agree; the man is a fool. To have wasted away the enormous wealth and the future of Iraq as he has done. Perhaps you ought to reconsider, Bobo, speaking as you are," Gaspar said.

"Gaspar!" Sarah sounded surprised, and hurt, at Gaspar's seeming appeal to Bobo to reconsider disclosing as much as he was.

"It needs to be told, Gaspar, and now," Bobo said.

"I don't think they will take it well on the Rue Mortier."

"That is right," Bobo said. "But so be it," he added.

"1980?" Sarah said. "We were in 1980–a great year for France."

"The Americans were beside themselves with the hostages in Teheran and all. I got involved in helping Kirney who ran the CIA then, to do an arms-for-hostages deal. Which, by the way, gave me a powerful lean on the newly elected American president because it was his crew that negotiated what I was later told was an illegal act–against their Constitution, you know."

"I am waiting for you to tell me that it was you who had brought about the Bible's flood and the demise of Atlantis," Sarah said.

"I had nothing to do with either because there was nothing for France in these. But when I maneuvered Saddam into attacking Iran there was plenty, great riches. I have seen tallies of eighty and ninety billion dollars, and I cannot argue with these figures," Bobo said.

"Will you say that again Bobo? You maneuvered, that was the word, Saddam Hussein into attacking Iran so that France would reap economic benefits? That is what you are saying?"

"Absolutely. To have not used my advantage to the maximum would have been unimaginable, Sarah."

Sarah was astonished and shook her head in disbelief.

"Bobo, in the name of merciful God, this is unimaginable! This war lasted ten years. A million, perhaps as many as a million and a half, humans died in it. Endless grief visited upon ordinary people on both sides. And you could not imagine another course of action?"

"Between 1980 and 1990 France thrived. Our public was happy, sated, clothed, our cultural institutions thrived as never before. Those who had set out to alter France, drag her into some leftist utopian horror, failed and were left out in the cold by a public that no longer wished to be rescued. This was what I had set out to accomplish; that is what I had accomplished."

Sarah reverted to a steady professional curiosity. "How exactly did you do it, get him to start a war? I mean, why would he have permitted a foreigner to push him into a war, which, as it turned out, he could not win?"

"Well, the man did much to make it easy for me. He and Khomeini started going at it without any assistance from me–just the age-old antipathy of the Persians and Arabs at work, only the players' names had

190

changed. And there was my information flow, Sarah. I was able to tell him how many Iranian fighter jets were out of commission on which airbase due to lack of spare parts. Iran's military was falling apart at the seams under Khomeini, and I was in the position to tell him which stitch frayed and when. Mind you, this fool considered himself a military mastermind, still does. For him the data I fed him begged for a single conclusion: my great foe is weakened greatly, the world is on my side, I can buy first-rate arms, Khomeini cannot. Let us go forth to victory. Once Saddam got going he kept going. After I gave up my job, after the Left won an election here, I had to keep our relationship with Saddam secure, our sales. They, the Left, actually considered pulling back from the Iraqi connection–this despite making public pronouncements to the contrary. So I had to keep it going on my own, supplying information to Iraq I mean. To do that *I* had to keep my Iranian contacts happy–that was how the Twanee came into play. 'I' because Gaspar knew nothing about it. Sorry, Gaspar. Anyway, I am certain the Twanee is about to be put out of business–that will undoubtedly be the Rue Mortier's new management's first move."

"And their second?" Sarah asked.

Bobo then fell silent. Gaspar stole a furtive, deeply anxious, look in the direction of the house.

Chapter Twenty-eight

Waiting time. Waiting for the arrangements that Paz and Harouni had made to kick in, to be put to the test, waiting for the calendar days to pass.

Sarah is staying in a hotel in Tibereas on the Sea of Galilee, east of Paz's village. She has moved there to relieve Paz and Shula from the burden of her edgy anticipation.

She visits ruins on the outskirts of the small, lakeside town, strolls its hodgepodge of a center: Third-rate clothing shops bearing absurdly grand names—Riviera, Monte Carlo, Broadway—, stands offering falafel, grilled lamb, fresh-squeezed carrot and citrus juices, cotton candy. She takes a taxi to the thermal baths nearby, then a bus ride onto the Golan Heights, the high plateau that looks down onto the lake. It is a pretty, windswept place that gives little hint of the bloody battles men have fought over it. She returns to her hotel to sit at its pool and re-read Waugh's churlish farces and two-day-old International Herald Tribunes.

A man named Ron Lapid, also staying at the hotel, starts out flirting with her, but soon calms down and becomes her friend. He turns out to be a producer for Israel's television evening news program. He is in Tibereas—built by Herod, named for the Roman emperor, he tells her—to research a story. And what, he asks, is she doing in this town that any self-respecting Israeli avoids?

Resting, she says, taking the hot baths, escaping a particularly stressful stretch of life in London. She leaves unsaid the cause of her stress. Her travel agent has suggested this as a place where no one she knew could possibly run into her.

Ron invites her to accompany him to a place just outside Tibereas, the ruin of a village as old as time now being reclaimed for the present by a group of young Israelis who have forsaken modernity and secularism in favor of mystical pursuits. Ron intends to do a news segment on them. She accepts his invitation, but only after checking with Paz, who tells her to go ahead, that she needs to take her mind off the upcoming day.

They climb a narrow trail that wraps around a mountaintop. They have already been to the ancient village's center and were directed to the ruined synagogue where they would find the community's leader. It's a country of many ruins, Sarah says to Ron, wrecks of the past are everywhere. For us, he says, they are more like memories in the process of going from black and white to living color.

The synagogue is constructed of large, rough-hewn, dark gray stones, perhaps of volcanic origin. Its walls are thick and liberally gashed and scarred, gouged by time and circumstance. Inside it is clean and quiet. A glistening concrete floor diffuses coolness. At the far end of the room a solitary man stands in front of a large pine closet draped in crimson cloth embossed with gold Hebrew lettering. His back is to them, his body in constant motion. It snaps back and forth, twists in small half-turns, bows and springs upright; the man is in fervent prayer. Suddenly, he roars and Sarah is startled and shaken, both by the suddenness of his cry and by its great intensity. His roar is words that cling to a long-winded sigh, a scream of a prayer. For all its noise and outlandishness, his act of worship rings true to her. She senses his demand to be heard, and his confidence that indeed the One is there to hear him.

When he is done, he collects himself for a moment, then approaches them. Sarah is astounded by his demeanor. He is aglow and appears at once elated and exhausted, an athlete who has just competed and done well in a spiritual contest. The rabbi, Abraham, greets them and she reads in his eyes a wish to say more about what they have just witnessed, and regret that a common vocabulary is not available to them.

Ron chats with the rabbi as they set terms for the filming of the segment he has in mind. A lengthy discussion ensues, marked by smiles and pauses and a certain tension. More issues are settled, and they leave Abraham at his synagogue ruin.

They drive on to Safed, some twenty minutes away, where Ron needs to do more location scouting. Safed is the seat of mystics and liturgical scholars, the burial site of holy men, and the locus of pursuit of knowledge of the deity. This particular pursuit is known as the Kabbalah, the Receiving. Ron tells her that Abraham was previously a science teacher in a Tel Aviv high school. Now he is a devotee of an earlier Abraham, Abulafia, who lived in Spain and elsewhere in the thirteenth century, who may have visited Safed, and whose brand of Kabbalah is greatly admired by newcomers to Jewish mysticism.

Rabbi Abraham has refused to speak to him about the pursuit itself, Ron tells Sarah. Instead, he advised Ron to inform himself as much as possible from scholarly sources. The Kabbalists, Ron explains, generally refuse to speak to the substance of their pursuit. They live by the ancient admonition that it is better that a man not have been born than that he take a dilettantish interest in the Kabbalah. Its pursuit might pose risks to his sanity, for should he truly come to know he will become his knowledge and can never again revert to his former self, though he might prove to be

193

unsuitable for his new self.

Ron notes the evident bewilderment on Sarah's face. Don't be overly impressed, he cautions her, in his time he has done numerous segments
on unusual people. The land abounds with them.

Like who?

Like the former firebrand leader of a radical political movement dedicated to tearing down this unjust state who is now a hack with one of the
mainstream parties. Like the woman who regularly foretold the future,
accumulating a large and devout following, and who is currently market-
ing creams that arrest aging and promote male potency.

How, Sarah wonders, would Ron have summarized Bobo?

On the drive back to Tibereas, Ron switches on the car's radio just as
the news is coming on. The news reader is a woman, her voice rich and
even. Ron's eyes flicker at what is being said and Sarah asks him what it
is about. Another operation has taken place, he says.

An operation?

A military operation, a raid into Beirut by Israeli commandos. A couple of Palestinian bigwigs were killed. The commandos have returned
safely to base.

As she listens, her heart begins to race. She stares at the lake that is
locally called a sea, fear for Gaspar making her rigid. At the hotel, as she
is about to bolt from the car, Ron observes that her efforts to relax are failing, that Tibereas is not doing her any good.

She races to her room to telephone Paz.

"I'm not God around here," Paz says defensively. "I'm a retired civil
servant. You think the studs in the Defense Ministry call to consult me
before sending their warriors out on a mission? Those two Palestinians
they killed today and the one they brought back with them—"

"I was told that two had been killed, nothing about one brought
back."

"Who told you?"

Sarah describes her drive with Ron Lapid.

"The military censor doesn't clear everything to be read on the news;
some items are blocked."

But what had this action been about? Sarah demands. Was it in any
way connected to Gaspar? Would it impact his situation?

"Nothing to do with Gaspar," Paz says. "About the rest, at this point
I just don't know. We have to hope it doesn't cause problems for him.
Probably these particular Palestinians have been on a hit list a long time
and maybe they hadn't been together under one roof until today—at least

194

not a roof that presented a feasible target. The opportunity was too good to let slip, so we hit. Did the planners care that one Gaspar Bruyn, a Belgian who chose his travel arrangements badly, is being held in Lebanon and that their operation might affect him? No, they did not. They cared only that the Palestinians they removed from the scene today have been trouble, have earned their punishment, and that our people got back in one piece. Did they know that this Bruyn is held captive by a Maronite lout whose girlfriend is half Palestinian and who consequently may become angry with Gaspar for having friends in Israel? I doubt it."

He is raising his voice now to make himself heard past her objections. "Look, Sarah, we're not talking about lives guaranteed by American Express here. We all take our chances, as Gaspar did when he went to work with de Bossier, as you did when you took up with Gaspar, me when I was running around Europe looking for people to help us. I suggest you go back to accepting that. In a few days we'll know one way or the other. Until then I'm sorry for your rough time, but I can't do a thing about it," he says, hanging up abruptly.

Gaspar is awakened by distant gunfire. At first he cannot identify the sound, nor its source. It is rather like the sound of wind-whipped rain pelting his tin roof. He stares at one of the perforations in the shed's wall. It is lightless, nighttime. He hears outside the shed the voices of his guards speaking excitedly. He deduces that they are talking about the distant sounds, that it is gunfire, lots of it. Somewhere in the vicinity a battle is underway.

With daylight Harouni arrives at the shed bearing Gaspar's breakfast. Ever since the day Mari told him that Harouni had gone to talk to the Jews in their security zone, his breakfast has expanded from tea to a pita, black olives, and a tomato.

"You heard the noise in the night?" Harouni says. "The Jews, they attacked some Palestinians in Beirut. Mari is making me crazy about it." He places the food at Gaspar's feet and offers him a cigarette, which Gaspar refuses. "All night after the shootings she says to me, 'Give up this dog Bruyn to the Hezbollah'—the fanatics, you know. They are the ones who now represent the Palestinians' bad feelings since the Palestinian fighters were thrown out by Shlomo." Harouni shakes his head in a sort of grudging admiration. "Mari is like a crazy person because now she knows that the Israelis also took away one Palestinian with them. They still live here, you know, Palestinians, not all went away. Some went and then came back from Tunis or Yemen or wherever. But she is making me crazy, she wants me to give you up to the Hezbollah, can you imagine? You know about them? Oh my God, they are crazy, these Hezbollah, truly. They love only their hatred, they hate all non-believers, they want the whole world for their own. When she is like this my Mari forgets about her father who was the Khatib, with our militia. She remembers only her mother who is from Lod—used to be Lod in Palestine, now it is Israel. On days like today she hates for her mother and for all the others who were thrown out. She wants me to give you to the Hezbollah so they can take care of you, maybe make business for you with the Israelis, get their people back. She says to me, 'I hate your money, Harouni, I hate you, I hate the Jews, their friends, the world.'"

Gaspar wonders whether Harouni expects him to sympathize, or merely to offer counter-arguments to Mari's tirade. Or to graciously suggest that for the sake of their domestic peace he will give himself up to Hezbollah.

Mari herself comes to the shed in the late afternoon. She is wearing a pale blue blouse, dark blue skirt, and black loafers. Maybe a school uniform, Gaspar thinks.

"One of the two men killed by your Jew friends last night was my mother's cousin, blood of my blood." She hisses her rage at him. "Do you think because I am with Harouni that I am not with my mother, with my people? I will not permit you to go free from here, Bruyn, if I have to kill you myself. You European asshole, you bloodsucker!"

One of the guards sticks his head into the shed. Gaspar, to his relief, realizes that they who are enforcing his imprisonment have become his guardians. It is the first overt indication that freeing him is being discussed. He is at once elated and infuriated: happy for the news, furious with Mari for interjecting her tribal peeves into the matter of his freedom, furious with the Israelis and the Arabs for being quarrelsome and bloodthirsty.

"I am a prisoner here," he says. "I have no idea what goes on out there—I've told you it's only that my wife has family friends in Israel. Not every Israeli's life is consumed with shooting Palestinians. Look, I'm sorry about your mother's cousin but I had nothing to do with it and neither had my wife. I think you know that. Keep your eyes on the prize, Mari. From what you've just told me it's clear that Harouni is on the verge of collecting a worthwhile sum for me. Isn't that the point here?"

She is no longer Mari to him. She has become a Deadeye-like creature, alien to what the people closest to her presumed her to be, nothing like the person Bobo had taken for granted—Bobo who had been good at manipulating minds but lousy at loving. In Gaspar's mind springs up a sweaty and edgy dread of Mari. Dread that she will prove his undoing, that her processes are unlike those of the other players. That her desire to see him dead will prevail.

Mari's eyes rake him, scour the interior of the shed. She is fury itself. Suddenly she kicks at his pile of letters and at the attaché case she and Harouni had presented to him a few days before. The attaché case topples and falls to the floor. She stomps out, and again the guards look in on him.

"Grow up, girl! They paid someone off, that was how!" Harouni shouts back at Mari. "One of your beloved cousins pocketed a bakshis from the Jews to sell out another. That is how they got those men. There's no other way. The Jews are not magic."

She is tired of losing to them, Mari whines. For a change she wants to be the one who takes, for a change she wants to do something unto them. Let them walk around with their hearts in the dirt, hopeless, knowing that no one cares about them, that they have become the world's street people, invisible. She wants Harouni to fix it so that they will see her, Mari, so they will gaze upon her with astonishment and terror.

"This I will do for you, my little lost kitten," Harouni says with a sudden tenderness. "Wait and see."

He grasps a fistful of her uniform skirt in his hand and lifts it well above her waist. He stares and grins, she playfully cuffs his face, says that she's not in the mood, says what a beast he is that this is all he can think about even at a time like this. But she takes care to remain playful. She engages him in a sham struggle for the bit of skirt he is holding, tries to pry it out of his crunching fist. But in the end she lets him win.

197

Chapter Twenty-nine

Deadeye met the two men aboard a bus parked in the maintenance area of the depot in Angres, a thirty-minute drive from Belle Marais. She'd spotted their cohorts as she was negotiating the feeder road that led to the maintenance area and she'd smiled a rare smile, wry and unforgiving. They were fools, she thought. In her day such rank stupidity would have been unforgivable.

Firstly, they were dressed in clothing meant to make them innocuous-looking, but which achieved the opposite result: one was a dandy straight out of Guys and Dolls, another a stained laborer whom Hugo would have adored, a third, an office-worker whose wash-and-wears came off the pages of a magazine ad. A fourth was a bus driver in a uniform that was making its debut that day, complete with white socks and black shoes, the fifth was his dispatcher, ever so busy though few busses were coming and going. In fact, they all fussed busily with blatantly ordinary activities—reading newspapers, making conversation, waving to fellow drivers, searching earnestly through posted schedules. And all of them, without exception, wore the same aviator sunglasses. And they call themselves soldiers, she thought. Crapheads is what they are. Action Branch? This is Dildo Branch!

She didn't keep this observation to herself. As soon as she entered the parked bus where the two waited for her she said, "You two from Dildo Branch or what? Judging by the guys you have posted out there the DGSE's head of Action Branch has a brother-in-law in the sunglasses business. I am Deadeye. Which one of you two assholes telephoned me in my car?"

"You are in deep shit, Miss Ironpants," one said. "You're up on Firm charges for multiple murders and that's the least of your problems. You are a traitor, a participant in a conspiracy to defy the nation's civilian leadership. You have been trucking with a declared foe of allies of the fatherland. Want to hear more?" He forced a smile onto his face.

The other craned his neck to search out their men and saw that indeed each wore identical shades. He grimaced.

"Fuck you and your charges," Deadeye said. "What do you want?"

"How long has Chardeau been working for Iran? Who else is in on it, besides the Count, Bruyn, and you?"

"Working for Iran? You guys better wake up. Chardeau wasn't working for Iran, none of us was. I think I'll leave now. Hanging out with amateurs gives me a stomachache."

"You murdered three of our finest," he hissed. "Men who were pa of the service, the same service you swore loyalty to. One was from a vi. lage not far from yours. Why did you do it?"

"I did it because you and your bosses are a bunch of stupid pinkos. Because you have put the service I loved to work for the enemies of France. Your bosses—or perhaps you are the bosses now?—were stupid enough to permit de Bossier to manipulate you into liquidating Chardeau. So why shouldn't I be with him? He has more brains in his toe than all of you together have in your heads. How is it that the man who was fired as Director five years ago can still order hits, and you can't put four guys on the street without me being able to spot them in a minute?"

"We are looking into it, Genvieve," said the one who had up to then kept silent. He was very different from the first, he spoke softly and gazed at her with tenderness, past her bluster and into her lonely misery. His eyes, behind wire-rimmed glasses that softened his image, displayed an array of life's lessons, as well as the message that he was not thrilled to have learned them. Now that they had been hoisted upon him, however, he would, with regrets perhaps, use them to his immediate purpose. "We'll find out how de Bossier managed, you can count on that—how it was that an outsider foxed the Firm into believing it was either do in Chardeau then and there or go down the toilet," he said.

"He's a hundred times smarter than you, that's how. And there are plenty of people left over in the Firm who feel about things as he does, so they help him."

"What does he feel about things? What do they all feel, Genvieve?"

She flagged. Perhaps his use of the word 'feel' threw her. Feelings as a factor in professional behavior and responsibilities did not often make it into conversations between herself and other Action Branch people. When she spoke again it was as if she had called on a reservoir of bluster, and she sounded slightly childish.

"That there are too many pinkos around. That France is being sold out to the unwashed guys of the Left. That's what."

"What do you really know of the Left, Genvieve? I mean, really know. I am a Socialist, I don't smell, do I? My grandfather was a Socialist too, a good guy, and you know what? Back then when the Right was getting fucked up the ass by the Nazis and liking it, my grandfather and a few other pinkos like him fought for the Fatherland, gave their lives for it. And all the while nice, pretty-smelling Right wingers were turning them in, ping people off to the camps for their Nazi masters. So you're wrong, ~nvieve. We're not selling the country to anyone, we have a different ~ke on things, that's all. This is tolerated in democracies, you know. Only ~ sounds like de Bossier has you convinced that it isn't, am I right?"

"Don't bother with her," the first said. "Let's take her in and get it over with. She's a murderous, disloyal bitch."

The second paid him no heed. "De Bossier tricked us into sending men to shoot Chardeau. He set us up. You too, right? He's been tricking you into doing his bidding, Genvieve. You know this now, I gather?" His voice took on the sympathetic tone of a tender father confessor taking a sinner to his worst sin to get him past it. "He tricked you into shooting fellow soldiers, didn't he? I know of you, Genvieve, I know your record. You wouldn't have shot those men in a thousand years had he not convinced you that they were enemies of France."

Again the first man interrupted. "What about this other asshole, the Belgian, Bruyn?"

"I think we ought to allow the Colonel to answer my question, don't you?" the second man said.

"Bruyn doesn't know anything. De Bossier was having him on. They're friends. De Bossier took advantage of him, too," the one in the wire-rimmed glasses offered. He gazed at her, took a deep breath, and spoke once more, still patient, still out to convert a sinner who had been conned into sinning.

"The point is, Colonel Greaux, that you and I and others like us remain loyal to the service. SEDCE, DGSE, what does it matter, it's the service and we've accepted that ours is to carry out orders and hope for the best, hope that our superiors don't muck things up too badly. You could even say that we love the service. Now your friend de Bossier, he's not like us. I don't believe he loves anything or anyone except himself, everything else is secondary. Worse, it's for his personal use, you know what I mean, Genvieve? So he concocted some fable for you, I gather, a bill of goods about the Left ruining the Firm, destroying the fatherland. I don't yet understand Bruyn's part in this, but that's another matter. The upshot is that de Bossier used you to his end, Genvieve, to enrich himself. We traced the documents Chardeau filched. That was how de Bossier panicked us into doing the liquidation. He somehow found out that we had become aware of Chardeau accessing the files and led us to believe that Chardeau was about to pass the information to an unfriendly party, that a world-class scandal would ensue. Well, you know how it is, we have to protect Matignon, Élysée, just like you guys had to do in your day.

De Bossier turned the good soldier that you are into a war profiteer, Genvieve, no more, no less."

By then she had fully reverted to being Deadeye, and she gave him short shrift.

"Much more than that, you fool," she said, and shook her head in disdain. "Much, much more. Better we go to the Mortier barracks together, my naive friend. And better grab hold of your testicles; they're about to be shaken."

Sarah was returning from a walk and had nearly reached the house when she saw Deadeye's old Rover approaching. It was Tuesday. The weekend at Belle Marais had elongated into an ongoing encounter session.

She watched Deadeye park her car, puzzled by the elaborate job she made of it, not nosing it into a spot among the other cars but maneuvering so that it faced the road leading away from Belle Marais. She watched as Deadeye walked to the house, waited a few moments, then went in herself.

Gaspar was asleep in their room. Since Bobo's proud confession, sleep had become his best escape. She decided to let him be and walked in the direction of Bobo's and Deadeye's room on the opposite side of the house.

She walked quietly but firmly past their door. If either of them should hear her footsteps in the carpeted hallway they would be the footsteps of someone walking past, not skulking about. Gently, she opened the door to the room next to theirs, removed her shoes, and made for the wall separating the two rooms.

She heard Deadeye's voice, and even before she could make out the words she derived from their tone an intense sense of recognition. Deadeye was making a terminal complaint, a final recounting of dissatisfactions—unmistakable to Sarah because she herself had made a similar complaint to her husband when she'd demanded a divorce, when she'd run out of willingness to settle. From beyond the wall came Deadeye's words and Bobo's silence. Sarah's husband, too, had uncharacteristically heard her out without interruption, as if he had sensed the gravity of the moment.

"I don't mind that you used me," Deadeye said, "I am a soldier, soldiers serve. In a way, serving is putting oneself up to be used. I only mind that you spun small lies for my benefit and kept from me your big lie. Who knows, Bobo, if you'd told me in the first place that you saw fit to start a war in a far-off place for France's good I might have gone along with you. Now we'll never know. Your small lies make me feel bad, Bobo. Killing fellow soldiers makes me feel very bad indeed, Chardeau's death makes me feel bad. I've been disloyal long enough—too long. And the shame of it all is that you don't even love me. Well, so much for my foolishness, Bobo, on to yours. A sentence of death had been passed on you, Bobo, at Mortier barracks. You're familiar with the procedure: you've been convicted of high treason and you're to be executed."

Sarah thought they must have heard her gasp, but apparently they did not.

"Are you the one assigned the task, then?" Bobo said. Deadeye must have nodded her confirmation because he continued, "Well, that was a bit over the top, don't you think? Just for the record, I didn't string you along, not in the personal sense. Personally, I gave you about as much as I'm capable of. I came away from this house not well-disposed to love others, you know. Besides, in one's life one can be sincere about only so many things. I spent my sincerity on France."

"You're a horse's ass, Bobo," Deadeye said. "I also didn't have it easy when I was a child. I grew up in a place where men thought women were merely cunts to hunt down. You had it rough? I lost my virginity because some lout from down the road outraced me one day. But I grew up. I worked at getting over it, and I did. I'm not saying I became perfect, I wouldn't have put up with you for as long as I have if I'd been smarter about these things. But I did teach myself to love and unfortunately for me I loved you. Perhaps I'll do better the next time. Anyway, I'm happy I was given the job. Do you want to write a note?"

"I did not string you along, Genvieve. There are things one can't help but do alone, solitary undertakings that must remain secret. I regret that you've taken this so personally, Genvieve, but there is such a thing as a need-to-know basis. You're certainly familiar with the concept. No, I don't want to leave a note, only to die at my river. And I want to speak with Gaspar."

Sarah scampered back to their room where she woke Gaspar and breathlessly whispered to him all that she'd heard. He leapt up, pulled on his trousers, and was about to leave the room when the door opened and two young men, lean and somber looking, entered. Deadeye and Bobo were behind them. Two more like the first leaned on the banister and peered with some curiosity in Gaspar's direction.

"You will be angry with me for a long time to come," Bobo said. "Still, you'll have time available. These fine folks," he glanced at

Deadeye and grinned, "my tender Genvieve and her true fami
mean to permanently deny me any more of it."

He spoke to Gaspar alone, the others becoming witnesses to his
administered eulogy.

"There are only so many things a person can do well in life, Gaspa
he said. "When I was a boy I read that Bismark's mentor, von Moltk
observed that the most fortunate people are able to see but a single choice
His point being, of course, that most are plagued throughout life with a
myriad of options and choices which, in the end, serve only to muddle
their minds. That's why most people never make much of themselves.
They are too mired in choices and options to devote themselves to a single pursuit. Mind you, Gaspar, at times I envy such people—people who
struggle with ordinary things, who love and fear along with their wives
and husbands, who love and are loved by their children. Every so often a
cloud of self-pity envelopes me for having forfeited an ordinary life. Such
sentiment is unavoidable, eh? However, I turned out to be one of von
Moltke's fortunates. For as long as I can recall I've been able to see only
a single choice: France. Surely, Gaspar, you will find it in you before long
to forgive me my shortcoming. How could I possibly have told you what
I'd done? You are not one of von Moltke's chosen. You would have seen
every side of the issue and then some. You would have thrown up arguments about law and legitimate elected authority at every turn. And
because you mean the world to me I would have had to answer and we
would have gotten all muddled up, Gaspar, become saddled with too
many choices. Think of the tortures of self-doubt I saved you from. You
would have wrecked your home life sooner and for different reasons.

"But take Sarah here, a charming and enterprising person for whom I
harbor nothing but respect. She caught up with you in Toulon, tossed
some disconcerting words at you, peppered you with Chardeau's accusations, and you soon came to see things in an entirely different light. On
my word of honor, Gaspar, I don't hold that against you, and I can see
how you would have come away with the feeling that I'd betrayed you.
The fact is, however, that I kept things from you only because I was true
to my single choice. I have had no friends but you, Gaspar, never confided in anyone else as much as I did in you, never felt as good about anyone else. But these feelings had nothing to do with the task I'd assigned
myself, and if I'd acted otherwise towards you my plan would not have
worked. But it did work. The bullet good old Genvieve intends to launch
at me will be, in a manner of speaking, financed by my success. The
salaries of these two wholesome young men whom Action Branch has

203

d to back up Genvieve during my execution are being defrayed ecause I loved France to the exclusion of all else. Because the fact without my little war France would by now be less than a has-been. ould have become the plaything of sophistic social theorists whose diwork would ruin our beloved country, would make sewage out of e finest civilization this world has known. I say bully for me, Gaspar. I ay France needs more like me and fewer like them."

"You can't do this, Genvieve," Gaspar said to Deadeye, his voice strained by the effort to control the panic welling up in him. "This is outrageous. Bobo hasn't had the opportunity to defend himself. He's half mad anyway, just listen to him. Surely he's as entitled to a defense as the next man. And what will you do after you shoot him? Shoot me, then Sarah, then who else? What happens when all this becomes known, as it inevitably will?"

Deadeye ignored him. "Are you quite done?" she said to Bobo.

There was a knock at the door, followed immediately by the sound of the lock being turned from the outside. One of the two young men who had earlier accompanied Deadeye to the river, and who had helped to haul back the stretcher bearing Bobo's body to a waiting van, entered the room.

After Bobo's body had been taken away, a sadness as dark and oppressive as an arctic winter settled on Gaspar. He lay on the bed in their room, where he and Sarah had been kept with the door locked and a guard posted outside. Sarah had attempted to comfort him. Bobo was another casualty of the war in the Gulf, she told him. In the high-stakes game Bobo had invented it was inevitable that the cost of losing a round would be extremely high. He needed to consider, she said, that Bobo may have been right, that within context Bobo, and therefore Gaspar, had done a great deal for France.

Gaspar, however, was not receptive to rational consolations.

When it was done, when the Firm's sentence had been carried out and Chardeau's "scandal for our times" eradicated along with Bobo, Sarah and Gaspar were escorted downstairs to the living room. There a gathering of polished and polite people waited to explain what would happen next and to inform Sarah that virtually all evidence that could possibly have been used to support an article about Bobo and the war in the Gulf was no longer available.

Perhaps the most disconcerting moment for Sarah came after they'd been away from Belle Marais and back in London for three weeks or so.

It happened during a conversation with Robin Colechester about her still-born article.

"Which one?" Colechester asked airily. "Not the one instigated by your disgruntled Frenchman?"

She thought, "Which one," Robin? How many have I been on in recent times? You, who never fail to spot a discrepancy between the color of someone's necktie as described during a story's progress briefing and its color in the final version, you say to me with such casual forgetfulness, "Which one?" My God, they've been here, haven't they? They've talked to you. Someone has laid down the law for you, too. Some British cousin of the polite chap from the Quay d'Orsay has been to see you or the Sentinel's owners to argue the case for public safety, to make certain that I will be shut down.

She searched Colechester's eyes, looking for Deadeyes's imprimatur, looking for embarrassment for having accepted the theory of curtailed truth and altered fact for the sake of the greater good.

"Too bad, that," he offered. "Sounded promising for a while. What went wrong?"

"The man proved to be a tall-tale artist," she said. "Spun one big fib after another and in the end was unable to get anyone to swear to his allegations. Wasted my time." She left his office with her heart pounding and the taste of something that has been spoilt for a very long time in her mouth.

To quell her racing mind and its loud and angry unspoken words that went clawing at each other she had but a single thought that she offered up to herself in the way of succor: Gaspar. She would live on with the awful taste and the heart that will probably never quite recover for the sake of Gaspar, to keep him safe and away from Bobo's fate.

For a long time afterwards Colechester avoided her. Not physically, not conversationally, on those levels they encountered one another at the office almost daily. Rather, he denied her full access to his regret, masking for her benefit his sorrow at having succumbed to the persuasive logic of coercion.

Three years later she and Gaspar were married and talking about a last-chance baby. They lived quietly in a large home in Holland Park, a few doors down from the one she'd lived in when they first met. Gaspar did small boat-design jobs and was pondering the wisdom of bidding on a shipyard that was up for sale in Cardiff. Then Saddam invaded Kuwait, was thrown back, and Colechester attempted to make amends.

"Can I get you to pay them a visit down there, ducky?" he said jaun-

205

tily over the phone. "You know, do a little digging, come up with bits that CNN missed. And what about taking along your worthy husband? Didn't you tell me once that he knew the area rather well? Did business in the Gulf, as I recall."

Correct, Robin, she thought, your memory is unerring. So how did it fail you that one time when I dropped Chardeau's tale?

"Do you think he'd like to do it? Sort of a technical advisor is what I have in mind," Colechester offered, then asked her to look in on the French angle in the Gulf. "They attempted a separate deal with Saddam, you know, just after he'd invaded and taken those hostages."

When Iraq's Republican Guard had overrun Kuwait, foreign citizens of several nations had been trapped there, and even as efforts had been underway to gain their release it became known in certain circles that France had attempted through PLO intermediaries to strike a separate bargain with Saddam for the release of its own nationals. The French initiative had folded under pressure from the anti-Saddam coalition and the matter trivialized, unity being more important than propriety.

"Perhaps we can splash a bit of color about France and the Iraqis. Must have been difficult for them to let go of Saddam, their golden goose. Wasn't your Gaspar once a partner in a French concern that had rather good ties to Saddam?" Colechester said.

Chapter Thirty

"The <u>Twanee</u> never existed, you see; the precautions Mr. Bruyn insti tuted when he first purchased the <u>Hydra</u> have been carried to their logical conclusion." The speaker's eyes flickered to one in his entourage from whom he sought acknowledgment of his bon mot. He received it, Sarah noted, in the form of an ever-so-slight stretching of the other's lips. "Forjieh, his navigator, Chardeau, de Bossier—all gone. Your story never was, Mrs. Tillinghast."

"You're making a mistake," Deadeye said. "They should also be liquidated."

"That is not for you to decide, colonel," the man said.

The others with him shifted their gaze from him to her to Sarah to Gaspar, ever so somber, ever so intent on not missing a syllable.

The polite man continued, "What is more, other information that you may at present consider proof of your claims will prove worthless. People you may assume will back you won't. What happened between you and Count de Bossier is our property, the public's interest and safety demand it. Everything having to do with this affair will now fall under this classification."

As soon as Sarah and Gaspar had taken their seats in the living room, the polite man had told them that they were being spared because it had been established that they had not been party to de Bossier's plot: that Gaspar had been duped and Sarah merely pursuing a story. Personally he, from that section of the Foreign Ministry on the Quay d'Orsay that was diplomacy's equivalent of the Firm's Action Branch, admired investigative reporters. Absolutely essential to a free society, he had always felt. But not as essential as the public's safety; that came first, surely she could see that.

The others in turn made their own small clarifications. One spoke of the legal justification and refused to acknowledge to Sarah that France, too, had an Official Secrets act. Another informed them that there were in force certain reciprocal agreements that would ensure that European democracies would view with favor France's wishes in the matter.

"Permit me, therefore, to make myself abundantly clear, Madame," the polite man summed up. "We expect you and Mr. Bruyn to cease and desist from any pursuit of further details of de Bossier's fantastical claims. I trust this expectation is fully understood and appreciated by you

He turned to Deadeye, as if confirmation of their comprehension uld come from her. Sarah and Gaspar too turned to stare at her and to ₂ that any acknowledgment there once might have been of their ₂quaintance, of fond feelings for Gaspar, had been obliterated. Her eyes ₂onveyed only a deadly contempt.

Captain Pandiakis was the last to climb down onto the rather incongruous tender that had brought out the Gulf professor—the name Pandiakis gave to the Bahairini pilot who became the Twanee's master for the last leg of her runs. The tender was an eighty-foot, gleaming white Hatteras yacht. The yacht belonged to Forjieh, the Bahairini had told Pandiakis the first time they met, his announcement accompanied by a proud and happy grin.

The Hatteras pulled away, turning back towards the coast of Bahrain, and the Twanee's screws were soon pushing back the Gulf's waters as she resumed her journey. It was nearly night.

By early the next morning the Twanee was on her way back. During the night she had dropped her containers in Busheher, an Iranian port that the Iraqis had been told was out of commission. Told by friends of Bobo's—a DGSE liaison team—which had showed the Iraqis satellite pictures of docks gouged and cratered by aerial bombardment, and gantry cranes looking like so many train wrecks. Told also by the CIA's Jerome Martindale Kirney. In truth, the port was out of commission to all except the Twanee.

The Bahairini pilot sipped his sweet morning mint tea, looked the new day over, and approved. He noticed a helicopter approaching, a Super Puma. He knew it was a Super Puma because he was a man who knew his war machines. He'd seen this helicopter pictured in Flight International and read the military gossip article which reported that the advanced, French-made machine had recently been lent to Iraq in small numbers, along with French crews to fly them. He was unperturbed by the sighting—the Twanee was a protected ship. Forjieh had explained to him at the outset that for happy reasons (that was how Forjieh the clothes horse had put it: "happy reasons") neither the Iraqis nor Iranians would harm him, Gulf War or no Gulf War.

The Super Puma flew low over the ship. It had turned upwind so that its engine and rotors were not heard on the bridge until it was virtually above the ship. It flew on a short way at altitude, then made a vertical ascent to perhaps a thousand feet and hovered, like an osprey tracking glints off the scales of a potential meal.

When the Exocet missile hit, the Twanee heaved for a brief moment, its forward momentum diverted, pushed sideways to accommodate the missile's own momentum. Then its bow ripped apart, bent and twisted sheets of steel peeling back like the foil cover of a yogurt cup ripped open by an impatient hand. Seconds later the second missile struck and the ship began to slip rapidly beneath the water's surface. Sailors who had been making frenzied efforts to lower a lifeboat abandoned their efforts and leapt overboard. The Bahairini remained on his bridge. There was a deep gash in his skull where his right ear had been before it was ripped away by pieces of disintegrating navigational instruments. He was dazed and in great pain, but still he assured himself that he hadn't been killed by the helicopter, which still hovered overhead. The missile had come from another French loaner, a Super Entendard, also flown by French pilots who had fired from somewhere off in the distance. The helicopter was there to insure that the target was correct and that it would be totally destroyed.

With what little presence of mind he had remaining, the Bahairini willed his body to climb down from the bridge, but his body and mind were too disconnected too effect locomotion. He saw the Super Puma descend from its perch. It hovered off to the side of the sinking ship, just above the water where the desperate sailors had leapt, and opened fire on them. It fired its machine guns for some minutes, then it lifted up once more and waited for the ship to disappear.

Atrash Forjieh liked the day, liked his progress within it, enjoyed the variety of food before him. He anticipated with pleasure his program for after lunch, when he and the Bahairini pilot he used to guide the Twanee through the Gulf's dangerous sealanes would meet aboard his Hatteras. There they would be joined by three young female flight attendants who augmented their salaries by catering to the special needs of a select clientele who appreciated their occidental colorings and textures.

Forjieh had a method all his own for ordering his meals, a method born of two irreconcilable features of his personality. The first was that he appreciated food in all its varieties, from a grilled, greasy sausage from a street vendor to the delicate, in-season shad roe flown in for his pleasure from North America. The second was his determination to retain his trim figure—else what use was his vast wardrobe? To this end, his table was laden with numerous selections from each of which he sampled small slivers; thus he got to have his cake and keep it off his waistline. So it was that day at portside in Bahrain.

His meal consumed, Forjieh paid his bill and headed for his customized white Mercedes parked in the small lot behind the soft drink distributorship he owned, one of his many businesses in the Gulf. The car was a 500 SEL with gilded trimmings where ordinary 500 SELs had only silvered chrome—yet another source of satisfaction to Forjieh on this day.

He unlocked the driver's side door and had only just inserted his right foot and leg and sufficient buttock to gain a purchase on the seat when something powerful and insistent grabbed his silk-hosed left ankle and yanked it in the direction of the car's underbelly. While his mind resisted wildly, his body buckled toward the ankle now mashed painfully against the car door's unyielding threshold, then toppled out of the car. His cry of pain and dismay as his head scraped against the rough asphalt of the cheaply-paved parking lot turned to a roar of futile anger as he saw that his ankle was being gripped by a man lying underneath his Mercedes, a man who held a pistol fixed with a silencer.

The man fired three times. Two bullets punctured Forjieh's skull through the soft under chin (where less fastidious men had by his age grown a double one) and exited through the back of his neck. The thrashing of his body resulted in the third bullet piercing his lower lip and exiting through the newly-made opening under his chin.

Chapter Thirty-one

Tomer has chosen the one named Yenukka, along with the one who asked the questions that annoyed Paz, another they call Madonna on account of his devotion to the singer's videos, and lastly himself. Staying behind during an action, even one as small as babysitting a hostage release, was for him not an option.

Early on the morning after Paz's visit to the Sayyeret's base, Tomer and Madonna surveyed the shepherd's hut where Paz's deal with the Maronite was to go down and concluded that to accomplish what Paz has asked of them they would have to bury themselves in the hut's vicinity the night before the release. The terrain offered no above-ground places suitable for hiding: no large boulders, no sufficiently deep crevasses, no thickets of bush nor stretches of clumpy grass.

After this visit, Tomer and Madonna went to see the commander of an artillery unit stationed not far from the site and described to him their requirements. The commander, a food machinery engineer in civilian life, demanded that they produce an authorization. Tomer made a telephone call and the authorization quickly came through. At ten o'clock that morning a single 120 millimeter Soltam mortar hurled twelve or thirteen rounds at the earth in the hut's vicinity, leaving twelve or thirteen craters, none either very deep nor very shallow.

"What is the matter with you people, so much nerves all the time," Harouni says with a mocking laugh. He points to the fresh craters in the earth near the hut. "What happened?" he asks Paz. "Everybody was coming to attack Israel?"

"Someone must have been trying to sneak in to steal our grapes," Paz says. "Like it says in the Bible, you know? The little foxes will come for the grapes. Our people must have shelled the little foxes. But not to worry, my good man, your money was not hit. It is all there." He gestures to the Blazer parked on a hillside about a quarter of a kilometer back, just inside Israel's border.

"And don't you worry, they did not hit your Belgian friend either," Harouni says, not about to permit the old spy the upper hand in the battle of thinly disguised insults.

Paz curses himself inwardly for engaging Harouni. He peers past Harouni to the Ford, in which Gaspar sits between two men. Mari is in the front seat. "I will ask him whether he is well, all right?" he says.

211

From the Blazer's front seat Sarah watches. Her binoculars only serve increase her frustration at not knowing what is being said below. She sees Paz put his hands to his mouth to amplify his words in the direction of the parked Ford. Her line of sight doesn't allow her to look into its windows, but when Paz is done shouting a hand and a bit of an arm emerge from the Ford's window signing a "thumbs up." Unmistakably Gaspar. She squeals her delight and pounds her fist on the thigh of the Blazer's driver.

"Fine," Paz says. "I will now go and get the money. As we agreed, it will be carried by another person, unarmed. He will come to where I am standing. You will send Bruyn over here. My man will put down the suitcase with the money, you'll look it over, then Bruyn will step across to me. You take the money and we go each our way. Good?"

"Good."

Yenukka, from his position in one of the painstakingly camouflaged craters, is the one to spot it. He is watching the woman in the Ford's front seat and sees her hands float up to a level where they briefly become visible in the passenger-side window. In one of her hands is an object that makes Yenukka ask himself why Mari would be playing a video game at a time like this. Because the object he glimpses is a joystick—well, not really a joystick. In actuality, it is a radio remote activator. Yenukka whispers his discovery into the ear of Tomer, his crater mate. Tomer whispers it into his tiny microphone so that the other two, in another of the disguised craters, will know what Yenukka has discovered.

The Blazer's driver walks down the steep hill. The money suitcase is heavy, and the man struggles to stave off the combined destabilizing effects of gravity and underfoot gravel. At the designated spot, Harouni waits until the suitcase is at rest on the ground. One of his men then kicks it onto its back, bends, and unfastens the locks. Harouni squats peasant-style and gazes at the dollars. He thrusts an index finger into the many packets and moves them around, drives the finger deeper into their midst, sends in his thumb to join the finger. Together they grasp a packet and retrieve it. He brings his other hand into use, fans the packet, his eyes making certain it is all dollars, that no fake fillers have been inserted. Still squatting, he swivels on his heels and looks to Mari and smiles. She cranes her neck and smiles back.

"Bring him," Harouni says to his man. The man walks to the Ford, opens the rear passenger door, reaches in. From the Blazer Sarah sees Gaspar step out. He looks thin but well, and appears calm. For a moment his eyes are trained on the people immediately around him. Then they

212

travel up the hill and find the Blazer. He gazes at it, then smiles a smile as happy as hope.

Harouni shuts the lid of the case, snaps its locks, motions his man to fetch it. It is taken to the Ford. Gaspar begins his walk towards the Blazer's driver. Paz, perspiring heavily now, shakes his hand, then turns to walk back up the hill. Gaspar falls in behind him and the Blazer's driver closes in behind Gaspar.

"Your love letters to your hot English wife," Mari gleefully yells from her place in the Ford. Before either of the men bracketing him can prevent him, Gaspar bolts and returns to the Ford. Mari hands him his gift attaché case, he grasps it and walks back to Paz and the driver.

Paz is appalled. He remembers agreeing that Gaspar could bring back his letters, but nothing had been said about an attaché case. Warning lights flash in his brain.

The Ford is in motion. Paz, in his consternation, is barely able to utter a question to Gaspar about the meaning of the attaché case, although it occurs to him that it may be Gaspar's own, that he may have had it with him when he was first taken from Beirut airport. He curses himself for not having gotten an inventory from Sarah of what belongings Gaspar had with him at the time.

The Ford makes its way back up the hill in reverse, neither fast nor slow, but seemingly bent on achieving some distance. Mari's hand appears thrust out through the passenger side window, grasping a device of some sort.

Then her hand is gone, then the stump of her wrist, then the car's door and its entire front passenger side. Yenukka and Tomer are on their knees, earth and dust trickling from them back into the crater from which they have emerged. They appear desperate to saturate the Ford's rear compartment with bullets from their Galil commando versions.

Their desperation is unnecessary. From the other hidden crater a single rocket-propelled grenade makes its way into the Ford where it hits the money suitcase and detonates.

Paz wrenches the attaché case from Gaspar's unwilling hand and heaves it as far as he can down the hill. He shouts hurriedly to the man behind Gaspar, who takes to poking Gaspar in the back to encourage him to climb faster. Paz trails them— his effort to keep up with the pace he had just demanded of them causes him to huff and to gulp for air.

Four grime-covered men in camouflage gear, their faces smudged with earth-toned paint, are now fully out of their hiding places. They close in on Gaspar and his escort, urging them into a smart jog up the hill.

213

When they reach the Blazer, one says, "Yenukka, esh." Yenukka lifts his short-stalked assault weapon and fires it at the distant attaché case, which explodes with a sharp report. The flames are jagged and brief, extinguished almost as the sound of the explosion fades.

Bits of paper go flying into the air, tiny remnants of Gaspar's letters. They remind Sarah of the feathers that trailed Deadeye's bird at Belle Marais.